D0173407

NO
LIMITS

No Limits

ALISON KENT

KENSINGTON PUBLISHING CORP.
www.kensingtonbooks.com

BRAVA BOOKS are published by

Kensington Publishing Corp.
119 West 40th Street
New York, NY 10018

Copyright © 2009 Alison Kent

All rights reserved. No part of this book may be reproduced in any form or by any means without the prior written consent of the Publisher, excepting brief quotes used in reviews.

All Kensington titles, imprints and distributed lines are available at special quantity discounts for bulk purchases for sales promotion, premiums, fund-raising, educational or institutional use.

Special book excerpts or customized printings can also be created to fit specific needs. For details, write or phone the office of the Kensington Special Sales Manager: Kensington Publishing Corp., 119 West 40th Street, New York, NY 10018, attn. Special Sales Department; phone: 1-800-221-2647.

Brava and the B logo are Reg. U.S. Pat. & TM Off.

ISBN-13: 978-0-7582-1757-8
ISBN-10: 0-7582-1757-9

First Kensington Trade Paperback Printing: May 2009

10 9 8 7 6 5 4 3 2 1

Printed in the United States of America

A land without ruins is a land without memories—a land without memories is a land without history.
　　　　—Abram Joseph Ryan, American poet, 1838–1886

They say this about the land. It owns a man. Heart, soul, and body, all the way to the bone. It breaks backs and bank accounts, reduces dreams to dust. It seduces skillfully, a demanding mistress, draining, mesmerizing, keeping promises only when the mood strikes.

And that owning? That hold? It can cause a man to do things he never would if he understood, if he cared about or considered the impact of his actions, if he knew who he was hurting and looked beyond the riches the land surrendered, to the value of human life.

This is the only explanation I can think of for what I've discovered. The details cannot be shared before I determine the implications. If I fail, if I'm found out, there will be little chance of anyone ever knowing the truth.

I can't let that happen. I can't let him get away with destroying the lives of those standing in his way. I can't let him live out his days without making amends, without paying restitution, without admitting to his crimes.

One

It was the perfect bedroom.

Truly it was.

The bed was queen size, the sand-colored sheets one-thousand-thread-count Egyptian cotton, the coverlet chocolate matelassé, the duvet imprinted with a scrollwork pattern in ebony and brown.

The nightstands and wardrobe, headboard, footboard, and five-drawer chest were hardwood solids, the cherry and walnut veneer inlaid with Italian marble. The lamps were urns of Venctian bronze with shades the same ivory as the handwoven rug of wool and rich silk.

The jewelry chest on the mirrored vanity held her signature onyx pieces—including the glossy ebony disk surrounded by lemon quartz and mustard-yellow petal pearls designed for her to wear at the Tonys. The photos had been splashed all over the Web. She'd never worn the piece again.

A social secretary handled all of her appointments, from luncheons to charity events to spas, nails, and hair. An executive assistant took care of her financial, legal, and business obligations. The two women shared an office on the first floor of the five-story prewar in TriBeCa, leaving her to her personal space on the third.

It was the perfect bedroom.

Truly it was.

Or it would have been had Michelina Ferrer not been thirty years old, still sleeping in her father's house, and sleeping there alone.

She slid from her perch on the end of the bed to sit on the floor, missing the rug completely and hitting the cold hardwood. Her purse followed, a plop of crushed leather at her hip. The contents tumbled out.

She groaned—not at that mess but at the other one she'd made before catching a cab to come home. Oh, but she was *so* not looking forward to the celebrity photos section of tomorrow's "Page Six."

What had she been thinking, ditching her underpants while at Slick Velvet and dancing bare-assed on the raised platform like some sixties go-go girl? Okay, she knew what she'd been thinking, but still.

She wasn't a pop star shaving her head and looking to shock the media into remembering her glory days.

She wasn't a celebutante seeking headlines through sex videos, music videos, DUIs, and reality TV.

She wasn't an actor feeding her drama queen need for publicity through breakdowns and rehab, fan sympathy, and peer critique.

She was the public face of and the spokesmodel for the family business, Ferrer Fragrances.

She was also her father's sole heir.

Micky dropped her head against the mattress, closing her eyes and fighting the need to weep. Papi was going to kill her when he saw tomorrow's edition of the *Post*. And he *would* see it. Greta would make sure of that.

Greta *always* made Papi aware of his "little Micky Mousey's" stunts—and for one simple reason. It was Greta's opinion that Micky had no business representing the Ferrer name across the globe.

Right now, at four a.m., on a Tuesday in April, more drunk than not, her butt sticking to the floor, her pedicure scuffed all to hell, Micky wasn't so sure the other woman wasn't right.

It wasn't that Greta wanted the job for herself, or even had anyone else in mind. She'd been Papi's personal assistant for fourteen years, and she made no bones about putting Ferrer's corporate interests above the family's.

Of the two women, Greta was the one with her priorities in order, her head on straight. But then Greta wasn't the one looking at a future with a man of Papi's choosing, a man she didn't even know.

It didn't matter what Micky was facing. Her streak of admittedly bad and self-destructive behavior had to stop, and stop now.

This recent old-school, arranged-marriage trigger aside, she didn't know where it had come from, this manic desperation. She didn't know what was going on with her. She did know this wasn't like her, wasn't who she was.

She never had been one to act out or throw tantrums. She'd only had to ask for what she wanted. It had always been that simple for Edoardo Ettore Ferrer's daughter, his "little Micky Mousey."

Either she didn't know what she was searching for, or worse. It was something she had no business thinking about, being in the position she was.

Whatever. She couldn't deal tonight, this morning. She'd had too many margarita martinis—like that was a good idea? Not her drinking them, just the mix of the two cocktails.

And with a gummy worm for garnish? She smacked her tongue to the roof of her mouth and tasted sour lemon and other things she couldn't place that quite frightened her.

She reached for her purse and began gathering the spilled

contents, contents that included her thong. She groaned, hooking the scrap of fabric with one finger and twirling it around before flinging it across the room.

God, but she wished she was more drunk so she could remember less of the night, or less drunk so she could remember more. As it was, she was gong to need her own copy of the paper to separate the brutal reality from the vodka-tequila haze.

No doubt Greta would be happy to provide her one to read at the breakfast table while Papi read his. . . .

Micky groaned again. She couldn't face him. She just couldn't. She'd seen the disappointment in his face too many times this last year as she'd strained against some weird boundary that had begun to constrict her.

What she needed was to blow off work and her shrink and spend a long weekend watching all six seasons of *Sex and the City* on DVD with Lisa, gorging on kettle corn and room-temperature Coke the way they had the last time her girlfriend had been in Manhattan.

When was that? Two years ago? Three? How had she let herself lose touch with someone who'd been such an important part of her life? Could it be because Micky herself had turned into a person she was really beginning to dislike?

Lisa Weston—now Lisa Landry—had stepped between Micky and a horny frat boy their first year at school, and the two women had been BFF—best friends forever—from that very day, even though Lisa later left college to marry a deputy sheriff down in Cajun country, abandoning Micky to the clutches of Greta and Papi and all the beautiful people Micky didn't care to know.

Poor little rich girl. All alone in her ivory tower. Making a mess of her attempts to escape. Wait. That's what she'd do! Escape! She'd take the Coke and the kettle corn down to Louisiana.

Lisa had written just recently; Micky dumped her purse

again and found the envelope she'd tucked inside after reading about Lisa's family keeping her out of some loop.

Some friend she was, not even checking back to see if the other woman was okay. Enough with the destructive behavior. Lisa would help her get her act together, and then Micky would make sure the Landrys understood that Lisa was a jewel and worth more than they obviously knew.

Drinking and driving was out of the question, but she was sober enough to dial. First she had to pack a few things. No, she decided, pushing up from the floor. Packing would take too long, though putting on her underpants wouldn't.

She had her credit cards, her cell phone, and the envelope with Lisa's address. She could get what she needed once she reached . . . She frowned, unfolded the envelope. Once she reached Bayou Allain.

Two

He was going to go.
His mind was made up.

He'd been putting it off for too long.

Standing at the window outside the wall of servers that hid the guts of the Smithson Group's ops center, Simon Baptiste stared across Manhattan toward the southwest and thought of Louisiana and Bayou Allain.

He hadn't been back in years. The realization that he had business there left dangling was making him restless, jumpy, irritable, like he'd popped back a handful of pills and been slammed with the backwash.

He'd joined the army at eighteen, boarded the bus for boot camp, and kissed the bayou country good-bye. That didn't mean the flavor wasn't still strong in his blood. Like his mother, he'd been born in that land of cypress trees and accordions, of alligators and boudin and swamps.

He'd seen a whole lot of the rest of the world since leaving the Gulf Coast. Twenty years had gone by, and he'd done as much traveling since his discharge as during his three tours. But other than going where Hank Smithson sent him these days, he was all about sticking close to home.

A studio on the Lower East Side had been his crash pad

since joining the SG-5 team. He'd figured it would be easier to stick close to headquarters than fly in and out the way Mick Savin did from West Texas, or the way Ezra Moore did from the Florida Keys.

The place was small, but it was all he needed, and lately, for weeks longer than was good for any man, he'd needed it a lot, holing up like an injured animal, tending his wounds in tight quarters, feeling safer in those few hundred square feet than he could in a larger town house or loft with too much exposed space, too much room to roam.

The billboard had helped.

It had gone up a month ago. He'd gotten used to kicking back on his small patio and telling the woman in the fragrance ad—Ferrer's Adria—about his day, giving her the rundown of what he had to do the next, where Hank was sending him, who the bad guys were this time.

She would smile, looking like all kinds of hot, listening to every word he said as if she couldn't wait for him to shut the hell up and take her to bed. She'd only started talking back when he'd been too drunk to stop her.

After the shit hit the fan on his last SG-5 assignment, he'd stayed that way for a week, her nagging voice ringing in his ears—or so he'd thought until Hank had quit the buzzer and started knocking instead.

Hank had told him it was fine to take a break and wallow, but he needed to be sober while he did. Not that Hank was wrong, but Simon had been the one walking in those particular shoes, the one to see the advantage in the bottle.

Speaking of Hank and shoes . . . Simon heard the older man's footsteps behind him only seconds before a meaty hand clamped down on his shoulder.

"Mornin', boss."

Hank moved to stand at Simon's side, staring with him at the financial district and the human ants on the sidewalk below. "When you just say mornin' like that? It leaves a man to wonder whether it's a good one, or whether the day has started off so wrong it'll never get back to bein' right."

Simon chuckled under his breath. "It's good enough; thanks for asking. I've just got something that needs doing that I'm not looking forward to."

He handed Hank the envelope that had hit his box after a series of forwards and courier drops; he liked that no one knew where he was other than those he wanted to know.

And then Simon waited while the man who had given him back his life took a look at the past Simon had hoped would resolve itself if he ignored it long enough.

Twenty years spent ignoring the property he owned but never wanted had accomplished nothing. The time had come to cowboy up, to get his affairs in order. He needed to see to the land. But of a higher priority was his need to make whatever peace he could with his cousin. After all, King was the only blood family he still had.

Hank scanned the documents inside that had come from Savoy Realty and included the property tax bills, the management company's maintenance records, the current appraisal and geological survey, the rental history that was out of date and sorely lacking in detail.

"Judge Terrill Landry, Sr.," Hank finally said, flipping through the pages Simon had fairly memorized. "I'm not familiar with the name."

Simon was familiar enough for the both of them. Judge Terrill "Bear" Landry, Sr. no longer served on the bench but worked as a land man instead. During his time with Division C of the Fifteenth Judicial District of Louisiana, however, he'd been the one who'd sentenced both Simon and King after investigators determined the fire that ate through the latter's family home to be arson.

"Le Hasard. That's what you call the place?" Hank asked, and after Simon nodded, added, "You going to sell? Hang on to the mineral rights? Unload the whole caboodle? Because I know you're not going to keep walking away."

And that was Hank, seeing through his SG-5 operatives' bullshit and never letting any of them slide. They were all good men, each with a lot to account for, to make up for. Yet Hank never played favorites, demanding they own up to their sins, forgiving them even when they might not know how—or be ready—to forgive themselves.

Simon scrubbed his hands down his face. "I'm not sure what I'm gonna do, but I do know I have to go, see what condition it's in and all."

"Then go." Hank hooked a forefinger and thumb around the stub of his cigar and pulled it from his mouth. "You'll figure it out when you get there."

"Might be I screw it up, sell it when I should keep it, keep it when I should sell." He didn't mention anything about King. "It's been known to happen. Me screwing up."

Hank knew what had gone down with Simon and Eli McKenzie, his most recent partner. Hank had been the one to bring Simon back from the brink. And Hank wasn't having any of it. "There's not a man here who hasn't felt the screwed-up fit of your shoes."

"Too true that, boo," Simon said, knowing they'd all spent time in their own versions of hell. "Maybe I should be getting one of them to go in my place."

He couldn't see Bear Landry—who had to be closing in on, what, sixty-five, sixty-eight by now?—knowing what to make of the fierce warrior that was Eli McKenzie. Or Lorna Savoy—and why was she still a Savoy?—putting up much resistance to Tripp Shaughnessey's charm.

And his cousin King knocking heads with Kelly John Beach would be worth the price of the ticket, since his cousin's head had no doubt grown harder with age. But this was one of those man-doing-what-he-had-to-do situations.

Hank folded the documents and slid them back into the envelope, tapping it against Simon's arm. "You know any one of them would. 'Cept that wouldn't be much in the way of a favor. None of them can kill off the bugaboos been keeping you away for twenty years."

Simon had never laid out the events of the past to Hank, but he wouldn't be at all surprised if the boss knew what had gone down with the fire, or why Bear Landry had wanted Simon and King out of the way and had meted out punishment that made it happen. Getting to the bottom of that mystery as much as dealing with King and the land was the very reason Simon had to be the one to go.

"You can run things around here on your own for a while?" he asked. "I don't want to leave you in more of a bind than I already have."

"We've got the bad guys under control, hotshot. You go and do what you need to do for yourself. We'll be here if you want to come back—"

Want to? Why wouldn't I want to? What would I do instead?

"—and we'll know where to find you if you don't."

"I'll be back. As soon as I can make it." That was a promise. "There's not a thing on the Gulf Coast worth stayin' there for." And that was a fact.

Three

"He's coming home, Baby Bear. He's finally coming home. I swear I don't know whether my heart's beating itself full of fear, or if it's fluttering from waiting to see what he'll look like after all this time."

Terrill Landry, Sr.—Bear to everyone living in Bayou Allain, Baby Bear to Lorna Savoy, who knew more of his secrets than his wife had ever been privy to learn—slapped a thick palm on a file folder to the right of the leather blotter centered on his desk.

"I've got a picture right here, Lorna, if it'll save you from peeing yourself," he told her, glancing to where she stood at his office window, the green paisley drapes more expensive than her outfit, her manicure, and her haircut combined.

For not the first time in the twenty years of their association, he found himself wishing he'd taken on someone who hadn't turned out so silly, so easily flustered, so goo-goo eyed when it came to men—except that particular bit of Lorna's being female had played well with his dealings and made the rest of who she was easier to overlook.

Then there was the surprising fact that inside all that fluff, she had a good head for his work. He supposed that had a lot to do with the pit of her existence before he'd plucked her out of her family's shack in the swamps, and knowing he was giving her a chance she'd never get again.

He looked her over.

Her hair was a nest of bottle-red flips and teased curls, her tits 100 percent real, still firm and high, and more than enough for any man's hands, mouth, or dick. Her hips, still trim, were curvier now than they'd been years ago when he'd crawled between her legs without help. Her stomach remained bikini flat above her shaved-bare pussy.

Even thinking of all that, he couldn't deny that these days he found more pleasure elsewhere. These days in particular it came from the impending culmination of what he'd been working toward for near on half his life. Being on the back side of sixty, it took more than what he could get from Lorna to keep his flames fed, even if once in a while it was nice to remind her of all that she owed him for.

She turned away from his office window, lifted a brow darker than her hair, and after a long moment, approached in that slow, easy way she had, using the bright white tips of her nails to pick at the loose end of the belt cinched around her waist, her lips pursed.

"If I pee myself, Baby Bear, it'll be because I'm scared out of my wits. When he called to tell me he was coming to look over the place, I thought I was going to die."

Scared of Simon Baptiste when she should've been worried about Bear himself. "All you have to do is follow the script. If he asks why Le Hasard has gone to hell, give him the reasons we worked out. You've done things a lot more fearful than that in your life."

He saw it in her bright blue contact lens–covered eyes when she snapped, "The minute he sees the place as run-down as it is, he's going to know something's up. Of course he's going to ask; wouldn't you? Or are you too feeble-minded to remember that he's been paying me to keep the place spruced up and rented out? And I haven't been doing either, thanks to you."

He waited, letting her think on what she'd said, on whom she'd said it to, on how much she should be wanting to take back her words. Then he reminded her of a few things, doing nothing more threatening than making one big fist out of his laced hands and making sure he had her eye. "My mind's as sharp now as it was twenty years ago. I remember everything, and you'd do good to do the same."

She knew where her bread was buttered and that helped her shed the attitude. She sunk defeated into the chair in front of his desk, wrinkles showing in her neck as she slumped. "That's the problem, B.B. I remember it all. I know every one of the things I've done, and especially what I did that night to Simon and King. . . ." She let the sentence trail with a shudder that took over her body.

Bear wasn't worried. He'd made sure she'd been as high as a kite that night. He doubted she remembered what he didn't want her to. And the only two people who'd been with her when the fire had started had no cause to question the past.

He stood by his admonition. "This is what you've been doing for years, Lorna. You're a professional. You make deals. You buy property. You sell property. You take your commissions and doll your gorgeous self up with the money you rake in. There's no reason to start second-guessing yourself this late in the game."

He planted both hands on the top of his desk and pushed out of his chair, standing tall, looking down. He needed this taken care of so he could get back to looking toward a future he'd never thought would come. "You can make Simon Baptiste believe anything you want him to, Lorna. Anything at all."

* * *

Later that night in his regular booth at Red's, his usual drink in one hand, his unlit cigar in the other, Bear found himself facing the most aggravating of quandaries. How in the hell did his son survive the life of a deputy sheriff with a goddamn limp dick for a spine?

"Jesus Christ, Bear." Terrill Jr.'s voice was scratched raw and brittle like all he'd done for days now was cry. "We should've found something by now. People don't just disappear into thin air."

The boy sat with his shoulders slumped, his hands wrapped around a near-empty mug. He hadn't gone home since Monday to do more than see if his wife had come home. Bear was fairly certain the boy hadn't slept but maybe an hour or two in the same expanse of time.

It showed in his eyes, which were bloodshot, his face, which needed a shave, his uniform, which smelled of sweat and long hours behind the wheel of his cruiser, driving aimlessly as if he'd find Lisa wandering the streets of Bayou Allain, or strolling through Vermilion Parish, lost.

All in all, Bear was disgusted. "Terrill, take yourself home and get cleaned up. You look like shit. That's no way to treat your uniform."

"I'm off duty," Terrill told his mug, rubbing at his rheumy eyes. "And if anything, I look like a man whose wife vanished without a trace. I doubt anyone is going to care about a few stains or wrinkles."

"I care, and that should be reason enough." On this, Bear put down his foot. No matter their personal trials, the Landrys would maintain a strong front. They couldn't have people talking, speculating, digging into their lives and their business. Not now. Not now. "If it's not, then you should look to the people who put you where you are today."

"One and the same, Bear," Terrill said, leaning his chin into the cup of his palms. "*You* put me where I am. You think I don't know that?"

Bear glanced away from his son and toward the two men sitting on stools at Red's bar beneath the sign for Abita Beer. He looked around at the tables clustered to the side of the dance floor. He took in the members of the band playing from the small stage near the door.

No one seemed to be paying his corner more attention than usual, so he turned again to his son. "What you need to know is that your appearance matters. Your appearance affects your reputation, and your reputation is what earns you the respect of the people."

"What matters is my wife," Terrill said, his voice getting louder with each word, his hands coming away from his face to slam against the table. "You may run this town, but you are not going to tell me how I should act when my wife is missing."

"People will see that you're grieving whether you're wearing a shirt that's wrinkled or pressed." Bear covered one of Terrill's hands with his own.

"Then at least they'll be seeing the truth." Terrill pulled away, signaled Red to send him another beer.

Agreeing it was time for a refill, Bear glanced in the same direction, catching King Trahan's eye in the bar's mirror. As if enough wasn't enough; damn his indigestion.

Dealing with Terrill and Lisa and Lorna Savoy already had his gut in an uproar. Now seeing King was souring the drink in his gullet. The Trahan boy hadn't spent near enough time behind bars to Bear's way of thinking, but then he had no one to blame but himself for the way that had worked out.

Still . . . Bear could read a whole lot of what King was thinking in his eyes. And there was just enough wild-man hatred there to give Bear a good solid pause.

When he finally tore his gaze away and checked in with his son, he decided the refill could wait. It was time for Terrill to call it a night. He reached for the mug, unexpectedly caught by the sadness twisting his son's face.

He shouldn't have been. He shouldn't even have noticed. Not emotion or sentiment or anything soft. And yet . . . "Go home, Terrill. Shower. Sleep. Then come by my office before you head for Abbeville in the morning."

"What the hell for?"

"I've got a man in Houston's done work for me in the past. We'll get him over here looking for Lisa," Bear said, knowing he was going to end this night in bed with a roll of antacids.

Terrill's head came up. "You didn't want anything to do with a P.I. yesterday."

The boy's petulance was plucking at Bear's last nerve, and he deserved it for making the suggestion—a show of support at odds with what he was feeling. "Yesterday I was waiting for the girl to get back from whatever shopping trip she forgot to tell you she was taking."

"You're kidding, right?" Terrill's question was rhetorical and dripped with sarcasm. "If anything, she would've gone back to the library. And she would have called."

"Maybe so." Bear had never imagined his daughter-in-law's genealogy research would turn into a time bomb. The ticking had become a relentless pain in his head. "But bringing in a P.I. before now would've been jumping the gun. You're law enforcement. You know how this works. Lisa being family doesn't change procedure."

"It damn well should," Terrill said, back to rubbing at his eyes. "Waiting lets the trail grow cold."

"My man specializes in cold trails. He'll sniff out any clues we've missed."

"We haven't missed a thing. There's nothing. She was here. And then she wasn't."

"Meaning, if she left of her own accord, someone somewhere has seen her or her car." How many times were they going to have to cover this ground?

"And if she didn't? Leave of her own accord?"

"Then someone somewhere would still have seen her or her car. All we have to do is find that someone."

"Needle in a haystack."

Bear wasn't about to disagree. But then, Vermilion Parish and Bayou Allain in particular were neither one population rich. "It's time to start thinking beyond what we know to what we don't, Terrill."

"What's that supposed to mean?"

It had to be the beers talking. His son was a deputy sheriff. He was not a deputy buffoon. "Do you know anyone who might want to get to Lisa? Anyone from her past? Anyone she might have talked to while doing her research?"

"No one," he said, shaking his head. "Jesus Christ, Bear. We've already been through this."

"We haven't been through enough," Bear told his son. "If we had, we wouldn't be looking for only the second person known to disappear from Bayou Allain."

Four

Kingdom Trahan sat bellied up to the bar, two fingers hooked around the neck of his beer bottle, his eyes shifting from the mirror on the wall to Red, the owner and barkeep who was busy pointing out to the eighteen-year-old trying to pass himself off as twenty-one how easy it was to spot a fake I.D.

King remembered eighteen all too well. It wasn't a year he looked back on fondly, and the several that followed hadn't been any better, spent as they were in Angola, where he'd been confined in Louisiana's state pen.

At the end of his time served and along with his freedom, he'd come away with skills that went beyond sorting laundry and stamping out license plates. One was a heightened sixth sense. Another amounted to a pair of eyes in the back of his head. And both were working overtime tonight.

He didn't know what it was in the air, but there was a buzz prickling at his nape that had nothing to do with his beer. He could see Terrill 1 and Terrill 2 in the older Landry's usual booth. Terrill 2 had just come off duty, the parish's finest, protecting and serving as long as doing so didn't get in Terrill 1's way.

It wasn't so much a case of like father like son, the off-spring turning out to be as crooked as the man who'd spawned him, but more a case of the spawn being as cowed by the Big Bear as everyone who lived in Bayou Allain. Most everyone, anyway.

King would've thought the Landry men were discussing news of junior's wife, except what he was feeling was bigger than Lisa. King didn't believe Bear's claims of knowing nothing about what had happened to his daughter-in-law. Bear Landry knew everything that went on in the parish whether the information was made public or not.

Whatever had the air humming, King was certain he'd find out soon because the strange energy wasn't confined to the back corner where the Landry men huddled. It was up front, blowing in on the wind along with the soft vanilla scent from the clematis every time the front door swung open.

If he came to town for a beer more often instead of drinking alone in his trailer at Le Hasard . . . maybe that's what the electricity was all about. How Simon would finally see for himself what had become of his land—land that by rights should've belonged to King but by law did not.

Then again, King didn't notice anyone paying him any more mind than usual. Red had greeted him with a cold beer, not a word about his cousin finally stepping foot back in Bayou Allain, just bullshit about work biting the big one and the well on Le Hasard sitting there waiting for the workover he'd been promising for years now to get to.

The life and times of a wannabe roughneck . . .

It was when Red's front door opened a couple of minutes later that King latched on to the fuss. Red's was by no stretch of any imagination a place a woman might come for a cocktail, and in a million years King couldn't see the one walking through the door palming a mug of suds.

Then again, he didn't have to think hard to picture the fingers toying with the ends of the scarf draped around her neck fondling the stem of a martini glass, or, for that matter, his dick.

That said, he figured his hands would be too callused to touch her in return, and why his thoughts were going to places he never would proved that he really did need more than one night a month out in public.

He raised his bottle to his mouth, kept his gaze focused on her face in the mirror, watched her take in the band in the corner, the three couples groping on the stamp-sized dance floor, the rows of booths and pool tables on the other side, and the bar against the back wall.

It was a weeknight. The crowd small. He and T-Beaux Gentry the only ones cracking their way through Red's basket of peanuts at the bar. All the other patrons gawking at her had someone at their elbow or across their table or in their arms to whisper with.

King did not. He was sitting there all by his lonesome, and roughneck or not, he knew he had a look that brought women close. Something dangerous, he'd been told. Something earthy and raw. This one, after meeting his eyes in the mirror and seeing that for herself, headed toward him—a fact that had ol' T-Beaux snarling at Red for another damn beer.

King, he just chuckled beneath his breath, cracked open another peanut, and swept the dust and the hull from the bar to the floor as she climbed onto the stool at his side.

"Let me guess," he said, taking in her cleavage and the lacy edge of her bra where the neckline of her black top gaped beneath her scarf. "A fruity martini or champagne."

She snorted. It was a sound he had to think back on to make sure he'd heard it right. He did that as she was saying, "Until I sweat out last night's tequila, I'm sticking to coffee, thanks."

"Coffee, huh?" King glanced toward the far end of the bar where Red huddled with T-Beaux, wadding the towel he used to wipe spills and making no move toward the princess who might as well have climbed into a fishbowl as onto a stool.

Pushing away from his own seat as well as from the imagined picture of her damp skin sweating out tequila, King stepped through the swinging gate into the service alley, where he lifted the carafe of brown sludge Red had brewed hours ago and brought it to his nose.

"This stuff's good for nothing but tarring roofs," he told her. "I'll make a fresh pot."

He went about doing so, waiting for her to tell him not to bother, it wasn't necessary, she'd pick up a cup at the first Starbucks she hit on her way out of town—since he couldn't think she was here on purpose; she had to be lost—instead of putting him out.

But she didn't.

She sat there wearing at least a grand in a designer's idea of casual duds, her black hair snipped and clipped to fall around her shoulders and down her back just so.

What? Just because he'd farmed, ranched, netted shrimp, worked on a rig, and collected unemployment he didn't know an expensive woman when one sat down beside him smelling like a field of flowers in Tuscany?

He finished with the coffeepot and turned to see her eyes on the mirror, searching through the reflections of Red's crowd. Interesting, he mused, leaning closer, his forearms crossed on the edge of the bar.

"Lookin' for anyone in particular or just a good time, *mon ami?*"

The look she gave him would have withered the balls on a lot of men. King took it as a challenge.

"I'm looking for a friend of mine." She left it at that.

King prompted, "That so, *chère?* Someone living in Bayou Allain?"

"Last I knew, yes. But no one answered the door at the address I have. No one answered at any of the neighbors' doors, either." She paused as if weighing the wisdom of what she wanted to say before adding, "Lots of drafty houses you've got here."

"What makes you say that?"

"The way the curtains swing back and forth in the windows."

King laughed. At the end of the bar, Red looked up. T-Beaux's glare turned to a grimace. Even Bear Landry, sitting across the room in his booth surveying all, shook his head.

No one liked it when King laughed. They'd come to know the sound, what it meant, and how the only one who would find the joke funny was him.

This was a good one. King knew all about folks here staying far away from all parts of a man's trouble save for the gossip.

"I'm glad one of us is amused," she finally said.

"What's your name, *chère?*" he asked, reaching beneath the bar for a mug he hoped was clean and pouring her a cup of coffee.

"Michelina Ferrer." She waited a few seconds, as if expecting recognition, before adding, "Micky. You?"

"Kingdom Trahan." He offered her cream and sugar. She took both, and he told her to call him King.

"Kingdom?" she teased—a stranger, yet she had to get in a dig.

"Michelina?" he came back with, used to the response. "Who is it you've come to Bayou Allain to see, *chère?*"

"A girlfriend from college," she said, and King tensed against barking out another laugh.

There was only one woman down here who could possibly have gone to school with someone who looked like this and was named Michelina Ferrer. "Oh, yeah?"

He didn't say anything else, just waited for her to confirm his suspicions.

She did, nodding. "Lisa Weston. Do you know her? Though she'd be Lisa Landry to you."

"Terrill's wife," he said, his voice stiff.

"I called the sheriff's office. The girl there told me he was already off duty and if he wasn't at home, he'd be here or at Bear's place, whatever that means. She didn't know anything about where Lisa might be."

That would be because no one knows what happened to Lisa. Or at least those who do ain't talking.

King thought it, but he didn't say it, casting another glance toward Bear Landry's booth and wondering if he should walk Micky Ferrer over, or if he could stretch out Bear's discomfort a while, because he didn't think there was anything he enjoyed more than watching the bastard sweat.

"Terrill was here. You just missed him. Bear's what everyone around here calls Terrill, Sr."

"So maybe Terrill," she paused, then added, "the son," as if he couldn't figure it out for himself, "is on his way to Bear's place?"

"I doubt that." He took another drink of his beer, his eyes on hers, watching them take his measure as someone she wasn't sure she liked, someone she wasn't easily going to trust. Someone she still wasn't ready to write off.

Not just yet.

"Why is that? Or do I have to jump through hoops for an answer?"

He didn't have the patience to linger any longer, no matter how much he enjoyed the game and her eyes. He wanted to see this woman go up against Bear Landry in the worst way, because for the first time that he could remember, King wasn't so sure Bear would win.

He shook his head, then gave a nod toward the room's back corner. "No hoops required. There's no reason for Terrill to head out to the old man's place when the old man is sitting right there."

Five

Terrill Landry sat behind the wheel of his patrol car in Red's parking lot. He was out of control. He knew it. The fact that he was about to drive home not caring about his blood alcohol level proved how far out in left field he was standing. But since he had nothing to go home to, no reason to be there, he really couldn't make himself give a shit.

Lisa was the best thing that had ever happened in his life. He'd grown up in this nothing of a backwater, raised by a father who ran every show in town. He'd spent four years at Louisiana State University, served four more at the feet of good ol' Uncle Sam.

Then he'd come back to Bayou Allain because this is where the Landrys lived. This is where they'd always lived. And right now, without Lisa, he couldn't think of anyplace he wanted to live less, or any reason to live at all.

He met her not long out of the service. He'd spent a week after his discharge on a Florida beach, wanting to get his game on, knowing the future he'd be returning to in Bayou Allain—a future his father would determine no matter any plans he made for himself. Living in the bayou meant living under Bear Landry's thumb. That's how it had always been.

It had been that way for his mother, too. It had been the reason she left. The people in town had seen a woman deserting her husband and son and called it abandonment. From his distance of twenty-five years, Terrill was now able to see more of the truth, that of a woman married to a man who gave her no say in raising their child, a woman never allowed to be the mother she wanted to be.

He didn't have to stay. He knew that, just as he knew it hadn't taken much to beckon his mother away. Yet he still hadn't been able to leave his father alone. Terrill hoped that made him a good son instead of a sucker, though feeling like the latter was where he spent most of his time.

He'd never felt the need for Bear's respect. No matter what his father said, Terrill had that of the town. More important, he had the love of his wife. The look on her face when he walked through the door every night, the expression of surprise at seeing him there when she knew he was coming, the pleasure that broadcast how much her love for him had grown since he'd kissed her good-bye that morning . . .

He stared up at the blinking lights of Red's sign, the blood-colored neon a watery blur, his breath a hitch in his chest. There was nothing he hated more than a cheap drunk, one who cried like a baby after a pitcher of beer. He didn't even have that for an excuse. Bear had put a stop to his drinking before he'd made it all the way there.

It just hadn't been soon enough to wash his head free of the picture of Lisa on that Florida beach sprawled across a blanket and reading a Civil War text. Spring break, and she was devouring details on the Battle of Shiloh along with the butter-bright sun.

What kind of woman wanted to read about war instead of flipping through a trashy beach read? He hadn't planned to stop, but walking by he'd been close enough to see a photo of Old Glory on the page when he'd glanced down to check out her cleavage.

She'd looked up, sat up, asked him about the scar on his shoulder that was nothing, a burn suffered years ago as a kid when he and his dirt bike had tussled and the dirt bike's tailpipe had won.

They'd talked until the sun had gone down, then talked for most of the night. He'd slept on the sofa in the living room of her beach house. He'd assumed it was a rental, learned the next morning when her parents walked in that it was family owned.

Her family was nothing like his. They cared. They consulted. They were close. No one ruled the roost, or set down laws they demanded go unchallenged. Was it any wonder he'd fallen so hard? Not only had he found the woman he wanted to be his partner, he'd found a second home that made his first almost bearable.

Knowing what she did about where he'd come from, she'd insisted repeatedly that the choice to live in Louisiana as his wife was an easy one to make. Digging into the genealogy of the Landry family had been her way of proving to him that there was a bigger Landry picture than the one painted by Bear.

Terrill scrubbed his hands over his face. Jesus Christ. How in the world was he going to tell her parents that he hadn't taken care of her as he'd sworn to do the day they'd exchanged vows? He couldn't think straight. He was no good for anything having to do with this case. How could he be when all he could see were Lisa's soft blue eyes?

She'd still been half asleep when he'd left for work on Monday. She'd smiled, her voice husky and low as she'd told him she'd be spending the morning going through the boxes in Bear's attic, but if he wanted to stop by for lunch, he could nibble on her in bed.

The attic. The boxes. Terrill's head came up. His men had gone through the room for clues, had canvassed the grounds with dogs, had turned over every piece of garbage hoping to find a trail. But no one had looked closely yet at the boxes' contents, at what Lisa might have found.

Someone needed to put the photos and records and multitude of stored documents under a magnifying glass. And other than Bear, the only person who knew enough about the Landry family to sort out the public lies from the private truths was Terrill himself.

He turned the ignition and put the car into gear, pulled slowly out of the parking lot, feeling not only sober but also hopeful. Bear never left Red's before midnight. Terrill had a good four hours to dig through the graveyard of his father's life.

Six

Micky Ferrer wasn't sure what she was doing or how she'd wound up in this dive. Oh, she knew she'd boarded her flight out of JFK Tuesday at five-thirty a.m., changed planes in Houston, arrived in New Orleans around one, and hired a driver to get her to the French Quarter.

She'd checked in early at the Monteleone and slept away the rest of the day. Then she'd slept away most of the night, but only after leaving Papi a voice mail saying she'd be out of town a few days, not to worry, and yes, yes, she was sorry.

All of that she knew. But none of that really answered the question niggling at her now that she was sober and facing what she'd done from a distance. Why had she thought that coming here was going to solve a thing?

First thing Wednesday, she'd rented a car in the city, found a small boutique with clothes she wouldn't hate being caught dead in when her body was found after Papi killed her, and then explained to the in-dash GPS where it was she wanted to go.

The rest of the day had been a wild-goose chase, taking her from one swamp to another—or so it had seemed while she'd been trying to find the hole-in-the-wall that was Bayou Allain. Once she had, the goose had been no easier to catch.

She'd explained to the guy named Kingdom how she couldn't get anyone in town to answer a single question. No one but the sheriff's office would even give her the time of day. She'd always wondered if there wasn't more lie than truth to the rumor of southern hospitality.

What in the hell was Lisa doing living here?

There wasn't a damn thing about this place Micky found welcoming. Red's itself was a dump. She'd been afraid she was going to fall through the porch boards or catch her heel in the gaps where they failed to meet. All she could hope for now was a quick Q&A with the man in the corner, the A part sending her on her way.

She took him in, finding his return scrutiny offensive, as if he were hoping to scare her away before she took a single step in his direction. And then she smiled to herself. It was time the man met the force that was Michelina Ferrer.

She dug into her hobo bag to settle her bill, the long strap across her body keeping the bag close. King waved her off. "It's on me."

She nodded her thanks, assuming that meant the bar owner would absorb the cost of the freshly brewed pot because King didn't strike her as the generous type, but she could hardly add that to her list of worries. Between Papi, her reputation, the family business, and now her best friend, she was all out of list-making ink.

The band was on break, so there was no fiddle or accordion or slide of boots on the worn wooden floor to cover the click of her heels on the planks.

She might as well have cha-cha-chaed her way to the man's booth and taken a bow. Every eye in the place was already boring holes into the back of her head—at least those that weren't focused on her tits or her ass.

Instead of acknowledging the stares, she kept her head up and her chin high, her eyes straight ahead. The man she wanted to see never looked away. But his gaze consumed her in a way that was different.

He was curious, yes, but he was also judgmental, pinning her against a felt backdrop and examining each and every one of her bones, her hair follicles, her teeth, and her pores. That look exposed her in ways being naked never could, yet still she walked toward him.

He was a big man, over sixty, she was certain. That much she determined by looking at his skin. His hair was gray and thinning, though she'd seen worse, and what had once been hard muscle was now not, his bulk soft, loose on his frame.

She didn't wait for an invitation but slid into the bench opposite his. "My name is Michelina Ferrer. Mr. Trahan at the bar tells me that you are Lisa Weston's—Lisa Landry's—father-in-law. She and I went to school together, and she told me if I ever made it down this way . . ."

Micky heard herself rambling and stopped. She supposed she should have considered where she was, whose company she was in, and whose help she wanted before jumping in with both feet. Jumping might not be the way things were done here in the swamps, but she was who she was.

And no matter how many people would be thrilled to death to see her change—Papi and Greta to name two—she didn't see it happening. Making herself miserable in order to make others happy was no way to live.

She thought about starting over, offering the man across from her a more thorough introduction and detailed explanation of who she was and why she was here, approaching him as someone needing his help, not someone demanding answers. But he held up a very large hand before she said another word.

"Welcome to Bayou Allain, Miss Ferrer. Any friend of dear Lisa's is someone we are very happy to have stop by. I am, as King told you, Terrill's father." He offered that same hand across the table. "Judge Terrill Landry. Known to my friends here as Bear."

Micky shook his hand. "My pleasure, Judge Landry. Your Honor."

"It's Bear," he said, covering their joined hands with his other, lingering a bit too long for her comfort while continuing to take her measure.

She took his as well. She could tell he was the sort of man who would respect her straightforward nature more than any show of meekness—especially when it would be just that, a show.

"Please, call me Micky," she said as she coolly extricated herself from his hold and sat back in the booth. "I apologize for intruding on your evening, and for keeping you from your nightcap."

"You're not intruding, *chère*. Not at all."

Chère. It sounded so faux when he said it, so Big Easy. She smiled as if finding it charming. "Thank you. It's just that I'm having no luck in finding her. The cell number I have for her isn't working. And she wasn't at home when I stopped by."

She left out the part about Lisa's curtain-peeping neighbors being of no help. For all she knew, they were this man's good friends and had already told him about the new girl in town nosing around.

He took a long moment to respond. She wasn't sure if he was using the time to fabricate a story or deciding if he believed enough of hers to help her out. If he didn't, she'd go home and face the music playing there.

She'd be fine without her father's approval. Definitely fine without his choice of a husband. Life would go on even if she had partied herself out of a job, though she would need time to come to terms with defending her life, with reconstructing her future from the salvaged remnants of her past. Lisa could help her get started. Lisa had always been the practical one of the two, Micky the impetuous other.

"I would love to put you in touch with our Lisa," Judge Landry was saying. "Unfortunately, neither Terrill nor I have seen her since Monday."

Just like that. No warning. No preparation. No easing her into the truth. No change to his tone of voice as if he was worried or mourning or simply used to her running off.

She hoped her face registered at least some of the shock that had stolen her voice because she couldn't think of anything to ask. "I don't understand," she finally came up with. "Are you telling me you don't know where she is? Or just that she's not home right now?"

The judge reached for his drink, eyeballed her over the rim of the glass as he sipped. "I remember you now. You're the one who wasn't able to make it to the wedding. You know, that was a big disappointment to our girl."

The ceremony had been a small private affair in New Orleans, one with very little notice—the couple couldn't wait—and Micky hadn't been able to reschedule a trip to Italy on behalf of Ferrer.

She'd paid for the couple's honeymoon as a wedding gift, knowing that the long weekend in St. Barts—the only time Terrill had been able to take off from work—hardly made up for missing her best friend's important day.

Lisa had told her not to worry, and Micky hadn't, because she had never heard the other woman sound so happy, as if her entire world had been out of balance until Terrill had set it to rights. "It was a big disappointment to me, too. I would have been there if I could."

"What was it I heard?" he asked, frowning. "You took a trip to Europe instead?"

What was he trying to do? What was he implying? "The trip was work and had been planned for months. There was nothing I could do."

"The way the newspapers reported it, work wasn't all that kept you busy while you were there."

The old codger. He'd known who she was all along. She was not going to get into *that* indiscretion with this man. Her irritation mounting, she crossed her arms, crossed her legs. "You haven't answered my question, Your Honor. Do you know where Lisa is, or don't you?"

He looked her straight in the eye. His eyes were hard, dark, and suddenly cold. "Neither Terrill nor I have any idea."

"Are you looking for her?" Micky asked, her stomach beginning to ache. "Is there anything I can do?"

"You can tell me if you've heard from her."

"Would I be here if I had?"

"I don't know. Would you?"

Unbelievable. "You mean would I come all the way down here and act surprised that she's gone just to cover for her and throw you off her trail?"

She'd met this man less than fifteen minutes ago, yet he was suspecting her motives? Questioning her honesty? Reading into her arrival a lot of underhanded scheming that wasn't there?

"First of all, no. I wouldn't do that for anyone. I don't believe hiding from a problem is a way to solve it." Oh, what a liar she was. "Second, that would assume Lisa has a problem to hide from, and in all our time together, I never knew her to hide from anything."

"Meaning?" he prompted, the tic in his jaw giving away . . . something.

She'd made him mad. She didn't believe for a moment that she had frightened him. She couldn't see this man being afraid of anything. She also couldn't see him brushing off what was effectively a challenge.

"Meaning, if anything was going on with her, you would know better than me. I haven't talked to her in ages. My last contact from her, in fact, was a note she dropped me a week or so ago."

"And that's what brought you here?"

That note had been what she'd latched on to, what she'd used as a reason to make the trip. But that wasn't what he was asking. And his question seemed less like casual conversation and more like bait dangling from a hook.

"She told me to visit whenever I could." That was the truth. "This seemed like a good time." That was another.

"Because of something she said in her note?"

Micky wasn't about to tell him that the timing had been spur of the moment, or that all she remembered Lisa saying was that she'd been left out of some loop. She considered asking him if that rang any bells.

Then she reconsidered, saying instead, "Because I had the time and was in the mood for a change of scenery. And because I miss her, and it's been too long."

"Do you have the note with you?"

Talk about a bulldog. She cocked her head to the side, wondering if he was playing hide, or if he was playing seek. "It might be in my things, but it might be on my dressing table. I'm not sure. Why do you ask?"

"You say she had nothing to hide from, yet you haven't talked to her in awhile. It's possible things have changed. It's possible there's a hint in that note of what she had on her mind when she left."

He tossed back the rest of his drink and swallowed. "I learned a long time ago with Terrill's mother that a woman will often share things with a close female friend that she doesn't want her husband to know."

Her husband? Or her father-in-law? "Some women, sure. Not Lisa. We might be best girlfriends, but she told me more than once that Terrill is her vault. She shares all of her secrets with him."

She paused, thinking of what she'd just said and growing

more than worried, reaching toward panic, her chest band-
ing tight. "Have you asked him if there was anything upset-
ting her? If she'd mentioned needing to get away?"

He slammed his fist on the table. "Of course I have. The
boy doesn't know a goddamn thing."

She was used to Papi's outbursts, his dramatic gestures
while he paced and implored the saints, asking them how a
man was supposed to handle a daughter like his "little
Micky Mousey," praying for guidance to understand why
he had been chosen for such a test.

This wasn't like that at all. This was . . . frightening.

Her stomach fluttering, Micky waited for the boom of the
judge's thunderous explosion, the loud crack of his hand
against the table to stop rattling in her bones. Even in the
bar's dim light, his face was the bright red of hypertension,
a cartoonish picture of a human balloon enlarging, expand-
ing. She wasn't going to wait around for him to pop.

She slid from the booth, got to her feet, adjusted the strap
of her purse across her body, and reached into a small inside
pouch for a business card. She set it on the table. "I'll be on
my way. Should Lisa get in touch with me, I'll relay your
concern. I hope you'll do the same."

She spun away before he could answer. From the stool
where he sat, legs spread wide, elbows propped on the bar,
King Trahan shrugged, his smile, his charm the only sign of
southern hospitality she'd seen since walking into the bar.

She tilted her head in thanks and turned toward the
door—then was nearly mowed down by one of the two
burly locals shoving past her as they headed for the corner
and the judge.

Once outside, she bounded down the porch steps and ran
for her car. Enough with fighting her way through the swamp
of good and evil. The faster she could get back to New York,
the faster she could hire a P.I. and get him on the case.

Seven

Simon remembered this drive. The road was in better shape now than when he'd made it last, but the trees still grew the same distance from the blacktop, rooted in the same marshy swamp that made pulling over to fix a flat the same iffy proposition it had been back then.

He'd done it enough times to know, hadn't gotten stuck more than a few, had ended up splattered with mud after pushing from the rear while King floored the accelerator to free them. He'd done the same to King a few times, leaving his cousin wearing a good chunk of the swamp. Most of the time they'd been just drunk enough to laugh it off.

For years they'd been inseparable, the best of friends, the worst of enemies, more like brothers than cousins—not surprising since each had been given a room in both the Baptiste and Trahan households, and they'd grown up together, roaming the fields of Le Hasard.

The land King still lived on.

The land Simon now owned.

He swerved to avoid the carcass of a possum that had run out of luck crossing the road. Having no idea how long he'd be in Bayou Allain, he'd made the drive from New York in his own truck, one outfitted with equipment he might not need but would never find in a rental.

The trip had given him plenty of time to think—not only about where he was headed and why, but about all of the reasons he hadn't been back to Louisiana since the day he'd shipped out for basic, the same day King had boarded a bus for Angola and four years in the pen.

He'd also spent a lot of hours wondering what their lives might have been like if he *had* returned to Louisiana after his discharge, if he *had* worked over the well their fathers had drilled, planted crops or an orchard, ran cattle on those four thousand acres.

If he and his cousin *had* ironed out their differences and found common ground for a new start. If they *had* settled the feud that neither of them admitted to starting.

Their fathers had made a living off the land, two roughnecks who'd married sisters and become brothers by law. They'd started their families at the same time, intending to establish a dynasty to rival that of the Landrys.

The gold coin Simon's father had found on the property had been the good-luck charm he swore would make it happen. Simon and King had gone along with the fun and grown as close as two boys could be. A large part of that was due to all the secrets they shared.

King had been the one to shoot out the windows in the junior high gym when he got benched for missing track too many days in a row.

Simon told no one else but King what he'd done to Judy Gaines in the corner of the stage during seventh grade rehearsals for *A Christmas Carol*.

King had nailed Patsy Thibodeaux before she liked it so much she gave it away to the whole high school football team at Christmas. Talk about a mascot.

And Simon, well, Simon had egged Principal Scott's car

for no reason but King betting him a week's worth of chores that he didn't have the balls.

It wasn't until the fire at graduation that the tension between them began. They'd been on their own by then, their parents gone, their closeness strained.

The last time he'd seen King had been in the courthouse for sentencing. Simon had chosen to enlist rather than serve time, but King had wanted to stay close to home and to be as far away from Simon as he could get.

He had gotten both of his wishes and had returned to Bayou Allain after his release, determined to make a go of Le Hasard. Simon had served three tours of duty, having no real home to return to, nothing calling him back to civilian life.

After his discharge, he'd worked private security for a firm that paid him more money than he'd ever need to provide protection for contractors and media types assigned to the world's hot spots.

That was where Hank Smithson had found him—specifically in Afghanistan guarding bodies in danger hell-bent on hitting the evening news. The offer he hadn't been able to refuse had included a move to Manhattan. The change of scenery had appealed—as had the thought of a home of his own, since he'd had nothing but a post office box for sixteen years.

That had been four years ago.

He'd been thirty-four, young enough to crave the adventure, old enough to know when to say no, experienced enough to get himself out of the scrapes that came with the job of being an SG-5 operative. The physical scrapes, anyway. He wasn't doing quite as well with the mental.

Shaking off the recent past and that even farther away, he slowed as he reached the bridge that crossed the swampland giving Bayou Allain its name. A fire truck, an ambulance, and three cars from the sheriff's department blocked all but one slice of road.

Simon could understand why. Hitting the abutment at too high a speed had not fared well for the car below, its front end buried in the muck, its underbelly exposed to the elements and covered in the detritus of the swamp.

The scene wasn't fresh. The car's wheels weren't spinning. He didn't see signs of a driver or passenger, though that could be explained by the ambulance. At least the parish coroner wasn't on-site.

He made it across the bridge without incident, sped up for the last half mile before the turn into his property, and headed for the house in which he'd grown up. Seeing King was going to require a concerted effort. He wouldn't know where to find his cousin's path to cross it.

So much for the family dynasty, he mused, his truck rolling to a stop in front of a two-story frame structure that he barely recognized as his childhood home. What in the hell was Savoy Realty doing with the money he sent monthly for maintenance? Why hadn't Lorna asked for more if she needed it?

No wonder she hadn't been able to keep the place rented. The gap on the most recent rental report was suddenly making a whole lot of sense. He took a minute to shake off the burst of anger, then climbed out of the truck.

He'd haul in his gear after he checked out the house, gauged whether or not it was livable or if his options for the night were sleeping in his truck or pitching a tent. He wasn't up to rooming with raccoons, possums, and rats.

The porch steps were solid enough, though the railing wouldn't have supported the weight of a bird. He shook it again. He'd have to round up a hammer and nails, pick up a couple of new two-by-fours. . . . Uh, no. He wouldn't. Not until he got with Lorna to see what was going on.

He was checking out the warped porch and the fit of the

screen door's frame when he heard a noise inside. The back door opened into the kitchen, and he knew critters enjoyed burrowing into cupboards, beneath old appliances, even holing up under floorboards.

Except how many of those critters had figured out pumping the handle to bring up water from the well to the sink?

He slid the Smith & Wesson M&P .357 he wore at his waist from its holster, took hold of the doorknob, and slowly turned it, pushing inward until he saw movement, then slamming the door open, swinging up his hands, gun at the ready.

"Who the hell—?" was all he got out before realizing he knew exactly who his trespasser was.

He'd just never seen her like this . . . standing at a kitchen sink, her dark hair caught on top of her head with a John Deere cap, a sheer push-up bra and a pair of rubber waders the only clothes she wore.

He engaged the safety and holstered the semiautomatic, chuckling under his breath with as much humor as disbelief. If only the guys from "Page Six" could see their favorite pair of tits and ass now.

Billboard or not, he couldn't help a smirk. "If it isn't Michelina Ferrer, heiress to the Ferrer Fragrances empire, in almost nothing but flesh."

Her lips trembled in response, the pallor of her face nearly the same shade as the shocked whites of her eyes.

He sobered, taking a closer look at the bruise on her right cheekbone, the scrape on the same shoulder, the duct tape on her arm that looked to be a makeshift bandage.

Then he remembered the accident he'd passed.

And he swore.

"It wasn't an accident, was it?" he asked, and she crumpled to the floor, shaking her head as a sob filled with fear shook her body.

Eight

Micky didn't care if she ever got up off this floor. She didn't care that it was sticky with things she couldn't name and smelled like ones even worse. She didn't care about the photos of her bare ass all of Manhattan had talked about with their morning bagels and coffee. All she cared about was not having a chance to tell Papi good-bye.

This man . . . When he'd burst through the door, she'd been certain he'd come to finish what his buddies had started. She hadn't been at all surprised that he'd found her. After being run off the road and bounced like a red rubber ball, she hadn't had strength to walk far.

It had been dark. She'd been more than a bit disoriented. Stumbling onto this place had been pure dumb luck. For a local, especially one wanting to know if she'd made it out alive, it would've been an obvious place to look.

It took another minute for her to realize this one wasn't a local. He had a Cajun flavor to his voice, but his presence and his attitude were more New York and the world. And then there were his clothes.

His boots were Mark Nason, his jeans designer chic, his black T-shirt silk instead of faded cotton stretched to accommodate a belly fond of fried catfish and beer. He didn't have a belly at all.

Whoever he was, she'd bet half her inheritance he knew the difference between Central Park East and West. The other half of the money she was going to need to get herself out of whatever this was she'd stumbled into.

Then she remembered he knew her name, knew who she was, and had been surprised to see her. Maybe her life was flashing before her eyes for no reason.

He knelt in front of her, his hand going to her cheek, the cheek that she was certain was the color of dead fish. She tried not to flinch, but he saw it, the fear that came with not knowing who he was or what he wanted.

She tilted her head to the side, away from his touch. "Who are you?"

"This is my house," was all he said, moving his gaze to the shoulder that hurt like the worst Brazilian wax.

"You don't live here." It was an obvious statement, but she didn't know what else to say.

She was the one who had no rights here, the one who had broken into a house she'd thought abandoned, looking for safety and shelter while she figured out what to do.

She didn't have a lot of experience with people wanting to kill her. She'd been skewered in the press, flayed on gossip TV, skinned raw by paparazzi who had no qualms about making her bleed.

But to be chased down a dark road while in an unfamiliar car with no clue as to where she was going . . . Dear God, when that truck had rammed her . . . when she'd seen the reflection of her headlights on the bayou below . . . the water rushing up at her . . .

Her skin grew clammy, and her heart rate, which had finally begun to slow, started up again, hammering harder than before. And now, again, here came her life flashing.

"No, I don't live here," he said, his voice distracting her, though she could still see the glare of the lights, the ripple of water. "This place isn't good for much but camping out, though you've probably figured that out on your own."

She nodded, repeated, "Who are you? And how do you know who I am?"

He sat back on his heels, and she noticed for the first time that his hair was pulled back into a low tail at his nape. She reached up to remove the cap she wore from her head. It had kept her hair out of her eyes while she'd scrubbed the bayou's mud out of her clothes.

But now it only made her feel ugly, out of her element. Oh, hell. Who was she kidding?

She wore no makeup, and nothing but the waders she'd found and her bra. Even her panties were hanging with the rest of her things on lawn chairs she'd placed to catch the breeze from upstairs windows missing their glass.

The chairs were far enough inside the rooms not to be visible to anyone outside looking up, and the broken windows wouldn't draw attention the way open ones would. Oh, good. She was thinking like a woman on the lam—a far cry from embracing the limelight.

And look where that had got her, she mused, then shuddered, wrapped her arms over her middle, the movement tugging at the tape serving as a bandage on her arm; she sucked back a breath in response.

"My name is Simon Baptiste. I know who you are because your face is on a billboard I can see from my patio." He took hold of her forearm and peeled the tape back, watched her face as she grimaced. "And if you don't get this stitched up, you're going to have a battle scar to put my dozen to shame."

"You have battle scars?" she asked, knowing he was right, knowing, too, that at this moment in time a scar was the least of her worries. That's why they made long sleeves.

"More than a few." He pushed up to his feet, offered her his hand, and helped her up. The waders squeaked and crinkled as she moved. "What happened to your clothes?"

"I washed them out. They were full of leaves and mud and squirmy things."

He offered her a kind smile. "I'm guessing you don't have others."

"I do. In the trunk of my car." Where they weren't doing anyone but the fish any good.

"Let me grab my gear. I've got soap and towels, and a pair of boxers I can donate to the cause."

"How about a T-shirt to go with the shorts?" The bra covered her, but it was still a bra—and the one thing she still needed to wash. "At least until my shirt dries."

"That I can do," he said, heading for the door.

"And coffee? I know it's asking a lot, but I am beyond exhausted."

"I hear sleep's good for that." His eyes flashed, but not with his smile as much as with the fire to right a grave wrong.

"You try closing your eyes when you see nothing but water ready to swallow you whole like some big gulping mouth." Not to mention headlights flying at you like bullets, or the grille of the truck they belong to grinning like the devil rising from hell.

Even worse was seeing it all with her eyes wide open, and feeling the impact in every one of her bones hours later. She'd lived a life of luxury, and Pilates or not, had no idea she could hurt this bad.

"I brought food for a week—"

"Food for one. I only need coffee." Even that was imposing, but she honestly couldn't find it in her to care. As long as he was one of the good guys and could get her out of this nightmare and back to New York . . .

"For one, yeah. But there are groceries to be had down here in the bayou, *chère*." He pulled open the door. "Let me unload the goods, get the generator going, and then you can tell me how the heiress to the Ferrer fortune wound up ass over end in the swamp."

Nine

By the time his guest returned, freshly showered and shampooed and dressed in his things, Simon had thrown together a breakfast of scrambled eggs, bacon, coffee, and toast. He didn't immediately turn around and greet her but focused on piling the food on paper plates, digging into his box of grub for sugar and powdered cream.

Concentrating on what was simple kept him from facing the complications that came attached like baggage to Michelina Ferrer. It was a different sort of baggage than what he'd been dealing with the last few weeks, but her being here was still going to weigh heavy on his mind.

Dealing with Bear and Lorna and the property would be enough to try any saint. Add King to the mix, and, well, Simon's patience wouldn't pass the first test. And now he had a mystery on his hands, a crime that needed more explanation before it would begin to make sense.

That was the only reason he finally turned around, the only reason he lifted his gaze from the food he carried to the woman standing in the frame of the kitchen doorway toweling dry her dark hair.

Her face was the same one he'd seen on "Page Six," on

magazine covers, on TV. The same one from his billboard.
The same one . . . but not.

Her skin was scrubbed clean. She wore nothing glossy on
her lips, nothing colored and glittery on her eyes, nothing to
smooth out her cool ivory skin. She had freckles on her
nose, two small red zits on her chin.

And her eyes were sad and scared, not sassy or sultry or
seductive. A big problem, her eyes. An equally big one, her
unbound breasts beneath his gray T-shirt, the curve of her
hips and thighs in his long-legged briefs.

He set the food on the table, cleared his throat, went
back for the Styrofoam cups filled with coffee and for plastic-
ware. He didn't turn back toward her until he heard her sit,
the chair legs scraping across the worn linoleum, the creak
of the wood beneath her weight.

The table hid most of her body. He could still make out
the shape of her breasts, the fullness, the upper slope that
made him wonder about the weight he'd feel beneath.
But there wasn't a damn thing he could do to avoid her face,
so bare and exposed, or her eyes.

He had to look at her to get her story. He had to watch
her expression, see the truth, her fear, find out how much
she knew or had guessed or thought about what had happened. This is what he did—gathered information, ferreted
out intel, zoned in on the pertinent details, used it all to
come up with a plan of action.

He needed one. Desperately. One that had nothing to do
with her body being naked under his clothes, one that ad-
dressed the fact that she was Michelina Ferrer. And she was
miserable, frightened, and lost.

He couldn't help it. He feared that juxtaposition—what
he knew about the celebrity versus what he sensed about
this woman with her armor washed away and fearing for her
life—was going to make it hard to keep this job from turning personal.

"Let's start at the beginning." He stopped, scooped up a bite of eggs. "You *are* Michelina Ferrer."

"Micky. Michelina is what my father calls me to make sure I know I'm in trouble."

"How old are you?"

She arched one of those famous dark brows. "My age is relevant how?"

"I wasn't sure if the being-in-trouble-with-your-father thing was past tense or present." Then again, he'd seen her antics reported in the press. The parties. The other women. The drinking. The men.

She looked down at her plate, piled eggs onto her toast as if she hadn't eaten in weeks. "I'll no doubt be in trouble with my father over something until one of us buries the other."

She said it matter-of-factly, and he wondered what her father would think about the trouble she was in now. If he would worry more about the reputation of Ferrer Fragrances or his daughter's safety should news get out about the danger she'd stumbled into.

"Micky, then. What could possibly bring you to Bayou Allain?" If he knew why she was here, he might be able to figure out why someone would run her off the road.

Then he wondered if whoever it was had fled once the car hit the water, or if they'd stuck around to see if she climbed free of the wreckage and followed her here. His stomach knotted around the bitter coffee and overcooked eggs.

She sighed, sat back in the chair, pulled her heels up into the seat, covering her legs with his shirt as she did so, and wrapped her arms around her knees. "I came to visit a friend. It was a spur-of-the-moment trip, and I didn't let her know I was coming. I wanted it to be a surprise."

Something in her expression, in the way she'd physically curled in on herself, made him wonder what had happened right before that spur of the moment, and if she'd headed south to avoid having her father call her Michelina.

"Who's the friend?"

"Lisa Weston." She shook her head. "Lisa Landry. We went to school together," she was saying when Simon interrupted.

"Landry? As in Terrill?" Whoa.

She nodded. "She's married to a deputy. Her father-in-law was a judge here, but then you probably know that, this being your house."

Simon was mulling over her connection to the Landrys and the odds of tying it to her accident when she added, "And neither one of them knows where she is."

His head came up and he frowned, watching as she reached for her toast, now sagging underneath the weight of the egg mountain she'd made. "What do you mean, they don't know where she is?"

She shrugged as she chewed and swallowed, then reached for her coffee and drank. "Just what I said. They haven't seen her since Monday."

Today was Thursday. Double whoa. "Has she officially been listed as a missing person?"

"Her husband's law enforcement. I'm assuming he's got that covered."

True enough. "What did he tell you?"

She continued to cradle her cup. "I haven't seen him to talk to. I only talked to the judge, if you can call what went on talking."

"What did go on?" He knew how Bear Landry operated, how intimidation was as natural to him as the tumbler of scotch in his hand.

She took on a look of disbelief. "I don't remember ever being bullied minutes after meeting any man. Or letting anyone I don't know so thoroughly provoke me that I say things I'm afraid I'll regret."

Eh, yeah. She'd definitely met the judge. "From what

I've read about you, that's not so unusual. That regretting business."

She narrowed her eyes, the glare not one of denial, just one letting him know she didn't care for the reminder, even if he wasn't too far off the mark.

"This was different. I've never been run down for speaking my mind. By the press, sure. Not by a truck the size of a small building."

"Tell me about the truck."

"It was big."

Uh, not helpful. "Color? Make or model?"

"I know taxis. I don't know trucks."

"A pickup with a bed? An SUV?"

"It was behind me. All I saw were the lights. And eventually the grille."

"No emblem in the center? Stickers on the bumper? More than one person inside?"

She shook her head, kept shaking it.

"What about a horn? Did the driver honk at you?"

She frowned, concentrating. "He might have."

"What did it sound like?" he asked, and when she looked at him as if she didn't understand, added, "The truck's horn. The sound."

"Like a horn. I don't know. Loud. That's all I remember, and I might even be imagining that. Maybe it was the sound of the impact, or the sound of hitting the water." She shoved away from the table, surged to her feet, was across the room and in front of the window before he could react.

Probably a good thing, her leaving the table, since he didn't know what his reaction would be. She was smart. She had snap. Even after what she'd been through, she hadn't been cowed.

But she was frustrating him all to hell, and he didn't know if that was because she couldn't answer his questions, or if it had to do with seeing her wearing his clothes.

He glanced over, saw her start to lean forward, her hands on the lip of the sink, then jump away, pressing her back to the side of the refrigerator.

Her face was pale, her brown eyes even darker with the surrounding skin gone white. "Does anyone know that you're here?"

That he was coming? Yes. That he was already here? On his feet, Simon strode to the window. A dusty white pickup had just appeared at the head of his drive. "I'll see who it is. You bag up your trash and haul ass upstairs. Take it with you. Breakfast for one I can explain."

He continued to watch the truck's approach while behind him Micky scurried around grabbing up the evidence of her presence. He turned back long enough to see her snatch two eggshells from the pile on the stove, as if he wasn't capable of downing the half dozen he'd scrambled.

The idea made him want to laugh. Micky's panicked movements made him want to smile. Both responses were way out of line. Nothing about this scenario should have inspired so much as the thought of laughter.

But then Michelina Ferrer had no idea who he was. Or that small-town criminal minds were nothing in the scheme of what he'd faced as an operative for SG-5.

Ten

Micky huddled on the floor of the closet in the second-story bedroom farthest down the hall from the stairs. She'd left the door cracked an inch for air and for light, but even that felt like too much exposure.

She wanted more than anything to close her eyes and sleep, but she couldn't. Not until he came back and told her she was safe. Not until she knew more about what had happened after she'd left Red's.

She hoped Simon would get her the answers. At least the ones that would explain who had run her off the road and why—and how Lisa's disappearance fit in, if it did.

Then there was the question of where she was, this house, her hideout. And the other one nibbling at her with tiny pointed teeth.

Who in the world was Simon Baptiste?

He owned this place. He lived in Manhattan. She lived in Manhattan. She'd taken refuge in this place.

She wasn't a conspiracy theorist, but this fluke was too close for comfort. If he'd followed her here, if Papi had sent him, she wanted to know who he was. A bloodhound nose that good would be a big help in finding Lisa.

His following her she could buy—with a really big stretch

of credulity. But her ending up in his house—out of all the places along all the world's bayous—she couldn't buy as anything but a quirk of fate.

And that reasoning made it a lot easier to accept that he wasn't in cahoots with the bad guys. That he really was on her side.

He couldn't have known about the billboard on East Houston if he hadn't seen it or had someone tell him it was there. And even Papi wasn't good enough to have hired a P.I.—should that be what Simon was—who owned property in the town where she'd gone to lick her self-inflicted wounds.

Unless Papi had made the connection in the past, anticipating that one day she'd run to Lisa—and had arranged to have Simon in his pocket just in case.

Or maybe Simon really didn't own the house at all.

Stop! No more analyzing the situation to death. Her instincts insisted that her questions about Lisa had made someone uncomfortable, and that that someone had taken pains to make sure she didn't ask them anymore.

She thought of Kingdom Trahan, Mr. Southern Hospitality himself. Had his Cajun charm been a ruse designed to get her to open up about her visit? How could he have known that having no luck elsewhere, she'd stop in at Red's—except that Red's was the only place to stop?

She thought back to the man who'd nearly knocked her flat on her way out of the bar. She wondered if he drove as recklessly as he walked, if he drove under orders to see that she met her end.

Now she was overanalyzing *and* overdramatizing. Except what she was thinking made too much sense not to be exactly what had happened.

And none of it would she ever be able to prove.

*   *   *

Simon leaned a shoulder against one of the beams flanking the stairs to the porch, tucked his fingers in the pockets of his jeans, and watched the approaching truck navigate the ruts in his road. He didn't know any of the local bubbas who had the run of the bayou, but he doubted this visit was about seeing if the prodigal son had come home.

He knew a whole lot of the folks in Bayou Allain blamed him for King's troubles. They saw his time in the service as a dodge to keep him out of Louisiana and Kingdom out of his hair, when the truth was, with his cousin despising his position as landlord, he'd felt it best to make his life elsewhere.

But, no. This bunch of rowdies wasn't expecting to find the owner of the property waiting to greet them. They braked the truck in its tracks when they saw his vehicle parked along the side of the house.

Simon pushed away from the beam—it was really in no shape to hold his weight, and falling flat on his face would kill his advantage—and moved from the porch to the top step.

At his movement, the truck started up again, though it seemed in less of a hurry than before, the occupants no doubt throwing together a quick story explaining why they'd ignored the posted NO TRESPASSING signs.

The truck rattled to a stop not far from where he stood, and two men he'd never seen climbed down from the cab. The driver left the engine idling.

Simon would've complained about the noise making conversation difficult, except the noise would also mask any sounds coming from inside the house. "Mornin', gents. What brings you out to my place?"

After a glance skittered between the two strangers, the beefier one moved his chaw from one cheek to the other, spit a dark stream of tobacco to the ground, and said, "Your place, huh? Guess that would make you Trahan's cousin. Baptiste, right?"

Simon gave a single nod. "That would be me."

"You got any identification?" asked the second one, a slender stick of a man. He slapped a palm on the hood of the truck, then moved his hand when the metal began to burn.

"You're the one trespassing," Simon said, biting back a laugh. "I could ask you the same."

The first man stepped forward. "I believe you're who you say. I've seen pictures from your trial."

"That so?" Simon crossed his arms, raised a brow. "That trial was near on twenty years ago, boo. You doing a research paper or something? Digging into the local past?"

The man didn't miss a beat. "You weren't around when your cousin came home after he was sprung from Angola. The TV ran the whole story again. With pictures of you and King both."

But no Lorna. Simon wondered if his cousin had even mentioned to anyone that Lorna had been there that night. "News around here must still be as slow as the bayou if that story got a rerun four years after the fact."

Another stream of tobacco juice hit the ground, this one only inches from the bottom step of the porch.

"A family that's suffered as much tragedy as yours tends to get a lot of attention. Not saying it's deserving, mind you. Just that here we see to our own. We don't run halfway around the world to solve problems others don't want us involved in."

If Simon had given a shit what these two yokels thought, he'd have been down the steps introducing them to Mr. Smith and Mr. Wesson, whom he'd charged with enforcing his NO TRESPASSING signs.

But the greeting he'd been given was no less than he'd expected, so he looked from one to the other and did his best to piss them off with a smile.

"Guess the years have been good to me seeing that I've stuck in your mind all this time." Simon watched the first man's face mottle up and grow red. "Now, since we've established that I'm who I say I am, let's get back to you two."

"We're working with the sheriff's department. Search and rescue." This from the man who'd been rubbing at his burned palm all this time. "Not sure if you would've seen it, but a car went off the bridge last night. We can't find hide nor hair of the driver."

Simon knew the bayou, knew if a body didn't surface, folks would assume that gators had eaten their fill. The idea of these two skunks getting away with murder because of Micky going into the water where she had rankled.

And realizing he hadn't pictured that scenario earlier, that of Micky thrashing her way out of her car and into those steel-trap jaws, made the eggs in his stomach curdle. He'd seen a gator take down a deer. Thinking of Michelina Ferrer being in that situation . . .

"Course that's not too surprising when you think about all the things that call that water home," the skinny one finished.

Simon's head came up. "Convenient for whoever it was who ran the car off the road."

The big guy butted in. "The sheriff's not saying she was run off the road. Who told you that?"

"She? If you haven't found the driver, how do you know you're looking for a she?"

"Car's a rental. Woman picked it up yesterday in New Orleans."

If they were truly working with the sheriff, that meant law enforcement was aware of Micky's identity—and very soon they'd realize they had a missing celeb. Before the story hit the press, she needed to get in touch with her family, let them know she was all right.

Unless keeping everyone in the dark would get her to the bottom of this mystery sooner than were she to announce that she was alive and well and slumming at his place. He needed to think about this, weigh all the options.

He glanced from Laurel to Hardy. "If you're here looking to man a hunting party, count me out. I've seen all the killing I care to for a lifetime."

"We're talking alligators, man. Not human beings," said the scrawny one. "But we're not going hunting. Not yet anyways. We're looking to see if the woman managed to get herself to shelter. Your place is about as close to the bridge as it gets."

"Then I'll keep an eye out," was all Simon said. He didn't want a lie to come back and bite him in the ass, so saying as little as possible under the circumstances seemed his best bet. "But right now, I need to grab the rest of my gear and get settled. If you'll excuse me."

Neither one moved. The larger one spoke. "That mean you're sticking around for a while?"

"Only as long as my business takes."

"So it's true, then. You're here to kick King out on his ass," the larger man said.

"Is that the story going around?" Simon asked, his mouth tightening around the words. "I guess anyone who's interested will just have to wait and see what happens. But since you've got an accident victim to find, I figure my business with King is none of yours."

The two strangers seemed conflicted, as if they wanted to stay and dig for more dirt but knew they'd blow their story if they didn't go.

And so they both took to nodding, backing toward the still-running truck, climbing inside, and taking a minute for a meeting of the minds. It didn't take long.

Big guy, the driver, finally leaned out his window to call, "Be sure and let the sheriff know if you run across any sign of the woman."

Simon raised a hand, not bothering to remind them that they hadn't given him any information about what he should look for. No description, nothing.

And so instead of answering, he waved them on their way, muttering, "Over my dead body."

A thud, then an echo, jolted Micky awake. The darkness was everywhere, enveloping, only a slit of light branding her eyes. She was sitting, the surface beneath her hard, not soft like the bed she loved so much.

And the smell. Stale, musty, . . . old. Unused.

Where was she?

Yet no sooner had the question entered her mind than she knew, she remembered. She was freezing, shaking, her skin crawling with things she couldn't see, but she didn't dare shake them off.

Something had happened, out there in the room, to jerk her awake. She held her breath, waiting, tears scalding her skin as they fell, as she wondered again if she was going to die.

And then the door opened, the light blinding her. She raised her forearm to shield her eyes, then felt his hand— Simon's hand—close around her wrist and help her to her feet.

She dusted off her backside and her legs, realizing if she was covered with anything it was only dust, though that didn't stop her from brushing at the clothes she wore, at her hair, at the tingles and tickles that she couldn't shake.

Then he was there, holding her, bringing her to his body, cupping the back of her head with his hand, soothing her, his voice soft and reassuring as it rumbled beneath her cheek.

"I'm getting you wet," she squeaked out, pulling her face away from his shirt and swiping her palm over the tracks of her tears.

"I want you to do something for me," he said, and as safe

as he made her feel, she couldn't imagine telling him no—a situation that was as unexpected as the way the heat of his body caused her heart to race.

She nodded, wiping her eyes, deciding it a more non-committal response than saying, "Anything." She'd apparently lost her backbone in the water. She could only hope it surfaced soon.

"Here, look." He turned her toward the room's bed, a mattress and box springs and cast-iron frame. He had spread out a sleeping bag on top, readied another to use as a blanket. The tiny camp pillow he'd added looked like heaven in plaid flannel.

She had never been this exhausted in her life.

"You need to sleep. You also need to see a doctor for that arm, but we'll take care of that this afternoon." He walked her to the bed. She climbed into it on her hands and knees, her eyes already closing again.

Once she was all tucked in—she tried to manage on her own, a small show of independence, not wanting to appear weak when that's exactly what she was, and oh my, but did his hands feel good and solid and warm—she asked him, "Who was that? What did they want?"

"Later. First, you sleep."

Her eyes drifted open. She looked up into his, which were green like willows, like springtime. "You'll be here? While I sleep?" When he hesitated, she reached for his wrist and added, "Please?"

"I'd planned to visit my property management company around noon, but I can wait. It'll give me time to take a look around this place and see what sort of repairs I'm going to need to do if I'm going to stay a few days."

That was all she needed to hear. Her stomach settled. Warmth followed, washing over her skin. The last thought to cross her mind before sleep took her was that if he was going to stay here a few days, then she was, too.

Eleven

L orna Savoy paced the width of her office so many times Bear found himself fighting off nausea. Her office was small, and she wore the worst god-awful perfume, always had, and if she thought bathing in an extra splash of the stuff today was going to lure Simon Baptiste into her web, she was wrong, because the truth of the matter was, the smell would probably make the man retch.

Even so, Bear couldn't deny that Lorna was a fine-looking woman. She'd kept herself tight, and she wore clothes that showed off her body. The skirt she had on was straight and gray, her heels tall and black, her blouse a pattern of red and white and black belted snug to her waist.

He watched the twitch of her hips, followed the bounce of her tits, remembered how firm her ass felt clutched tight in his hands as she rode him, her nipples pouting into his face, her pussy dripping all over his pole like she was trying to put out a fire.

He waited, shifted . . . nothing. Not a bit of stirring in his shorts. It was a sad day when a man could admire a woman like Lorna, when he could remember the smell of her twat, the taste of it salty and wet, but needed a pill to get hard enough to put himself up inside her.

She'd stopped in front of the window on the far side of the room, the one facing the parking lot of the strip mall where she rented her office space. Or where, in truth, Bear rented it, since the biggest part of her real estate income came from deals he sent her way.

"Lorna, *chère*. Do you really want him to catch you at the window drooling like some teenage girl in heat?"

"Oh, Baby Bear. What do you know about teenage girls?" A hint of humor in her voice, she cocked her hip and leaned forward, her palms on the window's ledge.

The way she was standing lifted her ass until it tempted him in a way he couldn't ignore. He'd always liked sticking it to her ass. "I knew you when you were eighteen, didn't I?"

She fluttered her fingers in his direction but didn't turn. "I don't want to talk about that. I just want him to get here so I can explain what we worked out. How it's hard keeping renters when they find they're sharing the place with an arsonist, not to mention living in a house where a woman took her own life.

"I mean, once he sees there's been no reason to keep up the place, I can give him back his money, right? And then pray he doesn't ask why I didn't tell him all this before." She pushed away from the window, circled the room to stand behind her desk chair, swiveling it back and forth.

Her nerves were getting on his nerves. "You never told him before because you have no way to contact him except through his post office box. And you didn't want to risk mailing a refund check without him knowing it was on the way."

She continued to rock the chair side to side. "I just don't know that he'll buy that. He's not a stupid man. Won't he want to know why I didn't just write him and tell him I needed him to call?"

Bear straightened the collar of the dress shirt he wore with his suit coat but without a tie. "He may have washed his hands of Bayou Allain a long time ago, but he won't have forgotten how we do things down here. He can want to know all manner of things. That doesn't mean he's going to get the answers he wants, or like the ones we give him."

The only one getting what he wanted here was Bear. And what he wanted was to keep everyone he could off of Le Hasard. He couldn't do much about King Trahan, but he was a known factor, one Bear had worked around now for years.

Another day or two, and he would have no need to work around anyone ever again. Two more days. Why the hell Simon Baptiste couldn't have waited two more days to descend on Bayou Allain . . . First that damn Michelina Ferrer and now Harlan Baptiste's spawn. And with everything Bear had been working for finally within reach.

Lorna stepped from behind her chair, came to perch on the loveseat cushion beside him. Her office was decorated much like her home, fussy and floral, with wall-to-wall carpeting in a periwinkle blue that matched the flowers in the vase on her credenza and the oil of an English garden above.

"I just want this day over with," she said, her voice wistful with a lust that was going to be their undoing if she didn't keep it in her panties, where it belonged. "I'm not going to be able to breathe or stop shaking until we're done here and Simon goes home."

A quick knock sounded on the door and Lorna jumped to her feet, patted at her hair, smoothed down her clothes. Bear was used to her fussing, but this obsession she had with Simon was going to do him in.

"Come in, Chelle," he called to Lorna's assistant, earning himself a panicked glare as Lorna shook her head and mouthed, "I'm not ready."

Paschelle Sonnier pushed open the door, looked from

Bear to Lorna, then glanced toward the phone ringing on her desk. She held up a finger, stepped away from the door to take the call. Air went out of Lorna like a punctured tire, but she puffed up again with Chelle's return.

"He rescheduled for tomorrow. Simon Baptiste."

"What?" Lorna gasped, sputtering out the word. "No. Oh, no." She shook her head, waggled a finger like a scolding teacher. "He can't do this. He cannot do this to me."

"I believe he already did," Bear said, turning to Chelle. "What time tomorrow?"

"He wants to come at ten. The calendar was free, so I penciled him in."

"Thank you, Chelle. That's all." He waited for the door to close before he added, "I'm getting tired of having my days upended. It's past time to eat."

"That's all you can think about? Food? You're not worried that he's discovered the truth?" Lorna's face had paled, her bright lipstick and cheek color looking more like it belonged on a clown.

Times like these he wondered why he still thought her attractive, why he'd chosen her as his ally all those years ago. Except seeing her reaction to Simon and the man not even here . . . he remembered the way Lorna at twenty had walked and talked, how boys for miles around had panted after her.

There was something to be said for the power a woman held over a man. She could take a deal a lot further, make a client a lot happier than Bear ever could alone. Too bad he'd never had the chance to see Michelina Ferrer at work.

He got to his feet and held out his hand, feeling the aches in his bones from the cushions that were as soft as the rest of Lorna's décor. "Let's get lunch. You look too nice not to show off around town."

She stood with her arms wrapped around her middle but finally gave in and wrapped her fingers around his. "I can't eat. My stomach feels like it's weighed down with a boulder the size of the Gulf."

"I've got a bottle with your name on it." He brought her fingertips to his mouth and kissed them. "It's just the thing to loosen you up. All you have to do is drink."

Twelve

Noon. Finally. Paschelle Sonnier had thought the lunch hour would never arrive. And even better, now that it had, was Lorna going to lunch with Judge Landry and giving Chelle permission to close the office until she got back.

Since Lorna's lunches with the judge usually involved more alcohol than food, it wasn't unusual for them to be gone two or three hours if they ever came back at all.

Chelle didn't have far to drive for her own lunch date, but she wasn't going to press her luck. She would keep her time away to ninety minutes, max. King, as anxious as the others to find out what Simon wanted, told her he'd meet her at her place today. He didn't believe for a minute the trip to Louisiana was to check out the old place, like Simon had said.

Chelle was probably the only one in town who didn't care why King's cousin had come back to Bayou Allain. She wanted King happy, that was all. And she was pretty sure he would be anything but when she arrived sans news.

She made a quick stop at the corner of St. James and State, then turned left, and in another half mile right onto Fern. Her cottage sat at the end of the long and winding road, and that's where King was waiting.

Her heart felt weightless in her chest, floating into her throat and making it hard to draw breath. Her tummy tingled, tightening up to send tiny shivers to tickle between her legs. She clenched her sex, feeling herself grow ready.

It had been like this since the first time she'd seen King that long-ago night at Red's.

She'd tended bar in the French Quarter when she'd lived in New Orleans, wasting her business administration degree slinging drinks the same way she was wasting it now working for Lorna. Then she'd been biding her time, checking the classifieds and Monster.com, though she didn't know why she bothered.

Working from early evening until two a.m., then partying until dawn was a lot more fun than a corporate nine to five. And then came Hurricane Katrina and the loss of her life as she'd known it.

She'd hit the road, dazed, confused, and run out of gas in Bayou Allain. She'd been here ever since, with no idea why she stayed. At least she hadn't known until the night she met Kingdom Trahan.

She'd been tired of spending her weekends alone. Lorna kept her busy enough during the week that she didn't mind heading home to a bowl of popcorn, her bed, and whatever DVD Netflix had sent from her queue. But there was only so much yard work and housework and reading she could do on her days off without going totally insane.

She did sew, and using the scads of decorating magazines Lorna let her take home every month, she'd turned her small rental into a funky *Project Runway*–styled *Extreme Home Makeover* showcase.

But she had no one to show it off to, no one to enjoy the wild mixture of colors and patterns and textures, and she'd avoided getting a cat because it seemed so desperately single-girl pathetic.

She knew about Red's, of course. The bar was a Bayou

Allain institution. But going out for a night on her own? Again with the desperately single-girl pathetic. She'd served a whole lot of drinks to a whole lot of women who were trolling, and she would not ever be one of them.

Then came the night when the popcorn turned into ice cream—one bowl, then two, then another. . . . And that was it. She'd had to get out of the house.

She'd worn blue jeans, a white T-shirt, Scottish plaid flats, and no makeup save for mascara. She hadn't thought about the apple-green mesh of her bra shimmering through her top's cotton fabric, but it had.

Men had noticed. Women, too. Apparently apple green only played in the Big Easy. A beer in her hand, she'd swiveled around on her stool, determined to enjoy the zydeco band and ignore the curious stares.

She hadn't been in town but a few months and probably remembered only a handful of people she'd met through her connection to Lorna. She knew the deputy and his wife, Lisa, who lived across the street, but that was because Terrill helped keep her Mustang running.

If she'd seen King Trahan before her visit to Red's, she would not have forgotten. He was older than her by ten years at least, and she loved what age had done to his eyes, the way he looked at her, the things he said without speaking, the potency in his gaze that was frightening.

He'd been sitting in the far corner, leaning back in the booth, both arms flung wide on the padded headrest, one long leg stretched out where anyone walking by could easily trip if the person wasn't paying any mind.

She could see it happening, someone caught by his full-of-bullshit-and-promises gaze and missing the big, bad challenge of his foot. She'd never been sure if it had been the shake of her head or the shimmer of her bra, but he'd slipped out of the seat and crossed the room with a roll of his hips that had left her needy and her mouth bone dry.

They'd talked at the bar for hours, their heads close, their breath a single exhalation of air, their laughter tangled up like puzzle rings, their hands touching, fingers and wrists and palms, once a shoulder, then his to her neck.

He'd walked her to her car, hovered over her when she'd stood with her back to the door, his forearms on the metal roof, where his fingers drummed.

She'd wanted to pull his body flush to hers. She'd wanted to melt into his skin, to feel his weight, to measure the length and width of the erection she was certain he had; as wet as she was, how could he not be just as ready for her?

It had seemed forever that they'd stood there like that, still and wondering and silent but for the need to breathe deeply and to stay. The moment had been magic, sex waiting, tension living, all in the air.

Finally he'd stepped forward, moved his hands from the roof of the car to the button of her jeans. He'd opened her fly, put his hand in her panties, and she'd let him, just like she'd done in junior high with Robert Benton when they'd cut study hall to make out in the locker room.

It was so much better this time. King was older and wiser and knew what to do. She'd dropped her head back, and as much as she'd wanted to close her eyes and do nothing but feel, she'd kept them open and locked on his, which were smoky and pleased and involved.

Thinking of it now . . .

. . . the way he'd finished her off without a word, how he'd helped her straighten her clothing when she was done, the sweet wail of a fiddle drifting out from the bar to carry him away, his leaving her there without a word, his only parting shot a wink that knew too much . . .

Thinking of it now . . .

She pulled into her driveway behind his truck, her palms wet, her hands shaking. Never in her twenty-eight years had she let a man get to her the way this one had.

He was a drug, and she was an addict, and knowing that her next fix was on the other side of her front door made it impossible to breathe.

Except he wasn't waiting inside at all. He was standing on the porch when she made her way there from the car. His jeans hung low on his hips, and he'd kicked off his boots. White crew socks covered his feet.

It tickled her, the way he made himself at home, tickled her in other ways, the way his chambray shirt hung open, the way the sun spun his feathered chest hair to gold.

"Well?" was the only greeting he gave her.

She was slow to climb the steps after that, the bubble of expectation burst. She'd been so caught up in the past that she'd forgotten King wasn't here for her.

He was here for news on Simon Baptiste.

She brushed past him into the house and made her way to the kitchen, calling over her shoulder, "He had to cancel. He rescheduled for tomorrow morning. And, no, sorry. No explanation for the delay."

King slammed the front door. Facing the kitchen sink, she cringed at the rattling echo. It wasn't fair, the ease with which he made her feel stupid, the fact that she let him get away with doing it, the reality that she was the only one here wanting more.

Women fell. Men fucked.

They'd been assigned their roles at the dawn of time. Why had it taken her so long to wake up?

Though it was bright outside, the sun shining down, turning her lawn to strips of glittering green, she caught a glimpse of his reflection in the window she faced. He was quiet, and only her senses told her he'd moved close. She knew he was there before he touched her.

Weak. That's what she was. Putty with no spine. Melted butter. Liquid Jell-O. She hunched up her shoulders, shivering when his breath tickled her neck.

He wrapped his arms around her, cradled her bottom with his hips, slid his hands beneath the hem of the tunic she wore over a gauzy peasant skirt that brushed the tops of her feet.

Covering her breasts, he pinched her nipples through her bra until the pleasure became pain. "How soon do you have to be back?"

She squirmed, but he didn't let her go, and she wasn't even sure that she wanted him to. "Lorna went to lunch with the judge—"

"We have hours, then."

He spun her around, grabbed the fabric of her skirt, and tugged. The elastic waist stretched over her hips, and the garment fell to the floor. She held on to his shoulders as he lifted her to the counter beside the sink. And then she leaned back on her elbows and watched.

She was a junkie, shameless in her need, at the mercy of her desire, mesmerized by the flex of muscles in his chest and shoulders, by the V of his open fly and the hair that grew thicker there, spongy where it pillowed his sex.

It was his sex that bewitched her the most, the bulk of his balls, his penis straining against the fabric of both his shorts and jeans like a compact spring waiting to uncoil and reach its full length and potential.

She knew that length, knew the circumference, the ripe knob on top, the slit that opened in the center, widening for the tip of her tongue.

He reached into his pocket, pulled out the knife he carried. Her breath left her lungs, her heart screamed with a fierce wanting.

He parted her knees, then her thighs, wedged his hips between and hooked her heels behind him. Sliding one index finger into her panties, pressing his knuckle into her entrance, he opened the knife with his teeth.

Anticipating, she widened her legs even more. He slid

the blade next to his thumb. The cool metal chilled her bare lips but only for the seconds it took him to slice through the fabric, exposing her.

He didn't even bother closing the knife, but just tossed it to the floor as he bent to cover her with his mouth. He sucked her plump flesh, one side, then the other, nudging her clit with his nose.

Oh. Oh. His breath was warm, his lips hot, his tongue nearly scorching. Oh, God, oh. She couldn't look away. She watched like a voyeur, her temperature rising at the sight of his open mouth on her pink flesh.

He used his thumbs to open her, pushing one inside to play, the other spreading her juices lower and slipping into her ass. Her eyes rolled back. It was too much, his tongue now flat on her clit, one thumb stroking her G-spot, the other filling her up the rest of the way.

She cried out, caught up in spasms, squeezing, contracting around him, her world spinning away. Her orgasm was all she knew. It was the only thing in her world.

He did this for her, took her apart in ways no one had ever known how to do. She hurt, she ached, he bruised her. She loved it all, wanted more, caught her lip between her teeth and begged him with a look.

He stood, his eyes firing like an engine running hot, and shoved his jeans to his knees. His cock jutted forward, impressive, intimidating, bold. She wanted it in her mouth, in her hands, the shaft thrusting between her breasts, the head pulsing in her ass.

He wrapped his fingers around it and stepped forward, drove into her with a stroke that she felt all the way to her spine. Quivering, she wrapped her arms around his neck when he reached for her, clinging tight, impaled.

He backed up two steps, turned, and fell with her to the kitchen table. He climbed onto it on his knees, his hands curled around the edges for purchase until the muscles in his arms, the tendons in his throat, bulged blue.

She gripped his wrists, crossed her ankles in the small of his back, and held on. As he rocked into her, the table shook, groaned beneath their combined weight.

His strokes were powerful, strong and fluid. Her sex swelled, her breasts swelled, her heart swelled to bursting with the emotions she couldn't release in words.

But she couldn't keep it out of her eyes, and he knew. His gaze locked with hers, he struggled not to speak, but the fire between them had set spark to tinder and was unable to be contained.

"Goddammit, Chelle!" he yelled, tossing back his head. "Don't do this to me. Not now. Don't fucking do this to me now."

And then he came, crying out, stiffening, shuddering, collapsing on top of her as he reached between her legs to make certain she found her oblivion.

How could she not?

She burned, flamed, exploded against him, beneath him, doing the very thing he didn't want her to do—loving him more than she should when she knew he didn't love her at all.

Thirteen

It was almost dark when Simon heard Micky stir. The house was old, worn, creaky. Even the sound of her feet hitting the floor as she rolled out of bed, the moan of the frame with the shift of her slight weight, was enough to rattle the beams and planks of old wood.

Not helping was the matter of how empty the house was. He'd come prepared with camp chairs and sleeping bags, a small charcoal grill, and a cooler for ice in case the place had been rented since Lorna's last contact and he had to find a campsite and make do. He'd made do in worse places and with less during his deployment, often dispatched with no more supplies than would fit in the pack he carried.

The house on Le Hasard had served as a rental for several years. There had been little he'd wanted to keep once he'd accepted that he wouldn't be living here again. He'd had his attorney handle things, retrieving a few photos, his mother's wedding ring, his father's dog tags.

The proceeds from anything sold—cars, tractor and tiller, power tools, rifles and hunting gear—were added to the rental income to pay property taxes and keep the place livable. For several years, a good chunk of the nearly four thousand acres had been leased as grazing land.

He wondered if the dearth of potential renters was a reflection of the Bayou Allain economy or if having King for a neighbor kept them at bay.

Whatever. The point was moot. The house wasn't worth the cost of the repairs it needed. That hadn't stopped him from spending most of the day shoring up the porch. It was busywork, nothing more, but working with his hands had always helped him think.

He hadn't planned on having to do that while here. He hadn't had a vacation in years. He was counting on getting his business done, then spending the rest of his time off recovering from his last assignment—and doing it while sober, so Hank wouldn't have to pry another bottle out of his hand and wonder if it was time to let him go.

He'd seen the toll taken on his fellow operatives, those who'd been working for Hank Smithson longer than he had, who had learned the value of downtime for keeping reflexes sharp and instincts humming.

He'd also seen the changes several of the men had gone through with a woman in their lives. That seemed the hardest act to balance of all, that of willingly stepping into danger with a wife or a lover at home holding tight to the hope that nothing would blow up in the team's face.

It was a commitment, an implied promise that Simon wasn't sure it was fair to make. Life wasn't fair, no, but putting his life in danger was one thing. Leaving a woman to deal with the fallout should he be killed, or putting her life at risk because of the job . . . After what he'd seen happen to Eli McKenzie's Stella, he wasn't sure he was ready to do that.

The thought now brought Micky to mind—no reason it should have, no reason at all—and when he heard her coming down the stairs, he stiffened, his hand too tight around the hammer he held, his teeth gritting against the shanks of the nails in his mouth.

Stupid, this reaction that was fitting of his twelve-year-old self, the one with feet too big and arms too long and a voice that hit as many bass notes as soprano. The one who couldn't find a thing to say to girls when his blood rushed from his head to his pants.

She materialized in the rectangle of the open back door. He didn't look up; he didn't have to. He could smell her, a hint of dark spice, and he wondered if the scent would ever wash out of his clothes she was wearing.

"Do you think I should stay inside?" she asked. "So I won't be seen? Or is it safe to come out since it's getting dark?"

It was, and he was going to have to hang up his hammer soon before he hit his thumb instead of a nail. Except the lack of light wasn't as much of an issue as was his lack of concentration, or at least his drift of concentration, since it was now all on her.

He straightened from where he'd been kneeling, tossed the hammer into his toolbox, and pulled the nails from between his teeth. "The porch is shadowed. You should be good up there."

She nodded, stepped through the door, her slender bare feet drawing his gaze. Funny, but he would never have pictured the heiress to the Ferrer fortune as the barefoot type, and whoa did he shut down that thought before it took him places he didn't need to go.

What he needed was to gather more information, just as he'd collect intel before heading into the field. It was the only way to find his footing, secure his balance.

"Are you feeling better? Rested? Head on straight?" Knowing that hers was would make it easier to get his back where it belonged. He hoped.

"I'd say I'm at eighty percent." She perched on the edge of the rocking bench, testing its integrity before she sat.

"Another eight hours or so, and I should be closer to a hundred."

"Good. You'll need that hundred tomorrow, but eighty tonight should be enough."

"Enough for what?" she asked, her forearms braced on her thighs as she hunched forward, her hair falling over one shoulder, her breasts full where her biceps pressed against their sides.

He glanced down, watched her curl her toes. One foot, then the other, then both. Her nails were painted a cinnamon brown. She had a small tattoo below her ankle, and a narrow gold ring on one toe.

He had never thought much about a woman's feet, but this woman looked so vulnerable already, having nothing but his clothes between the world and her skin, that the polish and the ring and the tiny tattoo all got together to make him wonder if she decorated more of her body parts.

This would've been a good time to be holding the hammer. He needed some sense knocked into his head. "To make a plan. See what we've got in the way of evidence. If there's anything we're missing that might prove your accident wasn't an accident."

"You mean like the paint from my rental on the grille of the truck?"

He found himself grinning. "Watch a lot of crime TV, do you?"

"Not really," she said, though she chuckled. "Or at least not by design. My assistant TiVos a lot of shows. I think she owns every season of every *CSI* on DVD. They run in her office constantly."

And had no doubt convinced Micky the fictional portrayal of that world was the truth. But her question was valid. "Paint on the grille would be good if he hit more than your bumper. Might be hard to separate the impact damage from what the crash added, though. Depends on what part of the car hit the water and if it rolled or bounced.

"Then there's the issue of the number of pickups and SUVs in the parish. Assuming the vehicle and the driver were local. And if this is all tied up in the disappearance of Lisa Landry, it's a fair one to make."

"A fair what?"

"Assumption."

"Oh." She rested her chin in the cradle of her palms, her elbows propped on her knees. "Are you sure you're not the one with a jones for crime TV?" She paused, cocked her head, a thoughtful consideration of her own remarks. "Or is that what you do?"

"What I do?" he asked, hedging.

"In New York. Are you NYPD? A federal agent?"

He had no intention of telling her what he was. He shook his head as he hunkered down to lock up his toolbox. "Nope. Just making use of my common sense and a dozen years of training on Uncle Sam's dime."

"You're not old enough to be retired military."

He stood, heaved the toolbox onto the edge of the porch, stayed there facing her. "I'm pretty damn old."

"How old?"

"Isn't that one of those questions you're not supposed to ask? Like weight and shoe size?"

"That's for women. And it's weight and bra size. I've already figured out your shoe size."

"You have?"

"From your waders."

"Those weren't my waders, *chère*," he said, laughing out loud when she screwed up her face in what looked like disgust. "You're just lucky I'm the one who showed up to see you wearing them."

She shuddered, but then her head came up. "What if this house had belonged to one of them?"

One of them. As in the bastards who if not joyriding and playing dangerous games had purposefully singled out Micky to guarantee her silence. "At Red's, when you were talking to the judge, was anyone else around? Could anyone have overheard your conversation?"

"There weren't a lot of people there, no. And with the dancing and the band, the noise level was pretty high. But my back was to the room. For all I know, there could've been someone listening from the next booth."

Something in her expression clicked. She sat up straight. "I met this guy who might know. He pointed out Judge Landry and seemed to think my talking to him was quite a show."

As a lead, it wasn't much, but it was more than the nothing he was holding. "This guy. Do you remember his name?"

She smiled. "Oh, yeah. Hard to forget a name like Kingdom Trahan."

Fourteen

Micky would have thought she'd poured a whole bottle of Veuve Clicquot on Simon's head. He closed down that coolly, that quickly, as if she'd delivered the cut direct. "Do you know him? Or where we can find him?"

The questions went unanswered as Simon jerked his toolbox off the porch and headed for his truck, his shoulders and biceps full and defined. He lowered the tailgate, slid the metal box in between what looked to be crates of supplies, then slammed the back end shut.

She expected him to stomp past her, pound up the stairs, and lock himself in the bedroom where she'd slept—the only one with a door that closed and windows left unbroken.

But he didn't. He just turned around and leaned against his truck, his backside on the bumper and his ankles crossed. "Don't count on him offering any help."

Hmm. King hadn't seemed the type not to help. He'd been very helpful, in fact. "So you do know him."

"I do."

"And you don't like him?"

"We . . . have issues."

Puh-lease. Who didn't? "And you think your issues would keep him from helping me."

"If he knew I was in the picture, yeah. They might."
Didn't say a lot for either of them. "Then maybe I don't
tell him that you are."

Simon didn't say anything right away, just crossed his
arms over his chest and continued to stare. He was thinking. Micky had no idea whether he was considering her suggestion, or revisiting whatever memories her mention of King
had brought to mind. She decided she wanted to know.

"How do you know him?" she asked at the same time he
said, "Tell me what the two of you talked about last night."

She pressed her lips together. Something was going on
here . . . something personal? Obviously so, if they had issues. But how deep did those waters run? And what did it
mean for her safety?

Would she be better off on her own than caught in the
middle of a man-on-man feud? Or was taking what she
could get better than nothing? "When I got to town, I had
no luck getting information on where I might find Lisa. If
her neighbors were home, they weren't answering their
doors. I stopped at the bar. He helped me."

"How so?" His question was curt.

Her answer was the same. "I told you. He pointed out
Judge Landry. I took it from there."

"Did you tell him who you were?"

"I introduced myself, if that's what you mean. I didn't
detail my whole life story."

"And I'm assuming you told the judge," he said, the shift
in his focus disconcerting.

What was he digging for? What did he want to know besides what he was asking? "Of course. I had to explain my
connection to Lisa. I didn't think he'd help me otherwise.
Not that he did." She decided she didn't like being interro-
gated. "Why? Does it matter that they know who I am?"

"It might have narrowed down the list of anyone out to
get you personally."

"Might have?" Now she was getting worried.

"The car was a rental. Everyone involved in the case knows who you are."

Ah, that. "Not really," she said, wondering what he'd make of her admission.

"How so?"

"The rental records only show who rented the car."

"And that's not you?"

"Yes and no. I always fly under my own name, but my executive assistant makes my travel arrangements and often books the rest of my accommodations under hers." Micky had a duplicate of Jane's driver's license—at a quick glance, they looked a lot alike—and additional copies of her credit cards in Jane's name. "The car was rented to Jane Mitchell. Not Michelina Ferrer."

Simon pushed away from the truck. "So as far as the authorities know, it's your assistant who went off that bridge and is missing. Though by now they've probably been in contact with her employer—"

And that would be me, Micky thought, afraid she might choke. "God. I need to let Jane know I'm all right."

She'd been so intent on keeping a low profile after the debacle with her underpants, hoping the press would lose interest—what fun would the story be if they couldn't track her down and hound her to the ends of the earth?—that she hadn't thought about the authorities searching for info on the missing Jane Mitchell. Or about Jane panicking when she realized it was Micky they were really looking for.

She needed to call her. She had no cell. "You don't have a phone, do you? I made it out of the car with my purse since I was all wrapped up in the strap, but everything inside was drenched and is useless."

"I'm not sure you could pick up a signal this far out anyway—"

She sighed. That's what she'd been afraid of.

"—but I do have a satellite phone."

He was halfway to the front of the truck before she registered what he'd said. Once she did, she started to follow, stopped when she remembered that she needed to stay on the porch in the shadows and that she wasn't wearing any shoes.

It occurred to her again while she waited for him that she still knew nothing about this man, who he was, how he happened to show up mere hours after she'd taken refuge in his house, which was obviously abandoned.

Very few people drove around with satellite phones. Very few people needed to access that technology. The few who had reason to . . .

"You never did tell me." And she doubted he would now. "Are you some sort of federal agent? Did you move from the military into government work?"

The phone in his hand, Simon looked at her as he powered it on and waited for a signal. "What makes you ask that?"

He knew exactly. He was stalling, avoiding. "Who else would just happen to have a satellite phone handy?"

He gave a careless shrug, the tail of his hair sweeping his neck. "Someone who might need to stay in touch with the civilized world even from the back of beyond?"

Again, with the logic, the evasion that made more sense than her wild imagination. "Who do you need to be in touch with? A wife and kids?"

He shook his head, fought a smile. "No wife, and no kids that I know of."

"That's not funny."

"It wasn't supposed to be." He handed her the phone. "Dial your number."

She took it, stared frowning at the keypad. "What do I tell her? I mean, besides the fact that I'm all right, how much should I say?"

"Find out if anyone's contacted her yet about the accident, who it was, and what she told them. Since she's the one assumed missing, they may have tried family and friends first."

"Or, like you said, her employer?"

He nodded. "The sheriff's department doesn't have a lot of manpower. They may still be out on their search and rescue and won't start in on the phones until they're forced to call it off for the night."

He was making a lot of sense—in that logically evasive and aggravating way that he had. She held the phone in both hands, punched the number with both thumbs, brought it up to her ear, and waited.

"You've reached Jane Mitchell in the Ferrer office. I'm currently unavailable but will return your call as soon as I'm able. Leave all the pertinent info. Ciao."

"Jane, it's Micky. I'm fine. I'm in Louisiana. I need to know if anyone has called about you being in an accident here, and what you told them. If you haven't talked to anyone, don't. Call it identity theft or whatever.

"Basically, you're in the dark. I'm out of town visiting a friend. I didn't tell you who or where." And that wasn't even a lie. "I'll call you later tonight or tomorrow and explain all."

She disconnected and handed the phone back to Simon. "Was that okay? Will that work?"

"Sounded like a pro."

"A pro what?" Liar?

"A pro at covering your ass."

She would've laughed if his assessment hadn't been entirely spot on. Then she wondered if it took one to know one. "Trust me. I've got it down to a science."

He looked at her curiously. "It's too bad that's something you've had to refine."

She shrugged. What could she say? It had been her life so

long it was second nature. "It's my own fault. I was born into the public eye. I just wasn't ever cut out for it."

"Charm school didn't take?" He headed back to the truck, stored the phone.

"Are you kidding? Miss Clare's Academy for Proper Young Ladies closed its doors rather than let me back in."

"Back in?" he asked upon his return.

She held up three fingers. "Miss Clare had her own three-strike rule. Unfortunately, Papi and his money insisted the strikes were mistakes easily corrected with a scholarship fund and a fully outfitted computer lab."

He had settled his back against the porch beam, obviously taking in and enjoying the true story of Michelina Ferrer. "She turned him down?"

What could it hurt to tell him more? He was listening. He seemed interested. A rarity in her experience that told her only sensationalism drew a crowd.

"She did. Apparently she was offered a position as a private tutor to the children of a Saudi prince. Even Ferrer money couldn't compete—though I heard my father telling Greta that the offer hadn't dropped into her lap. Apparently, Miss Clare had put out word that she was desperate to find work in a single-family environment."

"As long as that single family wasn't named Ferrer?"

"Exactly."

"Who's Greta?"

"My father's personal assistant."

"Where's your mother?"

"Good question. I haven't seen her since I was ten."

"Was that before or after Miss Clare's?"

"Around the same time, and yes, I'm sure my being a charm school dropout is directly related." Except that had been twenty years ago and she wasn't behaving much differently now, was she?

Running away instead of staying to face music she didn't

want to hear had nearly gotten her killed. Still, she couldn't regret what had happened. If she hadn't come to Louisiana, she never would have known about Lisa, and for all the efforts being made to find her, the other woman might have remained a missing person forever. At least Micky would be able to make sure that never happened.

She looked up, realized that she'd drifted away, realized, too, that Simon had patiently watched her go and waited for her to come back. This being contemplative wasn't like her at all.

There hadn't been much of her old self in evidence since she'd crawled soaking wet and sputtering through the open window of the rental, crouched on the higher ground as the nose was sucked into the same mud that had taken her shoes, the taillights flickering until the water extinguished all the life from the car's electrical system the same way it could so easily have taken hers.

Until Simon squatted in front of her and wiped his thumbs over her face, she hadn't realized she was crying. The hitch in her breath, her sobs, the moisture on her face, she'd thought those all in her mind.

She shook her head, murmured, "I'm sorry."

It wasn't what she'd wanted to say, but the words were the only ones that would come.

"It's okay. You have nothing to be sorry for. Being a charm school dropout is not the end of the world."

She tried to laugh. The sound came out as a hiccup, one that sounded so ridiculously pathetic that she buried her face in her hands to keep from breaking down completely, hysterically. But breaking down seemed the only thing she was able to do.

He was teasing, trying to lighten the mood, and she was reverting to the basket case she'd been when he'd pulled her from the closet—the one she'd never had time to be when she was fighting her way out of the swamp.

"All I wanted to do was spend time with my girlfriend. To eat, drink, and talk ourselves silly over a *Sex and the City* marathon. And look at me. My mind takes one wrong turn and I'm back at the bridge living through the accident again. And Lisa, God, if they were so ready to get rid of me, what did they do to her? I can't even think about it. I'm not sure I can handle knowing."

His hand was cupping her cheek, his thumb smoothing over her cheekbone. "You'll handle it just fine, but you don't have to think about it now. You need to take care of you."

"I need to make sure someone is looking for Lisa. Really looking." She shook her hair from her face, dislodging his hand, telling herself she was strong enough to deal with this, with it all. "I don't believe for a minute that the judge cares about anything but what she might have said before she went missing. He was more interested in her note—"

Simon stiffened. "What note?"

"It arrived in the mail about a week ago. She told me it had been too long and I should come visit if I could tear myself away from the wild life. She made it a point to keep up with what the press found newsworthy about me when I wasn't good enough to stay in touch."

She wasn't going to tell him about Monday night in case he hadn't yet heard. "But that was it. A don't-be-a-stranger reminder. She said it was bad enough that her family kept her out of the loop, that I didn't need to."

"What do you think she meant by that?" he asked, sitting back on the balls of his feet, his elbows on his knees. "Being out of the loop?"

It had seemed so innocent. An offhand remark. Or she'd been too caught up with herself to read between the lines. "I didn't take it as anything cryptic. Just maybe that southern hospitality ran out at the Mississippi River."

"How long have she and Terrill been married?"

She counted quickly. "Eight years."

"Any complaints before now about feeling left out? Or like not part of the family?"

"None at all." That she could say with no reservation. "It's only Lisa, Terrill, and his father. She always thought the judge was full of himself, but she adores Terrill. I don't think she's ever mentioned disagreeing with him about anything."

"What does she do?"

"Besides playing Martha Stewart inside, landscaping out-side, and lately working on the Landry genealogy?" Micky smiled, pictured her girlfriend in the various roles. "There aren't a lot of career ops for a marketing major in the bayou. I tried to get her to come to New York for a few months and brainstorm a new Ferrer campaign with our ad people, but she didn't want to leave Terrill."

"What about the genealogy? Has she mentioned any-thing about that?"

"You mean has she dug up any deep dark Landry secrets? Any illegitimate heirs birthed to young slave girls on the plantation?" She shook her head. "Not a thing."

"So being left out of the family loop . . ."

"Your guess is as good as mine."

Simon thought for a minute, got to his feet. "I'd like to see her research notes. Find out what she might have un-covered."

She snorted. "Oh, I'm sure you'll have no trouble getting permission."

He didn't miss a beat. "Who said I was going to ask?"

Okay. This was interesting, this confidence, this entitle-ment, this cheek. "Who are you, Simon Baptiste?"

Laughing, he headed for the door, gesturing for her to come inside, too. "Someone who's been sitting behind a wheel too long, unloading double his weight in supplies, swinging a hammer in a shirt that doesn't breathe, and needs a shower before he can even think of rustling grub for dinner."

He sounded like a cowboy. It made her smile. "Fair warning. The water pressure is pathetic, and the hot-water valve needs help," she said.

"That's okay. A cold shower sounds like just the thing."

She cocked her head. "I hope you're not saying that needing one's my fault."

"You never know," he said, his grin a devilishly delicious thing.

The whole world is my native land.
  —Seneca, Roman philosopher, mid-first century A.D.

  The Landry family Bible held an amazing secret, a secret neither my husband nor his father had hinted at knowing even once during the eight years of my living in Bayou Allain. I let that bother me for a while, let myself pout privately about being left out of the loop. I pouted semiprivately as well, dropping a note to my best girl-friend, knowing she'd pick up on things not being quite right.

  But then I realized how stupid that was. Terrill shared everything with me. He told me personal things I knew he'd never trusted anyone else to know. Since he hadn't mentioned that a Civil War treasure was buried on the family's land, it made sense that he, too, was in the dark. Before telling him, however, I needed to know more, to figure out exactly how the code pointing to the cache of gold worked.

  The inconvenience of having to go to the parish library so often was minor. The Bible, though the family's property, was considered a historic find, having been unearthed during the razing of a tumbled-down barn that was part of the original Landry homestead. The judge had agreed to let the book remain on public display.

I have no idea why the letter in the binding hadn't been discovered before. Maybe it had. Maybe the decision was made to leave it where it had been found. Or maybe the lack of resources for restoring the worn leather meant no one had ever looked at the cover carefully.

The minute I read it, I knew what I had—but only because I'd been looking through the boxes in Bear's attic, and the list of codes the letter referenced was fresh in my mind. It wasn't a complicated cipher, but a series of dots and dashes resembling Morse code that referred to books, chapters, and verses in the Bible instead of representing the alphabet.

Alone, the markings meant nothing and were virtually worthless, but the handwritten letter in the leather binding made them worth, well, whatever the key to a buried treasure was worth! And, honestly, it wasn't that hard to figure out how they worked after I read the note. . . .

My name is Ruth Callahan Landry. I am the lawful wedded wife of Samuel Jonathan Landry. We have not been blessed with children for me to tell what has happened, and my Samuel will be dead and soon in the arms of the Lord, though I would wish him to stay on this earth as my husband for fifty more years were the Lord willing and had not the gangrene set in before he got himself home for me to tend to the gunshot wound.

I know what he did was sinful but I am a woman alone and I am not of a mind to face the Union soldiers even now in New Orleans to return the gold my Samuel took when he knew he was going against the Lord. The satchel is safely buried in the ground, and I have made markings in the Old

*Testament books of Ruth and Samuel 1 to serve as a guide
to the location should I have a need to settle monetary
obligations I am unable to satisfy with the fruits of honest
labor. The clarification of how the markings are to be read
have been recorded with this letter.*

*If no such need arises before I am joined again with my
beloved Samuel at the feet of the Lord, the gold will remain
in its final resting place until it is discovered and returned
to whom it rightfully belongs.*

After reading Ruth Callahan Landry's words, I couldn't
wait to work out the symbols for myself. I wasn't sure if I'd
be able to find the treasure, or if almost a hundred and fifty
years later there was anything left to find, but I wanted
more than anything to surprise Terrill with an amazing
inheritance that was by all rights his.

When I went back to the attic for the codes, a newspaper
clipping slipped loose from a folder containing several
more. I picked it up, glanced at the story, and that's when I
knew the puzzle was bigger than a cache of gold—and
more than I could solve on my own.

Fifteen

Having realized four hours wouldn't be enough time to go through even half the documents boxed up in Bear's attic, Terrill had carried all he could find to the trunk of his patrol car last night. His father would never miss them. He would never even know they were gone.

Bear wouldn't be able to climb the stairs or haul himself through the narrow opening into the top of the house if the place were on fire and his life at stake. He was too wide, too old, too dependent on the cane he swore was a decorative accessory like the cigars he never smoked, his only vice being his nightcap.

Well, the scotch, and Lorna Savoy. Why the old man was still keeping company with that woman was beyond Terrill's grasp. She was young enough to be Bear's daughter, though his relationship with her had never been paternal. It was strictly business, with sex thrown in for good measure—a fact that made Terrill question Lorna's motives more than Bear's.

What either of them got out of their association—and such a long-running one at that—was something he'd never understand. He remembered Lorna being at the house off and on when he was in high school, and more than a few times when he came home on leave.

He'd chalked that up to the secretarial work she'd done for Bear, work that had started out as a part-time job during a vocational program her senior year. She'd stayed on with him at the courthouse after graduation, had never done more than a few hours at South Louisiana Community College in Lafayette that Terrill could remember.

Yet, for some reason, she and Bear had never parted ways. Terrill knew that her real estate business kept her plenty busy even in the small town of Bayou Allain, and that his father had helped her get started.

She handled a lot of seasonal rentals, folks wanting to tour the swamps before hunting season, others taken in by the bald cypress, the alligators, and the snowy egrets that made the bayou their home.

Her brokerage also held the contracts for a lot of the storefront leases in the small town, and she was the Realtor anyone wanting to sell looked to. She was a pro when it came to turning over private property.

And then Terrill got to wondering what was at the root of Bear and Lorna living in each other's back pockets the last few days and if it had anything to do with his father being such an asshole last night.

Not that he really cared; he was just curious. All he had time to care about right now was his wife. He would've thought Bear would've felt the same.

Today had been shot to hell as far as making any headway in finding Lisa. He hadn't even made it to Bear's for the promised meeting this morning with the P.I. The car that had gone off the bridge and the subsequent search for the driver had eaten up all of his day.

He was only taking the break now to do something with the boxes in his trunk. Keeping them in his patrol car as long as he had wasn't smart, but last night he'd grabbed them without thinking things through.

It had been close on midnight when he'd made it home, and he didn't want to be seen that late carting the boxes inside. He had neighbors who'd been friends of the judge since before Terrill had been born, and he wouldn't put it past any of them to slip that tidbit of info to Bear.

He'd thought about transferring them to his personal vehicle, but the Jeep didn't have enough hidden storage space to accommodate his haul, and it made no more sense to keep them there than in his patrol car.

What he needed was privacy and space to dig through the contents of them all. With his father stopping by unannounced the way he often did before going to Red's in the evenings, laying them out in the spare bedroom wouldn't work.

He'd finally thought of a solution when he'd seen his father and Lorna out on the town at lunch and had wondered how long Paschelle Sonnier had been holding down the fort. She lived right across the street from Terrill, and her cottage had a detached garage with an office built into one corner.

The CPA who had lived there before had used it. Terrill knew from Lisa that Paschelle did not. When he'd called her late this afternoon, she'd told him he was welcome to store anything he needed to in the space.

Her Mustang was sitting in her driveway. He pulled into his and backed across the street, angling his car so that his open trunk would act as a shield. He hit the latch to release the lid, then climbed from the car just as Paschelle opened the office door on the side of the garage.

"I set up the folding table so you could stack the boxes there instead of on the floor," she said, walking toward him, her long skirt swinging around her ankles, her black hair swinging against her chin, her earrings dangling from her earlobes to her shoulders like wind chimes.

"Appreciate it." He hefted up the biggest box. She grabbed a smaller one and led the way. "And if anyone asks, can you tell them these are some things friends found from your place after it was wiped by Katrina?"

"Sure. You got a story to explain how you wound up with them?" Once inside the garage, she set down her box, turned to face him, a smile on her face that told him how much he sucked at telling lies.

He scrubbed a hand over his head, scratched a spot at his nape. "Here's the deal. I don't want Bear to find out I have these. Lisa was going through them for her genealogy project. She wanted to surprise him on his birthday with a photo album. I thought I'd try to work on it some. In case, for some reason, she's not back in time to finish it."

Paschelle didn't say anything right away, and Terrill was glad. It was hard enough dealing with the things he was feeling. He didn't want to have to answer questions or share his thoughts.

Bear getting in his face last night had been bad enough. Paschelle and Lisa being friends . . . he knew whatever she might want to know would require he dig too deep. He just wasn't ready.

But when she spoke, it was only to offer a solution. "If anyone asks, these are some things my folks sent me. They don't have my address, so they sent them to your office because I'd mentioned we were neighbors. How's that?"

He stood, nodding, finally found his voice. "Do your parents really not have your address?"

She shook her head, set her hair swinging. He missed Lisa's hair, the soft blond strands slipping between his fingers, tickling his chest. . . .

"Not the house number, the street, the city, or the zip. They don't even know that I'm still in the state, much less that I have a peace officer for a neighbor."

"Why don't they know? Why haven't you told them?"

"I'll tell you"—she arched a brow—"if you tell me what you're really hiding from the judge."

Smart girl. "You didn't buy my genealogy story?"

"Not so much. I mean, I do know about the photo album. Lisa told me. But she also told me she'd picked out all the pictures she wanted to use and had them stored in Tupperware at home."

He called her bluff. "You first. Let's hear about your parents."

She paused a minute, and then she laughed, her earrings jangling along. "Why don't we just grab the rest of your boxes and admit that our secrets are safe?"

Sounded like a plan to him. He motioned for her to go ahead, then followed her back to the car. "You're good with me coming and going, then?"

"Not a problem. The key's hanging on a nail inside the door."

"Is it going to be a problem for King?"

"Shouldn't be," she said, once they'd hauled in another load. "I don't anticipate he'll be here much anymore."

"Sorry to hear that." It seemed like the thing to say when he didn't have an opinion one way or the other. Lisa had always thought King too old and hard for a girl like Paschelle. But since Terrill had never known how he himself had won Lisa's heart, he kept his mouth shut.

"Thanks, but it feels like the right thing to do. That's not to say I won't weaken and have him back, but he'll never know the boxes are here. If he does see them, he won't give them a second thought."

"I just need to be sure they're safe. I'm hoping to find a clue about what happened to Lisa." *And after all that effort to make up a story, here comes the truth.*

"What do you mean?"

He'd said too much, but that didn't stop him from saying

more. Some things were hard to keep bottled up. And Chelle, well, she was Lisa's friend. He trusted her. "Maybe something got her curiosity up. She could have mentioned it to someone, or gone asking questions."

"And asked something she shouldn't have."

"Or talked to someone who didn't want her talking." He felt his jaw go tight. Even thinking that might be the case was enough to make breathing hard. He backed toward the door. "I've got to go."

"If you want help looking through things, just knock, okay? Or if you'd just like the company, or a pot of coffee." She smiled, shrugged as if she knew there was really nothing more to say. "Anything, just let me know."

"Thanks." He started to make a joke about giving the neighbors more gossip to chew on, but he couldn't find the words.

All he could think about was how much Paschelle's generosity reminded him of Lisa. And how very much he missed—and feared for—his wife.

Sixteen

When Simon finally climbed the stairs, long after Micky had turned in for the night, he walked the length of the hallway quietly, hoping to find her asleep. She wasn't, of course, though she was doing her best to pretend otherwise, and he saw no reason to rain on her parade.

Since she had both of his sleeping bags on the bed, he dug a sweatshirt from his duffel, used the pack for a pillow, the shirt for a blanket, and stretched out on the floor.

He would have camped out in his truck; the seat was a lot more comfortable than the floor's worn hardwood, but he didn't want Micky wandering around in the middle of the night making sure he hadn't left her alone.

That was part of it. The rest was that he didn't want to. Leave her alone. She'd been through a lot. She needed a long and good night's sleep. By staying close, he could make sure she got it. Or at least make sure that she tried, that she had no reason not to stay put.

"I talked to Jane," she said, her voice coming out of the darkness like a beacon.

That didn't make sense. He wasn't lost, didn't need a guiding light to show him the way. He'd known that she was awake; that didn't surprise him. He was surprised that he was glad, that he had wanted her to be. That hearing her voice pleased him the way it did.

This had been the longest, strangest day he'd ever spent on what was supposed to be a vacation, but was reminding him too much of work. "What did she say?"

"That the rental company did call looking for an emergency contact and was surprised to reach her instead."

"She followed your script?"

"She told them that she hadn't made the reservation. That she was alive and well and in Manhattan. She's very good at doing her job."

He hadn't thought anyone in her position would be otherwise. "And at lying by omission?"

"If that's what it takes to cover both her ass and mine."

He let all of that digest. "That may have worked to put off the rental company for now, but it won't satisfy Terrill and crew so easily."

"I was thinking the same thing." She took a deep breath, tugged at the sleeping bag. He heard the zipper teeth scrape the mattress ticking. "She'll be screening her calls until she hears from me again. I suggested that this would be the perfect time for her to take a week off. And that it would be a good idea for her to pay cash for any shopping or traveling or sightseeing she does."

So no one could trace her by her credit cards. "You and your crime TV."

"I imagine they'll eventually want to talk to me. Papi and Jane both know I went to visit a friend. When Terrill realizes who it is Jane works for, he should easily be able to put two and two together. He won't buy that he's looking at identity theft. He'll know I was behind the rental's wheel."

He liked her mind. She was sharp. It made him appreciate the rest of her that much more. "Hopefully, he's good enough to do the rest of the math and realize it's too much of a coincidence that both his wife and her good friend are nowhere to be found."

She shifted on the bed, the frame squeaking. "And if he learns that there were only two people who knew that I was here to see Lisa, his father and your cousin, well, case solved, yes?"

"Your case, anyway. Or at least the right questions raised, the list of suspects narrowed down."

"Like was it his father who came after me, or was it King Trahan? Who had the motive and who had the means?"

Simon couldn't see King having either. Bear, on the other hand . . . "Assuming they determine the car was run off the road and you didn't fall asleep at the wheel and drive yourself off the bridge."

She snorted. He noticed she did that a lot, noticed it made him smile.

"Do they even have investigators here with the tools and the training to tell the difference by looking at the car?" Again with the squeaking bed. "God, it makes my head hurt to think about all of it."

"Then don't. Not now, anyway. Not until you get some sleep."

"Do you think they'll bring in the state police? Do they have state police in Louisiana?"

A dog with a bone. "Sleep, Micky. We'll get back into all of this tomorrow. After we get you to the doctor and your arm stitched up."

He heard the catch in her breath. "You want to take me out in public? Is that safe?"

He'd been thinking about that off and on all afternoon. About keeping her hidden or using her as bait. Luring out the bad guys, letting them know she hadn't been the main course for any alligator picnic might make them nervous. And careless. Enough so to come after her again.

He didn't have to tell her that was the plan, or that such situations were where he did his best work. But he did need to tell her something, she being the crime-solving millionaire heiress that she was.

He rolled to his side, tucked the duffel beneath his arm, and rested his head in his hand. She turned toward him in a similar position, the light shining through the window reminding him that he was looking not only at the face from his billboard but at the face of that heiress, at the face of a woman used to being in the public eye.

He wondered if she'd ever been threatened before, if she'd ever been in danger. If it came with her job, as it did with his. "You'll be safe. I'll be with you."

Her expression wasn't exactly dubious, but her eyes did question what he'd said.

"You don't believe me?"

"It's not that I don't. It's just that I have no reason to. Besides your word."

"Then you doubt me?"

"I don't know you. You say all the right things. . . ." She paused, searching, as if she didn't want to insult the only person she had on her side. "But I don't know why you say them. Because they sound good, or because you know what you're talking about."

Ouch. Okay. How to ease her mind without giving himself away. "As far as keeping you safe, I know what I'm talking about. I did private security for a while after the service."

"Like a bodyguard?"

"In a way. But think Afghanistan and automatic weapons. Not men in black behind tinted shades."

"I think I'm feeling better already."

A smile. Good. "Now you can relax and get some sleep."

She was quiet for a minute, then, "Since I'm going out in the public eye as myself, then there's no reason I can't use my credit cards, right?"

"You didn't lose them when the car went under?"

"I was wearing the strap of my purse across my body. The purse stayed put, but I lost all the things I'd bought the day before in New Orleans. And as much as I appreciate the loan of the clothes, I've learned my lesson about what's appropriate to wear, or not wear, in public."

Now this he needed to hear. "I must have missed this one. What did you not wear and when?"

She flopped onto her back. "I don't want to talk about it."

"Consider it rent. Your story for the use of the house as a hideout."

"If you want rent, find me an ATM tomorrow and I'll pay you in cash."

Uh-uh. He wasn't that easy. "I've got cash. I don't need cash. I'm more interested in what drove the Ferrer heiress off her Manhattan mountain and into the swamp."

"Why would that interest you at all?"

"I told you. I look at your face every day out my window, though you're not quite who I imagined that woman to be."

"Oh, I'm definitely her. You're just seeing her on a very bad day. I'd like to see that Hilton chick drag her ass out of the swamp and look any better."

She didn't get it. He didn't know if he should explain. "It's not about the way you look."

A puff of breath. A chuckle. "Since I can't do anything about that with what I have here to work with, that's good to know."

"That's what I'm saying." Did he know what he was saying? "You blow it off like it's nothing. That's not what I thought that woman would do."

"You fantasize about that woman a lot, do you?"

"Let's just say that she and I have a lot of interesting conversations," he said after weighing full disclosure against keeping his big mouth shut.

"One-sided, I hope. Or have you been putting words into my mouth?"

Putting things into her mouth. Nope. He wasn't going there. "What can I say? You looked like you'd make a good listener. And like you might have a thing or two to say."

"And what did I tell you?"

Well, hell. This wasn't where he'd planned to go, either. "One night you told me that I'd had too much to drink. To put down the bottle, take a cold shower, and get into bed."

"And did you?"

"Two out of three. The shower started to sober me up, so I took the bottle to bed." *Since I couldn't take you. . . .*

"Why were you drinking?"

Tit for tat. "Why were you running around half dressed?"

"I was fully dressed when I went out. I just got rid of my underpants on the dance floor at Slick Velvet."

Underpants. That didn't seem like a Michelina Ferrer word. But dancing bare-assed in public? Yeah, that he could see. That he would *like* to see.

And now that he'd met her, he understood her chagrin. "Who noticed?"

"I don't know. Someone with a cell phone camera and an up-skirt fetish, I guess. Or just a member of the paparazzi devoted to his art."

He didn't want to accuse her of inviting trouble, but the obvious question was still sitting there unasked. "Why did you take them off?"

She pulled the sleeping bag closer to her chest, held it there. "You first. Why were you drinking? And why did I tell you to stop?"

"You told me to stop for the obvious reason. A weeklong drunk never did anyone any good." Though it had seemed the perfect solution at the time.

He'd been on assignment with Eli McKenzie, one that

should've been a quick in-and-out package retrieval for a friend of Hank Smithson's. The members of the Russian mob hadn't been amenable to letting it go.

When Simon and Eli had learned the package was living and breathing and had a name, it was too late into the operation to regroup. The girl had taken a bullet in her shoulder, but she was returned to her grandfather without further harm.

In retaliation, the mob had gone after Eli's woman, Stella Banks, holding her hostage and demanding a trade everyone involved knew would never happen.

Stella had choreographed her own escape, chiseling loose the mortar from between the cinder blocks of her basement prison and shorting out the building's electrical system with the wires she'd found behind the wall.

Unfortunately, she'd started a fire, and suffered smoke inhalation and burns that still had her confined at Weill Cornell. It seemed like a lifetime ago. It had been less than three weeks. Simon had spent the first on a bender, refusing to take Eli's calls.

It had been Hank who'd finally gotten Simon to open his door, but it was Michelina who'd heard his confession, who'd brought him back from the dead. Michelina who'd told him to go see Stella, to deal with the guilt and the grief like a grown-up.

Knowing that she had as much trouble facing problems as he did made the whole thing even more of a joke than it was. They were some kind of pair, even if that pair was nowhere but in his mind.

"Hey," she said softly, as if she'd given Simon all the time she thought he needed. "Where'd you go?"

He wondered how long he'd been gone. "Not to sleep, which is where we both need to be."

After a long quiet moment, she said, "You don't have to sleep on the floor, you know. This is a full-size bed."

"If it was a king, I might consider it. I take up most of a full by myself."

"You can wrap up in one sleeping bag, and I'll wrap up in the other."

Someone, anyone, deliver me from temptation. "I think I need more personal space than that."

"Then at least take one of these," she said, balling up the sleeping bag she'd been huddled beneath.

She tossed it to him, squirreled around, and wrapped up in the one covering the mattress, lying on her side rolled up like a bug in a rug. He sat up and arranged the second bag similarly, half of it as a mattress, half as a cover to keep off the chill.

They laid like that for a long time, awake but not speaking, close but distant, aware of the big empty house around them and how the two of them were sharing the same small space, breathing in and out the same air.

For however long she stuck around, he needed to think of her as the victim of an accident, as someone who'd asked the wrong questions and found herself in someone else's way. He couldn't think of her as the woman who knew all his secrets, the one he'd told things he didn't want anyone else to know.

If he made that mistake, thought of her as his, he wouldn't be able to keep a safe distance, maintain his objectivity, or give this mystery the attention it deserved. Then again, were he to be honest with himself, he'd have to admit it was already too late.

He'd lost anything resembling detachment the moment he'd seen the fear in her eyes—eyes he'd looked into for his own salvation so many times they were the only eyes he ever saw in his dreams.

Seventeen

Chelle could not wait for the weekend. There'd been enough office drama the last few days to spread out over a month, and today was going to be just as bad as—if not worse than—all the others combined.

After today's meeting with Simon, things would settle down, and Chelle wouldn't feel like she was sitting in a basket of eggshells, wincing every time the door opened or the phone rang, waiting for them to crack.

It wasn't that she had a problem doing her job or dealing with the public. She'd tended bar in the French Quarter long enough to get over any people issues she'd had. But if Lorna didn't stop hovering, Chelle was going to snap.

Her boss gave her a lot of autonomy, and the atmosphere at Savoy Realty had been great, but taking Simon's phone call earlier in the week had Lorna so on edge, Chelle had been feeling the pain.

The waiting had sucked up her emotional energy, leaving her spent to the point where she feared making a mistake at work, or making a bad decision that would impact the rest of her life.

Like telling King Trahan they were through.

Letting him know of her decision was not going to be

easy. Hell, coming to the decision had been no piece of cake. But after yesterday, in her kitchen, the decision was one she'd forced herself to make.

In reality, the sex they had and the way they had it should have been enough. She'd never planned to stay in Bayou Allain forever. She'd never planned her time here at all. It was a case of having nothing better to do and no compelling reason to move on.

But those words King had cried out had been weighing on her heart ever since. She'd put herself in a position she'd have steered clear of in the past, a position she'd have smacked her friends silly for putting up with.

A relationship, even one that had never promised to be more than sexual, had to go somewhere. It couldn't remain stagnant. It had to get better or get worse. It had to grow or die.

She knew that, and yet she'd still thought it possible to keep her heart from getting involved with what her body was doing with King. But oh, their encounters. Their second had been even more incendiary than that first night in the parking lot at Red's. . . .

She'd run an errand for Lorna to Lafayette and had blown a tire on her way home. She wasn't incompetent. She knew how to change it. But until she had the back end of the car ready to jack and the lugs on the flat loosened, she hadn't realized the spare was in no better shape. She was stuck in bumfuck nowhere with no cell service and a five-mile hike to town.

She had known Lorna wasn't going to be happy about the delay, but Chelle had been even more unhappy about having to leave her car. It was a classic, and there were too many itchy fingers living along the bayou for her to trust that she'd find it in one piece when she got back.

She'd been standing there, her hands on her hips, cursing her stupid car, her stupid life, and herself for being so irre-

sponsible, when a big diesel crew truck had come into view
and slowed, pulled over to the side of the road, and stopped
on a dime.

The sun had been bright, reflecting off the windshield,
making it impossible for her to see the driver. She'd bent
for the tire iron in case she found herself needing to bash a
skull and kept a tight grip on it even after the door swung
open and the driver climbed down.

She'd seen King Trahan only the one time, a night in-
volving a lot of alcohol, very little light, and a complete loss
of inhibitions. But something about this man . . . Oh, yeah.
One and the same.

Dark sunglasses had covered his eyes. A white T-shirt
had stretched to cover his chest and shoulders. His long legs
had been covered in worn denim that showcased the lean
muscles of his thighs and the thickness behind his fly.

In the bar he'd been devastatingly handsome. In the
parking lot he'd shown her how easy he could take her
where he wanted her to go. But none of that was real. Life
was not a fantasy. Life was a big flat tire and a worthless
spare five miles from civilization.

She'd kept that in mind as he'd walked toward her, saying nothing while assessing the situation, returning to his
truck for a pump and a plug to fix the hole left by the nail
she'd run over. He'd made the repair, done the same to her
spare, inflated both of the tires.

She'd hated feeling helpless, so she'd begun packing
things into her trunk while he carried his tools to his truck.
She never heard him come back, hadn't known he was behind her until his shadow fell over hers.

When she'd turned to thank him, he'd stopped her, moving close, lifting her skirt to her waist, exposing her backside and her panties to the sky. He hadn't held her against
her will, not at all.

But when she'd heard the rustle of denim as he'd opened

his fly, she hadn't been able to move. They'd been parked on the side of the road in broad daylight. Granted, his was the only vehicle to come by since she'd pulled over, but that didn't mean a thing.

Her last thought before he'd torn her panties away had been that at least they were shielded by her raised trunk and the massive bulk of his truck.

She'd felt his hand as he'd held on to his cock, as he'd rubbed the bulbous head between her legs, smearing and spreading the moisture she'd released and coating himself for entry.

His first stroke had been slow and sure. He'd filled her completely, his length and his girth immobilizing her. She'd widened her stance, kept her palms braced on the car's bumper and her eyes closed.

He hadn't moved right away. She'd kept waiting, wanting him to fuck her fast and furiously, wanting him to come so they wouldn't get caught. She hadn't expected him to care about her pleasure. But she'd known nothing then of who he was, of how her response was as vital to him as his own.

So when he'd dipped his knees and reached around with both of his hands, she hadn't even been able to think about the fact that he'd just changed a tire. All she could do was let him touch her, and relish her body's response as he did.

He'd rubbed her clit between two fingers, pulled back the protective hood with a thumb, opening her to the butterfly flicks he'd learned their first time drove her wild.

She'd squirmed back into the cradle of his hips, contracted around him, and caused him to groan. She'd liked that, liked feeling it rumble through her, liked knowing that he was human, a man, and not a mechanical hard-on.

She'd shifted her weight to one hand, brought her free one between her legs, reached behind their joined bodies to fondle his balls. The skin around them had been tight, his testes hard and drawn close.

And it had suddenly become imperative that she take charge, that she delay getting hers, that she make him come. She'd begun to move, sliding forward on his cock, sliding back, repeating the slow stroking motion and refusing to stand still even when he took hold of her hips to stop her.

She wasn't going to be stopped. He'd caught her off guard the first time. She'd been determined to own their second encounter. It hadn't taken much in the way of persuasion to convince him.

All she'd done was use her hips the way they were intended, rolling them, a sultry figure eight that pulled and squeezed and played his cock until he was a mass of nerve endings and barely able to breathe. When he came, his cry had sent birds out of hiding and into the air, sent her into mindless spasms.

To this day, she was still surprised she hadn't stripped down to her bare skin and sprawled across the hood of her car, her heels pulled to her hips, her legs spread wide. It was as if she could think about nothing but sex when he was around.

Which was why last night while in bed alone she'd made the decision to cut him out of her life. Terrill had been out in the garage and strangely had made the choice easier. He'd lost his wife and was coping. All Chelle would be losing was sex. She'd done without before. She could do without again.

When the door to the lobby swung open, she gladly buried all thoughts of King to focus on work. It was ten, meaning this was most likely the appointment Lorna had been anticipating. Chelle forwarded the switchboard to voice mail, wanting to give the client her full attention and not miss a word.

Two people walked through the door. A man and a woman, when she had been expecting only the first. The woman was wearing clothes that had seen better days. Blue jeans, a low-cut black top with what had once been the funkiest scarf, and nothing but socks on her feet.

Her face was free of makeup, her dark hair pulled back with a red rubber band. Her eyes were dark brown, her forearm wrapped in gauze, and strange appearance aside, she was one of the most gorgeous women Chelle had ever seen.

But the man . . . if he was Simon Baptiste, Chelle better understood Lorna's nervous behavior of late. He was big and dark—his hair, his scowl—and in charge of whatever was going to happen. Chelle couldn't even imagine Bear Landry standing up to this man.

He wore an aura of authority as casually as he wore his T-shirt and jeans, and in a really twisted and psycho way, he made her think of King—which wasn't so twisted and psycho when she thought about them being cousins.

"Good morning," she finally said as the door closed behind them and the room filled with tense expectation. "Can I help you?"

The man stepped around the woman. She took in the small lobby, her scrutiny making Chelle wish she'd worn her Donna Karan knockoff today instead of her usual long skirt and tunic—the wardrobe she'd adopted since coming here, because it was as far removed as she could get from the leather and metal she'd worn during her other life in New Orleans.

"Simon Baptiste. I'm supposed to see Lorna Savoy. If you can tell her—"

Chelle held up one hand and reached for the phone with the other. "I'll tell her you're here."

Simon pressed a finger to the disconnect button. "No need. Just let her know something's come up and I'll have to get back with her later."

And he couldn't have called to let them know? Saved

them all this stress? Chelle didn't know what to say. She returned the receiver to its cradle, her gaze shifting from Simon to his companion.

She scrambled. Lorna would have her hide if she let him leave. "I'm sure Ms. Savoy would like to talk to you. At least to say hello personally."

But he was shaking his head, on his way to the door, the woman with him fighting a smile. "There's no need—"

The door to Lorna's office opened and interrupted him. "Why, Simon Baptiste. Don't tell me you're going to walk out of here without so much as a word. After all these years?"

Chelle watched him stop, watched him turn, swore the temperature in the room turned from polite and cordial to a bitterly personal cold.

Now this was interesting. And oh, didn't she wish she could turn on her cell phone's video recorder and capture this fly-on-the-wall moment for King.

Simon took in the hitch of Lorna's hip where one hand rested, the other resting against the door frame head high. It didn't matter how long it had been since the two had seen each other. There was no way he could miss the strain around her eyes.

Quite frankly, Chelle didn't think she'd ever seen Lorna look worse. As always, her outfit and body were killer. But her lips were tight, the wrinkles at the edges dry, her face too pale for her makeup—all of it making the worst sort of contrast to the woman standing in the corner by the door.

Lorna suddenly realized Simon wasn't alone. She seemed to deflate where she stood, as if she'd put more stock in seeing him than in seeing him about business.

But she was a pro, no matter her personal disappointment, so she walked closer to him and extended her hand. "It's wonderful to see you again, Simon. Is this your wife you've brought with you?"

"She's not his wife, Lorna," Bear Landry said, following her into the lobby and standing in front of Chelle, blocking her view. "This is the woman I told you I met last night at Red's. A friend of Lisa's. Michelina Ferrer."

Michelina Ferrer? As in Ferrer Fragrances?

Chelle rolled her chair to the corner of her desk and peered around the bulk of the judge. Without her hair dressed in the wild mane she wore in the ads, and her face lacking the soft matte glow that showed off the vibrant colors her stylist used on her eyes, it was hard to tell that's who she was, but Chelle wasn't about to question the judge.

Besides, he'd said she was a friend of Lisa's, not a celebrity spokesmodel . . . except how many women could possibly be named Michelina Ferrer and look this amazing, even without the makeup and hair she was known for?

"It's good to see you again, *chère*," Bear told the Ferrer woman. "I wasn't sure I would ever have the pleasure, or an opportunity to deliver the apology I owed you after speaking to you so rudely."

"Any particular reason you weren't sure, Bear?" Simon asked, stepping between the judge and Ms. Ferrer. He didn't acknowledge Lorna at all.

Bear inclined his head. "It's good to see you, too, Simon. And no reason other than I assumed Miss Ferrer was already on her way home."

Michelina lifted her chin, spoke softly. "I'm not ready to leave yet. Not until I learn what happened to Lisa."

"Why don't we all step into my office? We can sit and talk, catch up on old times." Lorna waved her hands as if directing traffic. "Chelle, make some fresh coffee, or would you all prefer iced tea?"

Simon put a stop to that. "We're not staying, Lorna. Some things have come up that I have to deal with now. I'll have to get back to you on the property and the maintenance fees. I figure the delay will give you time to fine-tune your story, seeing as how you're going to need a good one to explain the condition of my place."

"There's nothing to fine-tune, Simon. And it won't take but a minute to explain." Bear moved closer to the door. "Surely you've got that much to spare."

Chelle could see the Ferrer woman's face, and her expression as she looked at Bear was enough to make Chelle wish she'd left the room when they'd entered. The other woman might have been one of the most beautiful and wealthiest in the country, but there was nothing of privilege in her face.

She was furious, and she was frightened, and Chelle couldn't help but wonder what Bear had said to her last night at Red's, if it had been more than rude, if it had been somehow . . . threatening.

And then she wondered how the two of them had met, Michelina and Simon, if they knew one another away from Bayou Allain and had come here together, or if they'd met as strangers in the same place at the same time.

Chelle tuned back in to what Bear was saying.

"I know you haven't kept in touch with your cousin, but King hasn't exactly been welcoming of the folks who've rented the house over the years. Learning they're living next to a convicted felon has sent a lot of them running." Bear let that slap in the face sink in, moved his cane to his other hand and leaned on it heavily. "Those who have stayed, well, they haven't stayed long after finding out what happened in that house with your mother. It's the sort of thing that gets around and keeps renters away."

He reached for his handkerchief then and wiped it over his brow, pausing for a moment as if delivering such a blow had worn him down—or else pausing for effect and giving Simon time to take it all in before conveying even more bad news. "Lorna and I discussed the situation and decided no one should hear such a report through the mail. Unfortunately, having no other way to reach you, we felt our chosen course of action the best."

Wow. Chelle knew the judge could be a jerk, but that was just cold. And cruel. And a lot of it a big pack of lies. She'd lived here a while. She dealt with renters all the time. She'd never heard anything sordid about Simon's mother. Not even from King.

And Bear didn't get involved in Lorna's rental business anyway. What was that all about? They'd discussed? They'd decided? Their chosen course of action? Whatever was going on, she could tell by the look on Simon's face that she wasn't the only one who didn't think much of Bear's speech.

"So . . . what now? You're going to try to sell me a time-share in the Everglades?" Simon asked, muttering some not-so-nice words under his breath. "No, wait. I'd rather bend over and take it on my own terms. And thanks, but I'll show myself to the door."

His hand was on the handle when Lorna reached him and placed her fingers over his. "If you wait, I'll cut you that check right now. It won't take but a minute. I should've had it ready, but I wasn't sure if you were going to want the money back, or want me to use it for repairs even though the place has been empty so long."

His expression was priceless, just the right mixture of fury and disbelief and loathing. "Oh, I want the money, *chère*. You'd damn well better believe it."

Nodding, she looked down to where she held him, sighing as if the picture of her skin against his was a masterpiece. It made Chelle want to roll her eyes. "Putting a check that size in the mail just didn't seem right. Not without you knowing to keep an eye out for it."

Simon barked out a laugh. "Certified mail, Lorna. Return receipt requested. Ever hear of it?"

"I'm so sorry. I should have sent it. I should have been in

touch about the problems with the place. Forgive me? Please?" Lorna's plea was desperate, her skin gone ghostly and clammy looking.

Something was going on here that was way over Chelle's head, something that had nothing to do with any amount of money Lorna might owe.

But Simon wasn't swayed. He pushed open the door and held out a hand for Ms. Ferrer, ignoring Bear completely, looking at Lorna only long enough to say, "I won't be needing your services any longer, but I will be by for my check in the morning. Have it ready."

Chelle watched him go, remembered the switchboard was set to voice mail, and managed to remove the forward before her boss noticed. Not that Lorna would have.

Lorna was standing at the front door, her fingers wrapped around the metal crossbar, her gaze following her visitors' departure through the window as if she were watching her dreams drive away.

Bear had already returned to Lorna's office, and his voice was none too gentle when he called for her. Twice. The third time she finally let go of the door, wringing her hands at her waist as she crossed the lobby.

"Oh, Baby Bear. What are we going to do now?" was all Chelle heard before the office door closed. Chelle sat there for a minute, not moving, her heart racing as she tried to process what had just happened but failed.

Lorna was obviously disappointed, but Chelle couldn't think of any reason for her to have dissolved into tears loud enough to rattle the office walls. She did, however, know one person who would love a rundown on this turn of events, and reached for the phone to dial Red's so she could get a message to King.

Eighteen

"Let me get this straight," Micky said, one hand flat at her hip on the truck seat, the other holding on to the armrest for dear life. "You've been paying that woman money to keep your house in livable condition, and she's been doing nothing? Taking it and letting the place fall to the ground?"

"That's about the size of it," Simon bit off in answer.

"Why?" was the only question that came out when there were so many others swirling in her head . . . namely, what had Judge Landry been doing there, what was Simon's connection to him, and why had he failed to mention it? "What was that cryptic stuff about the things that happened there with your mother? And about living near King? A convicted felon? What does he have to do with this?"

"He still lives there."

What? "In that house?"

Simon shook his head. "He's got a trailer about a mile away."

A mile? "How big is your piece of property?"

"Four thousand acres, plus or minus," he said, slowing the truck as they approached the first intersection past the real estate office.

Micky wasn't sure what had just happened, but she knew it was big. Yes, she was viewing the incident with her recent history coloring her perceptions. But that was neither here nor there. As much as the others might think her an innocent bystander, she wasn't. She might not know Lorna Savoy, but she knew enough about Judge Landry to know she didn't care to ever learn more.

What she did want to know was, what in the world of soap operas had just happened? Simon's agitation was clear in the way he had driven out of there: backing from the office's parking lot into the street without checking for oncoming traffic, slamming on the brakes before shifting gears and tearing forward in a squeal of burned rubber.

He wasn't the same driver who had gotten her safely from his house to the small medical clinic and then to the meeting without jarring her tender arm even once. Was it because of the judge's remark about his mother? Hearing that bullshit story about getting in touch?

"When did you change your mind? About putting off the meeting?"

"Last night. After you'd gone to sleep. We never got your arm looked at yesterday, and that couldn't wait," he finally said, sitting at the stop sign long enough to make up for the other infractions. "The meeting could."

She appreciated his concern. She would have appreciated it more if she believed that was all of the story even knowing he didn't owe her a thing. If anything, she owed him. He'd saved her life, after all.

"There's a small clothing store next to the pharmacy," he said. "Or there was when I was last here. They won't have anything fancy. Blue jeans, sneakers, work boots. Oxford button-downs, T-shirts. Will that work, or do we keep driving and find a boutique more to your liking?"

His question wasn't that big of a deal. She knew who she was, the way she dressed, how people saw her and the expectations that came with that. But his attitude, his sarcasm, yeah, those she could've done without.

"I spent yesterday in your boxers and T-shirt. Today I'm wearing clothes I rinsed within an inch of their life and they still smell like dead fish." Really. It was gross. "And you think I need something other than jeans, tennis shoes, and a clean top?"

He didn't say anything right away, but she saw the edge of his mouth quirk toward a smile, and she felt better realizing that his anger was short-lived and compartmentalized outside this truck.

Still, if he had something going on that was going to get in the way of keeping her safe, she needed to know. If he was going to guard her body, he needed his head in the game.

"Then let's drop off your prescriptions and see what we can find in your size."

At this point, size was less of an issue than the clothes being clean, and her need for the meds. The doctor had not been pleased that she'd let the gash go unattended for more than twenty-four hours. Neither had he liked her use of duct tape.

But the topical he'd used before stitching her up had worn off before they'd made it past his billing clerk, and hiding the pain was getting harder to do.

Simon pulled his truck facefirst to the curb and parked between Schott's Pharmacy and Day's Dress for Less. He killed the engine, turned toward her, his hand on the door handle when she made no move to get out.

"You change your mind?" he asked. "This was a good idea until you actually saw the place?"

She arched a brow. "No, I haven't changed my mind about anything, though if you don't kill the attitude, I'm going to change it about you."

He looked forward again, blew out a long, slow breath. "I've got a lot going on."

"You and me both."

"You're right. I'll find someone else to use as a punching bag. Sorry."

His punches had all been verbal, but she wasn't in sparring condition and wasn't sure she would be until she had answers to the questions turning her life upside down.

"Tell you what," she said. "If we can get my medicine and find a few things for me to wear, I'll buy lunch and let you punch all you want as long as you don't have a problem with me punching back."

The look in his eyes nearly sent her to the mat. "You're playing awful loose with those credit cards."

He had no idea what a shopaholic she could be. And no idea of the flutter in her belly that had nothing to do with it being empty. "As long as I get something to wear that doesn't smell like it's been hanging in a fish market, you can max me out the rest of the way on food."

He laughed at that. A laugh that sounded so real, so true. "Not sure you'd be saying that if you'd really seen me eat."

"That's okay," she teased back. "You haven't seen me punch."

Nineteen

Simon was glad for the truce even if they hadn't needed one. At least Micky hadn't. He, on the other hand, was ready for a time-out, especially since he'd just been handed a reminder of why he'd kept his distance from Bayou Allain.

The judge's reasons for letting the house go to shit were lousy. Simon hadn't heard anything that lame in a hell of a long time—maybe since the last time he'd been here . . . the day the judge opened his big mouth and announced to the courtroom he was sending King to prison and Simon to war.

Seeing Lorna again today had triggered the memory of the fire. A couple of years older than Simon and King, she'd been there the night of the blaze. There'd been a lot of sex and a lot of alcohol and most of what happened was a blur.

But something in her expression today—an edgy case of nerves hidden beneath too much blush and begging—brought it all back and had him thinking of this thing with Lisa and Micky. He couldn't say why.

The two incidents were years apart and unrelated—or as unrelated as anything could be with Bear Landry's fingers in both pies. That's what was bothering Simon the most.

The judge had shipped Simon and King away, leaving Le Hasard temporarily abandoned.

And now, except for King, it was abandoned again. No renters, no livestock, no agriculture, nothing. Four thousand acres virtually uninhabited. What did anyone have to gain by keeping it that way? And how was Bear Landry involved?

"What do you think?"

He looked up. Micky was on the other side of the chest-high rack of hanging clothes holding a blouse to her body, a blouse that made him think of a fifties housewife vacuuming in heels and pearls.

He pretended to consider her choice when he was in no shape to shop or keep from speaking his mind. "You buy that, I'll spring for the heels and the pearls and the vacuum to go with it."

She frowned, but she did hook the hanger on the rack. "That's not funny. I remember my mother wearing heels and pearls."

"While she ran a vacuum?"

"Well, no. I'm not sure she ever ran her own, but she dressed up for everything. Playdates, shopping, school events."

"And she always wore a Ferrer fragrance, no doubt."

Micky nodded, wistful, and Simon breathed deep and let the morning go. "Trapani. She was the epitome of the Ferrer woman. One who wore the fragrance like a signature, making it a part of who she was, of everything she did."

He followed as she scooted hanger after hanger along the rack, watched her face as she studied the selection of out-of-date garments. "Do you wear the one on the billboard? The Adria one?"

"Of course." She tossed her head, sending her ponytail flying. "It is who I am."

He'd thought her beautiful. He hadn't realized she was

also so cute, or such a good sport, or so brave. "And you've made it a part of everything you do."

"I have, yes." Another hanger. A frown as she returned the selection.

He wasn't even sure what that meant, making a scent part of everything she did. "Because you wanted to? Or because it was expected of you?"

She cut her eyes toward him and glared. "I thought we were saving the deep shit for later," she said, tugging at a black polo shirt faded along the shoulders from too much time spent exposed to sunlight streaming in through the store's windows.

He wondered if Micky felt similarly exposed, down here in the South, away from the protection of the Ferrer machine and the Ferrer people who kept her toeing the company line. Or if—crimes against her aside—she was enjoying the freedom of being a public figure unrecognized.

She tossed the polo over one arm. "I'm buying this one, the one with the nautical stripes, and the gray baseball jersey."

They were all big and bulky men's shirts. They would cover her well, hide her assets, keep him from trying to sneak a peek where he didn't need to be looking, though nothing would stop him from thinking what he had when she'd come downstairs in his clothes.

He shrugged. "Your call."

"Or my call as long as it doesn't make you picture me doing housework?" she asked.

And because he was in the mood he was in, he answered, "You can do all the housework you want, but a short skirt, fishnets, and a feather duster would be my outfit of choice. If you were asking. Or wondering."

"I wasn't, and I wasn't." Surprisingly, her face colored. "And no, I'm not going to keep it in mind for future reference. I don't do the costume thing if I get the urge to strut my stuff."

"That's right. You're more the full-monty type." And what a picture that brought to mind. "I'll remember that next time I'm in town to hit the clubs. Maybe I'll give Jane a call, check your schedule."

"You don't have to check in with Jane," she said blithely, completely serious. "I'll be happy to share my full itinerary. All you have to do is ask."

Well, hell. That was unexpected. He wasn't sure where they were going with this. He'd thought it harmless flirting, a back-and-forth way to relieve the tension both had been feeling since earlier today.

Except the banter seemed to be more, edging as it was into territory that had nothing to do with missing persons and auto accidents and long-ago fires, and everything to do with the conversations they shared on his patio when he was the only one talking, and her one-dimensional eyes were open to her soul and staring into his.

"I'll remember that," he said and left it at that, not certain he was ready for whatever truth had prompted the comment, especially if it turned out to be a lie. "Are you going to need more things?"

She glanced from the shirts she'd chosen to the stack of folded jeans she held to her chest. "Three changes of clothes and the ones I'm wearing. That should be enough, don't you think?"

Depended on what she was planning. He'd been talking about unmentionables, but her question begged another.

Why hadn't she left the investigation to the authorities and caught the first plane home? "How long are you thinking to stay?"

"I'm not sure. I haven't done anything yet about Lisa. So however long that takes."

"What were you going to do?"

"To start with, hire the best private investigator I can."

Money would be no object in that regard. And a good P.I. could turn over the stones that needed turning and let Simon do his job. And it was his job. He couldn't walk away from what was happening, either.

His first vacation in how many years? And it had turned into just another assignment—only not, because he had a personal connection, a personal investment, a personal reason to see justice served. He hadn't been able to do anything about Stella . . . yet. Micky's case would serve for the moment to slake his need for revenge.

Revenge. A word Hank Smithson didn't allow his operatives to use, believing revenge got in the way of getting things done right, and was a dish best served cold. That chill time gave a man room to think, a chance to make sure he was being smart and acting instead of reacting. It could also give him room to hone his plan, to be certain he knew what he was up against and how to bring the enemy crashing down.

Simon looked up a moment later to see Micky still standing opposite him, the rack of clothes between them, her expectant expression losing patience. "A P.I. wouldn't be a bad idea. You have one in mind?"

"I can call Jane as soon as you can get me to your phone. Or any phone. Even better, a store that sells phones, so I can replace my cell."

She said it, but she didn't sound overanxious. Curious, that. "We can do that, sure, as long as you don't expect the same service here that you get at home."

"What about you and your bodyguard work?" she asked, getting back to business. "Even if you've worked overseas primarily, I would think you would have contacts in the States who could recommend someone? Maybe the type of someone out of Jane's reach?"

He had contacts, all right. He could always call on one of

the Smithson Group team members to do the digging he couldn't do from here, the type of digging he might not want Micky to know he knew how to do.

"I can make a call, yeah, but I can't do it from here. And if that's the plan, I might as well stick you on a plane after that. There won't be anything more for you to do here, and I can keep you updated."

He knew that she was going to want to stay, that she had a vested interest in finding Lisa, not to mention discovering the truth about what had happened to her. They were both legitimate reasons. But they were emotional reasons. There was no physical reason for her to stay.

In fact, there was a physical reason, a very large and potent physical reason, for her not to. But that would require him explaining the distraction of attraction, and that was one thing Simon wasn't ready to do—no matter her invitation to come see her dance.

"I'm going to the cashier to check out now," Micky said evenly, her calm belying the anger simmering around her. "And then we're going to get you to a place where you can make that call."

"And after that?"

"After that, it's gloves up. Because I'm not going anywhere."

Twenty

Lorna Savoy was rapidly becoming the biggest liability to the rest of Bear's life. He'd carried her all these years because he was able to use her devotion to him—a devotion he'd earned by putting her in a position to live a better life than 90 percent of Bayou Allain's population.

He'd made it possible for her to be a queen, to have her name be known when most of her classmates and contemporaries had vanished into the oblivion of poverty. She hadn't lost her figure popping out swamp brats for some unemployed felon who kept rabbit, squirrel, and gator on the table and called that providing for his own.

But all of what Bear had done for her was fast coming apart because of her obsession with Simon Baptiste, and her fear her part in the fire that had destroyed the Trahan home would be discovered.

It had obviously slipped her mind that Bear himself had even more to lose than she did. She had been complicit in that single crime. His had been conceived then but had been ongoing since.

As surprised as he'd been by Simon's appearance in Louisiana after half the other man's lifetime spent far, far away, he'd been shocked to see Michelina Ferrer in the man's company. As far as Bear knew, those two had never met and had no reason to be together now except for the obvious.

Simon had been the one to rescue the woman following her plunge off the bridge.

She would have told him about the vehicle that had rammed her from behind. She would have told him about their conversation at Red's and her interest in finding out what had happened to Lisa.

What Bear wanted to know was whether or not she'd told him why the car had been rented in a name other than her own. Who was this Jane Mitchell whose name had been on the agency agreement, and who Terrill and his men had spent the day dredging the bayou to find?

Bear hadn't talked to his son since last night. He'd seen no need, being quite certain that the driver's body would never be found, that she'd drawn her last breath as she'd fallen.

Not only was she still drawing breath, but she was keeping company with the very man Bear was doing his damnedest to extricate from his life.

So now, not only did he have to deal with Simon and shut up Lorna, but he had to figure out what to do about Michelina Ferrer who was not Jane Mitchell and, like Lisa, knew too much for her own good.

Twenty-one

Micky listened to Simon give his lunch order to their waitress, thinking he could feed a small country for a week on that amount of food, not to mention max out more than one of the credit cards she'd offered.

She started not to order at all, and instead tell the waitress she'd be eating from his plate. But her arm was already hurting. She didn't want to lose a finger or a hand should he not be willing to share his fries or his onion rings or a bite of his pecan pie. So she settled for a club sandwich with a pickle, no chips, no shake, just coffee.

He'd been quiet on the drive from the pharmacy after they'd gone back for her meds. Granted, the trip to the diner had been short and hadn't allowed for a lengthy conversation. Neither had he had time to make the call he'd said he would make. That wasn't a problem. She'd taken him at his word then, and nothing had happened since to make her doubt him.

What she didn't like was his assumption that she would go quietly back to New York. That there was nothing more here for her to do. That might have been the case when she'd first arrived and been unable to locate Lisa on her own. But things had changed since she'd run into Bear

Landry at Red's and he'd given off a vibe that made her feel like she'd stepped in a pile of shit that wouldn't wipe free from her shoe.

She and Lisa might not have been the closest of friends since the other woman's marriage, but that's what matrimony was all about, wasn't it? Spending less time with the girls and more with the man in her life. At least that's how Micky would want it to be.

She had no idea if Lisa agreed, because they'd fallen out of touch—a situation that was primarily Micky's fault. She was the one always telling herself they'd catch up the moment she had the free time. Lisa, on the other hand, wrote, e-mailed, sent Hallmark cards that made Micky giggle, then had her eyes welling up with tears of guilt.

So, no. There might not be anything she could do here, but she wasn't going home just yet. Not until she was sure that a real search was under way, that there was someone in Bayou Allain on Terrill Landry's side. . . .

"Have you thought about talking to Terrill? Feel him out, see if he suspects anyone in Lisa's disappearance?" Facing Simon across the booth that sat next to the window and being this close in the light shining through, it hit her for the first time how old he was.

His crow's-feet were deeper than she'd realized, fanning out from the corners of his eyes to his temples. His face was scarred. Not in some dramatic exhibition, but he'd been hit or cut badly enough to need stitches in a couple of places.

Her hand went to her arm. The doctor who'd closed up the gash had recommended that she see a plastic surgeon instead, that he was an old sawbones and didn't have the same equipment or experience, that his handiwork would leave a permanent mark.

Greta would kill her. Papi, too. But she'd told the doctor to go ahead, that a scar was the least of her worries. And that much was true. She'd been thinking about the mess surrounding her, not about taking home a souvenir to remind her of all she'd been through.

But now she wondered if the marks on Simon's face brought back the battles he'd fought, or if he even noticed them anymore. If they'd become part of the landscape of his face, as familiar as his nose or his mouth.

"Don't you think if Terrill had any suspects he'd have brought them in? It's not just that Lisa's his wife. He's the law."

"That's not what I asked you," she said, making sure she had his attention before saying more, delaying another few seconds while her coffee and his milkshake were served. "I know that Lisa's his wife and that he's the law. I asked if you'd thought about talking to him."

"Considering we probably know more than he does?" He shook his head. "Why?"

"Well, crime TV fanatic that I am," she finally admitted, "it's not hard to tie together the happenings of the last few days. I mean, there's only so much coincidence that can be a coincidence. After that, there's always a trail. One thing leading to the next. Like my questioning Judge Landry about Lisa's disappearance and then ending up in the bayou less than an hour later."

Simon straightened in his seat, his full attention caught by something she'd just said, the vein at his temple throbbing, the tendons in his neck popping into relief.

She frowned, unsteady. "What?"

"Less than an hour later. That's what you said." His words were clipped, his tone harsh.

"It could have been more than, but I don't think so. I hadn't been back on the road very long at all."

"Tell me everything. After your meeting with Bear, what did you do? What were you on your way to do?"

Micky didn't want to think back to that night, to the judge's anger, to the feeling of being threatened even if he'd never put a threat into words. But she could almost feel herself pale when she remembered those headlights bearing down, getting closer and closer and brighter.

She cleared her throat, uncertain if she'd be able to pry words past the gravel tearing at her throat. "I went out to my car to catch my breath. I was furious and didn't want to drive around in circles and wind up lost. I knew I was going to hire a P.I., but I decided I might as well drive back to New Orleans before doing anything else."

"That late?"

"I'd expected to hook up with Lisa. I didn't think I'd be needing to hunt down a room. And there aren't a lot of local vacancies, in case you haven't noticed."

"So you left Red's and that was it. The end of the world as we knew it."

She started to accuse him of exaggerating, then realized his assessment was pretty damn close to the truth. She nodded. "I left Red's . . . and here we are."

That was it for the next few minutes while their waitress, Annette, worked to situate all their plates on the small table. Micky's gaze took in the double meat-and-cheese jumbo burger, the pile of fries, the roller coaster of onion rings, the side salad drowning in dressing, the slice of pecan pie oozing sticky sweet sugar.

He was a big guy, her Simon, but that amount of food tripped every one of her celebrity spokesmodel, the-camera-adds-ten-pounds eating habits, not that she'd been sticking to her diet the last couple of days. . . .

Wait a minute. Had she just called him her Simon? Wow. That had come out of nowhere. And it wasn't true. It just wasn't, she mused, reaching for her pickle while he grabbed up his burger with one big hand and speared his fork into his salad with the other.

He wasn't hers, not her Simon, not even her rescuer. She'd rescued herself, climbed out of the sinking car and climbed to the shore, where she'd huddled against a cypress trunk, moss hanging spongy and pungent in her face, while she waited for the truck to come back and the driver to shine spotlights down on his handiwork. He never did. Either he didn't want to hang around and get caught and questioned, or he didn't think anyone could have survived that fall.

Simon had arrived at his house just as she was deciding between hitching a ride to the sheriff's office or flagging down a trucker to take her back to New Orleans. He'd fed her and clothed her and given her a safe place to sleep.

He'd run interference when strangers had come looking for her even before he knew a thing about who she was or what had happened. He'd taken her to the doctor, and shopping, and now here they were. But, no. He wasn't hers. Even if he was the first man to have done so much for her without asking for anything in return.

They always wanted something. A job at Ferrer. Their photo in the paper. An intro to someone—whoever they thought could advance them in the fashion industry or society. Whatever cachet they could get by dating her. And it was rarely about her. About sex, yes. About her, no. Yet Simon, who wasn't hers, hadn't asked for a thing.

He set down his burger, reached for his shake, caught her staring at his mouth. "If your accident wasn't an accident, then that's our working timeline, and where we'll find our suspect."

She brought her gaze up to his. "I've been thinking the same thing since I first saw the headlights."

"Did Bear know where you were going after leaving Red's?" he asked before sucking on the shake through his straw.

"Did I tell him specifically?" She shook her head, waved the pickle from which she'd just taken a bite. "I told him

I'd let him know if I heard anything from Lisa and I hoped he'd do the same."

"That was it?"

She nodded. "I made it to the door without incident but for one burly beast nearly knocking me to the floor."

"One of Bear's men?"

No doubt. If only she'd paid attention to what he'd looked like. "He and his buddy were walking in that direction, but I didn't look back, so I can't say for sure."

Simon continued his feast, obviously thinking as he chewed. She didn't want to be caught staring again, so she picked up her sandwich and took a bite, surprised at how good the simple fare tasted.

Or maybe it was just that besides yesterday's breakfast of bacon and eggs, she'd eaten nothing but camp rations—her own fault for sleeping as long as she had under her not-rescuer's watchful eye.

But as good as the sandwich was? Oh, what she wouldn't give for pasta drizzled with garlic butter and sprinkled with Asiago and Parmesan cheese. There was nothing that made her tummy happier or her breath smell worse.

"I'd say a penny for your thoughts, but that look in your eye?" He lifted a brow, his laugh lines crinkling. "I'm not sure it's safe to buy."

She grinned. "It's safe. I was thinking about how hungry I am. I'm a serious foodie. I just have to be careful of what I shove in my piehole, being a public figure and all."

Simon sputtered. Ketchup dotted his plate and more than a little bit of the table. "Ah, *chère*. You're ruining my fantasy here."

She loved that she was his fantasy. "You mean that woman on the billboard would never be so crass as to say piehole?"

"That woman wouldn't even think it."

"I'll bet there are a lot of other things that woman would

never think to do that are on my list of favorites," she said before she could plug the very orifice in question.

"Such as?"

In for a penny . . . "Showering naked outside."

This time he almost choked. "When have you ever showered naked outside?"

She really was disappointing him, wasn't she, she thought with a laugh. "More than a few times, actually. In Manhattan and in Italy both."

He let that sink in, waited. "Is this an exhibitionism thing, or are you just a nature girl?"

"Which do you want it to be?"

"I don't think we should go there."

"Why?" she teased. "You don't have an inner voyeur wondering what all I exhibit?"

"If you're showering naked, I'm going to assume it's just about everything. I don't need an inner voyeur to figure that out," he said, chomping down on his burger again.

He wasn't going to play, or to bite into more than his food, for that matter. She wondered what it would take to get him to see the woman sitting in front of him and not the billboard he'd juxtaposed her against. And then she wondered why that was what she wanted, *if* that was what she wanted.

After today, was she really going to see him again? "The reality never does live up to the fantasy, you know."

"What are you talking about?"

"The multidimensional me. I'm not the embodiment of the billboard. I am who I am, not who you created."

He set down his burger, wiped his hands and his face, challenged her with his gaze. "You think I'm disappointed?"

She shrugged off the question. "You close down any conversation that gets personal."

"Jesus, Micky. Everything we talk about is personal. We weren't thrown together to talk about the weather."

"Maybe we should. It's neutral, impersonal. Hardly a subject to make you twitch," she said only to find him frustrated, shaking his head.

"You think our conversations make me twitch?"

"Yes." She didn't say anything else. He aggravated her, the way he changed topics, as if they had nothing to talk about but the web of mysteries in which they were caught.

"Maybe you're right. But if I do it's because I get tired of reminding myself that you're real, that you're not what I expected, that I have to keep my hands to myself no matter how much I might wish otherwise. And if I don't want my dick to snap in half in my pants, then yeah, the weather might be a safer subject.

"Except the weather isn't going to solve a thing, so I guess I'll keep shutting things down when the road gets too bumpy. If you think that means I'm disappointed in who you are, then that's your problem to deal with, not mine." He said the last while leaning across the table, his forearms on the edge, his face as close as he could get it to hers with their plates of food in the way.

She forgot that they were in public. Forgot it on purpose and mirrored his position, leaning as close as she could and then even closer, until she was breathing the same air that he breathed. "I only see one problem at this table. It doesn't matter whether our association is personal or professional. The only one saying you have to keep your hands to yourself is you."

"Don't think I'm going to forget you said that, *chère*." Forgetting their deal, he grabbed the check before grabbing her wrist and pulling her to her feet, his eyes smoky hot. "When the time is right, I'm going to remember it plenty."

Twenty-two

Kingdom Trahan turned onto the long dirt drive that led to the abandoned house his cousin was apparently now calling home. He stopped his truck just inside the gate and sat there, idling. There were a lot of trees between here and there blocking his view.

He didn't know if Simon was there, and if he was, if he was alone or had the Ferrer chick with him. How those two had hooked up was a question for another day. The only thing King had on his mind at this moment was what Chelle had told him when she'd called after lunch—that Simon had been given the shaft by Lorna Savoy for years.

By all rights, King and Simon should have owned the property jointly, the way their mothers as sisters had. But King's parents died without having changed their will to provide for his future. His aunt, Simon's mother, had petitioned the court for custody and won, walking away with not only her sister's kid but his share of the four thousand acres that had been in their family since the Civil War.

The oil had been discovered before Simon and King were born. The production hadn't been astronomical, the barrels enough to provide for the Trahan and Baptiste families. Then came the accident that had taken King's parents and the tragedies that had followed to take Simon's away as well.

The cousins had stuck together through all of it, running the place on a smaller scale after Simon's father took off after their graduation. Or they had until Simon had managed to burn down King's house and they'd both been sentenced to serve time.

When King had come home, he'd wanted to pick up the drilling where they'd left off. Things hadn't worked out the way he'd expected, and somewhere along the way he'd stopped caring. Why should he be the one doing so when the place wasn't even his? When he'd heard Simon was coming to check out the property, he hadn't been surprised. No reason for his cousin to hang on to a losing proposition that hadn't interested him since his discharge.

But what was Simon doing with Michelina Ferrer?

The night in Red's when King had met her, she hadn't said a word about knowing Simon, or traveling with him to Bayou Allain. But then they hadn't done a lot of talking. She'd come there to find someone who could tell her where to find Lisa.

The way she'd stormed out of the bar, she obviously hadn't been happy with what she'd found out, or the way the information had been deep-fried and served up with a side of Bear Landry's bullshit. She'd flown out of the place as riled up as Terrill had only minutes before.

King had pressed Chelle for answers. She hadn't been too thrilled when he hadn't wanted to talk about anything besides what had gone down between his cousin and the judge.

If the woman didn't understand his fixation, that was her problem, not his. Sex wasn't worth the hassle of having her get up in his face over something she didn't understand—

though he wasn't much for understanding things himself, it seemed.

If he was, he'd have an answer to why he was still sitting here wasting time and wasting gas instead of shifting into drive and getting the answers he'd come here to get—even if doing so meant facing the man who had ruined his life.

Twenty-three

Simon needed a bigger truck. That's all there was to it. He used this one in the field, kept it garaged when he was working at SG-5's Manhattan ops center. Cabs, the subway, his feet—they all made a lot more sense than trying to maneuver this beast through the city.

But driving back to his place from town, his second row of seats filled with Micky's purchases and Micky taking up the passenger side of the front, well, he needed more room. He was surrounded by her, and it was making him crazy . . . the way she smelled so rich, her attitude that was so full of bite, her fingers right now clenched tightly in her lap.

All the time that he'd talked to her billboard, he'd thought about her hands. They weren't visible in the picture, hidden beneath her hair as she lifted it, the mane just ready to fall in thick glossy waves. He'd thought about her hands because he'd thought about touching her, about her touching him, and they hadn't been nice thoughts at all.

The drive back to his place took thirty minutes. They were only halfway through and all he'd thought about since the diner was not having to keep his hands to himself unless that's what he wanted to do. Right now he had to keep them on the wheel, but once they were back at the house—

"Do you think Judge Landry is capable of harming Lisa?" Micky interrupted his musings to ask. "Do you know him well enough to say?"

Shoptalk. That he could deal with. Question was, could she deal with the truth? "Bear Landry is a lot of things, and none of them particularly nice. Whether or not he'd hurt Lisa? I don't want to think he has that in him, but I'd be lying through my teeth if I told you I didn't think the man's involved somehow with her disappearance."

"She was just mad about Terrill. The kind of mad that's intoxicating. I've never seen anyone else that much in love." She grew silent, sighed deeply, then, "I can't stand to think her father-in-law might be the reason she's gone."

And Bear was most likely the reason Micky had almost been gone. . . . "You've never been that much in love?"

Well, hell. That wasn't what he'd meant to ask.

"If I had a relationship like that, do you think I'd have run away from home to commiserate with a girlfriend?"

Relationships didn't always last, no matter how perfect they seemed at the start. Surely she knew that. She couldn't be that naïve, not with the life she'd led, the things she'd seen. But since he wasn't much of a relationship guy, not wanting to deal with exactly what Eli McKenzie was suffering now with Stella, all Simon said was, "It'll happen. When it's time."

She snorted. "You're kidding, right? Do you know the baggage I come with? The things anyone who wants to be with me has to deal with? That's assuming a man might want to be with me and not just my name. Trust me. Half the time even I don't know if it's worth it. And now with this latest . . ."

He waited for her to go on, but she didn't say a thing. She sat with her elbow braced on the door, her chin in her palm as she stared out the window. The bridge was coming up. She hadn't breathed a word when they'd crossed it on their way into town, but they'd been going the opposite direction.

Heading toward the bridge now, he didn't see how she could help noticing the spot where she'd been rammed from behind and sent flying. He picked up the conversation where she'd dropped it, hoping to distract her for the rest of the drive.

"What latest? The case of the missing underpants?"

She shrugged as if the incident that had brought her here had lost its stranglehold in light of what she'd been through since. "The case of the missing underpants was a smaller manifestation of a much bigger problem."

Yeah. He'd say she was distracted. "Your girl-gone-wild tendencies getting out of control? They probably make a pill for that."

"What's getting out of control is my father's insistence on running my life his way. I get it when it comes to my position with Ferrer and his wanting final say on everything to do with the company image. But now he's messing in my personal life, and that's just not going to work."

"Messing how?"

Micky buried her face in both hands. "God, it's so archaic. He brought me a man from the Old Country to marry."

Simon found himself grinding his jaw. "Old Country?"

"To him it's the Old Country. Where he was born and raised. Where he met my mother. Where Ferrer Fragrances was established by my great-grandfather. To me it's just Italy."

Now he wanted to laugh. She made him want to laugh. Her sarcasm. Her self-deprecating nature. The way that he had yet to see her put on anything resembling airs.

But he couldn't laugh because there was some guy out there expecting to marry her when she'd belonged to Simon since the morning he'd first looked up from his patio and seen the billboard with her face.

"Who is this guy? This future husband of yours?"

"I don't know. I haven't met him. And, no, I don't plan to. The arranged-marriage thing is not going to happen. My father says I have no choice. I have a duty to the family and the Ferrer name."

"And you thought losing your underpants in public would get him to change his mind."

"Or at least disinherit and fire me."

"But he didn't."

"Actually, I haven't talked to him to find out. I've had too many other things going on."

That was some kind of understatement. "If you wanted him to fire you, why did you run? Or were you trying to give him more ammunition?"

"Mostly I just didn't want to face him," she said softly. "I'm thirty years old and I still fear my father's wrath."

More like she feared disappointing him, and the panty stunt was an easier pill to swallow than refusing the man he wanted her to marry and her father by extension. This way the man could refuse her, and if her father was smart, he'd see that's what she was doing.

"Of course, the fact that I still live in his house doesn't help matters any."

Wait a minute. "Wait a minute. You still live with your father?"

"It's a long story."

"One that's got to be a big wet rag for your dates." Was she really surprised that she'd never had a serious relationship?

"It's not something I tell them."

"What do you tell them?"

"That I have a policy about taking men home—I don't."

"You go home with them instead?"

"I'll rent a hotel suite if things go that far."

"If you decide to sleep with them, you mean."

"No. What I mean is that if a relationship progresses to the point of needing quality time, then the suite is the next step. I don't need it to have sex."

"And if they pass that test? You move on to telling them about living with daddy?" No wonder she'd never experienced intoxicating, living in this bizarre reality that was as bad as his obsession with a billboard.

"I don't know," she said, reminding him that he'd asked her a question. "None of them have ever gone that far."

He started to press, curious, wondering, until he realized they were heading for twitch territory. Her living situation seemed a safer conversational choice, and yeah, he was doing exactly what she'd accused him of. "So what's the long story? About you living with your father?"

"We don't have time. Your driveway is right up ahead."

She hadn't said a word about the accident when they'd crossed the bridge. He didn't know if she'd been lost in thought and hadn't noticed, or if she had noticed and decided mentioning it would only open the wounds that had started to heal.

"You've got time for the short version."

"Not everything lends itself to being condensed."

"Try," he said, coaxing, not wanting to examine too closely the why of his insistence.

"I don't like thinking about my father living alone. He's perfectly capable, in excellent health, has all his faculties and wits. My rational side knows he'd be fine. He's told me repeatedly that he'd be fine.

"But then I start thinking about him being there by himself and I imagine all sorts of ridiculous scenarios, like he's fallen in the tub, or impaled his heel on a golf tee, and I go nuts. Besides, he has plenty of room. We rarely even see each other. But I know I'm close, and it makes me feel better."

Simon started to point out the contradiction she was living, but Micky was a smart cookie and had no doubt figured that out for herself already. He decided not to say anything, just to let her stew.

And then anything he might have said was lost as his house came into view, and along with it his cousin's truck—and King himself cocked back on the porch steps as if he alone owned every one of Le Hasard's four thousand acres.

Twenty-four

Terrill knew he was spending too much clock time working Lisa's case, but he would turn in his resignation without notice if anyone gave him grief and never miss his position. His father would undoubtedly miss having the personal connection to law enforcement, his own inside man.

Lately Terrill didn't much care what his father thought, or wanted, or expected of him. Anytime Bear called or came by, he made mention of Lisa only after he'd taken care of business. Because it was always business. Every single time.

Terrill couldn't get over the change in his father's behavior. Maybe it was just Bear's way of dealing, but it seemed an awfully strange way to deal.

Up until Lisa's disappearance, his father had been nothing but devoted to his only daughter-in-law, warm even, oftentimes joking with her or taking her into his confidence in ways that left Terrill feeling like a third wheel.

And at Christmas or on her birthdays? Bear spoiled her worse than he could possibly have spoiled a grandchild. Lisa had taken it in stride, never letting it go to her head, but his fondness for her had played another part in her tackling the family genealogy.

She'd wanted to know more about where he'd come from, to share with him anything of interest she'd found. She'd also decided the photo album would be the perfect way to show her appreciation for his unconditional acceptance of her as a Landry.

And now this.

Terrill pulled into his own driveway, sat in his cruiser just long enough for the curtains on the Picards' windows to flutter back into place before climbing from the car and jogging across the street to Paschelle's garage. He'd slipped the key on his ring last night and had come back late, staying only thirty minutes or so for fear that he'd disturb Paschelle.

The boxes were labeled by dates, so he'd arranged them chronologically, figuring starting at the beginning was always a good move. He knew that's what Lisa had done, working her way forward and sorting through memorabilia dating back before Bear's parents were born. Her notes told him that she'd made it to nineteen eighty-eight before she'd vanished, and Terrill had been thinking about the last twenty years off and on all day.

Which was why he'd changed his plans. Instead of starting at the beginning, he would start where Lisa had stopped. If her disappearance was the result of what she'd discovered, the timing could be the clue. Not only the timing of the two events coinciding, but the timing of the Landry history she'd been digging into.

He laughed to himself, a weak cackle that was more of a cry than anything else. How sad was it that his wife had learned more of his family's secrets than he'd ever known. And that if he'd paid more attention to Bear's nefarious dealings, rather than turning the expected blind eye, he might have done a better job of keeping his wife safe by holding his father to the letter of the law.

Yeah, he knew that blaming himself for something without even having all of the facts wasn't particularly smart, but he couldn't help thinking about all the things he could have done differently, or better, how he could have been a better husband, protecting the precious life that had been given to him like a gift to share.

"Need any help?

He glanced over his shoulder at the sound of Paschelle's voice. She stood in the doorway, her arms crossed, one shoulder braced on the jamb, wearing flip-flops beneath a long skirt that barely showed her ankles. She looked like a girl, not a woman of twenty-eight, and he thought again about Lisa worrying that she was too young and soft and in-experienced for King. Terrill had to say he was glad the other man might not be coming around anymore. King wasn't a bad guy, just . . . rough, and who he was.

"The company would be nice, but I figure I'd better do all the digging myself since I'm not even sure what I'm looking for."

"Company I can provide," she said, then walked inside, boosted up to sit on a two-drawer file cabinet.

"What are you doing here this time of day?" he asked. "You home sick?"

She shook her head. "Lorna closed the office for the after-noon."

"Made the day's million before one o'clock, eh?" He didn't bother to hide his sarcasm. He knew Lorna was only Paschelle's boss. There was no love lost between them as friends. "Must be nice."

Paschelle snickered like a kid with a secret. "You haven't heard, then. I figured the news would be all over town by now."

He closed up the folder of papers he'd just thumbed through, slid it back into place in the box, and gave her his full attention. "What news?"

"Simon Baptiste came to the office. He was supposed to sit down with Lorna and go over things about the maintenance on his place."

"You mean how it's not being done?"

"Exactly. Lorna and your father gave him some B.S. about no one wanting to live near a convicted felon in a house where a woman committed suicide, though he only implied the suicide part."

That sounded like the sort of crap Bear would pull. "What did Simon say?"

"Not much. He told Lorna to get his refund check ready and to consider their contract canceled. He'd be handling the property himself from now on."

Finally protecting his own interests. Seemed like more than a few of them dealing with Bear were finally wising up. "Baptiste has always been a straight-up guy, from what I hear."

"You didn't know him?"

"I knew of him. I was in junior high when he and King played high school football. One a receiver, one a back. Everyone in the district knew Simon and King."

"What went wrong between them?"

"You mean the fire?"

"Was that it? I've read the stories in newspaper archives, but I didn't see anything other than the facts. And they don't seem enough for this feud."

"What has King said about it?"

She shook her head. "Nothing. We don't talk much."

Terrill felt his ears begin to burn. If they weren't talking, well, he didn't want to know. "I don't know anything for certain, but I hear tell it had to do with the blame, neither of them admitting to lighting the match, though the fire was a clear case of arson."

"So they both had to pay."

"In any other parish, I doubt it would have happened,

but Bear ran his courtroom his way back then. Neither one confessed, both were there, drunk on their butts."

"Meaning, neither one remembered what happened."

"And Bear wasn't going to buy an amnesia defense. The only thing he considered reasonable doubt was who poured the gasoline and who lit the match."

She pulled up her legs to cross them. "Do you think neither one really remembered, or one didn't want to confess and the other didn't want to rat him out? I mean, you said Simon's a pretty straight-up guy."

"And King might be a little more questionable?"

"Yeah, well, straight-up isn't exactly an adjective I'd use to describe him. I'm not saying he's a criminal at heart, no matter his record, but, well, you know."

Terrill knew. He wished he didn't. But King Trahan was almost as familiar with the workings of the sheriff's department as Terrill himself. "To tell you the truth, I doubt anyone but Simon and King will ever know the truth, and since both did their time, I don't see how it really matters anymore."

"Except for the fact that they're finally here in the same place after all these years. You'd think they could let it go, bygones being bygones and all that."

Terrill didn't have anything to add and really had no investment in whether the cousins ever kissed and made up. The two had been a source of gossip for years, the mysterious fire one more element feeding local curiosity. Had any families ever suffered as much as the Baptistes and Trahans and not provided a town with fodder for years?

"I guess all families have to deal with their baggage in their own way," he finally said, getting back to work.

"How are you dealing?" she asked after a couple of minutes spent watching him. "Not with baggage, just with things?"

He wasn't eating, was barely sleeping, turning into a grieving cliché. But he wasn't lying down and giving up. He was working it, living and breathing it. He knew Lisa was waiting for him to find her, to come get her and take her home. And that tore at his heart like nothing else, leaving him feeling like 180 pounds of raw meat.

What he said to Paschelle was, "Not great, but it could be a whole lot worse."

She nodded toward the table. "Are the boxes helping? Or are they mostly trips down memory lane?"

"My memory doesn't go back as far as some of this stuff, but there is a lot here that I'd forgotten about. My kindergarten award for perfect attendance. A book of coupons I made Bear for Father's Day one year." He snorted softly. "None of them redeemed."

"Save them. Give them to your son and you can redeem them for him."

He loved the idea, the hope for the future it gave him, the assumption that he would have a son, that Lisa would return soon and safely, that they could get back to the discussion they'd been having the night before she'd vanished about how much longer they wanted to wait before starting a family, and whether or not they wanted to do it here.

He stuck the coupon book in his shirt pocket, pushing away the fleeting thought that he'd never have need of it. It was Bear's voice in his ear, hurtful and negative, a voice Terrill had heard often as a child but thought as an adult he had learned to ignore.

He needed to go back to work, move away from this past that Lisa had found fascinating, but that gave him a burning and heavy heart. "I've got to get to the office, but I'll probably be over again tonight."

Paschelle hopped down, dusted her hands over the back of her skirt. "No problem. I can even throw dinner together if you'd like."

"That's too much trouble," he said, folding in the box

flaps, then stopping as a loose piece of parchment caught on one corner fluttered to the garage floor.

"It's no trouble at all. Trust me. I have to eat anyway, and fixing enough for two doesn't take any more time and effort than fixing enough for one."

Terrill knew she was saying something and he was probably supposed to respond. He had no mind for anything but the document in his hand, the one that didn't explain everything in clear-cut details, but sure as hell raised his eyebrows and gave him enough of a charge that he knew he'd found exactly what he'd been looking for—a solid place to start.

He opened the box back up. He even pulled up a folding chair. "On second thought, food sounds good, since it looks like I'll be here a while. Just be warned that I'm a starving man and might eat you out of house and home."

For where your treasure is, there will your heart be also.
—Matthew 6:21

Like the code sheet pointing to the words in the Bible that spelled out the treasure's location, the newspaper story alone wasn't telling. A man's body had been found. The sheriff's department in a neighboring parish had asked for the public's assistance with the identification. He had a remarkable tattoo on his chest and a uniquely shaped wound from the assault that had cost him his life. They were hoping someone would recognize one or the other and come forward.

After discovering the existence of the gold, I dug up what I could about coins, trinkets, and historical artifacts found in the area. One coin that everyone seemed to remember and was mentioned several times belonged to Harlan Baptiste. He carried it everywhere, considered it a lucky charm.

Unfortunately, his family's luck was far removed from charming. They'd suffered more tragedies and disasters than anyone I'd ever known. According to Mr. DuPont down the street, Harlan Baptiste made sure the entire town of Bayou Allain knew once Simon and King graduated, he'd be hitting the road. He'd kept to his word and hadn't been seen since.

It was the sketch of the wound accompanying the article about the dead man that drew my attention, though it took days before I again ran across the photo with what I thought might be the murder weapon. I was curious why the judge would have saved the article when the others he'd clipped all referred to cases he'd been involved in.

My mistake was to ask him about it. His reaction was the polar opposite of the joy he'd displayed when I'd shown him the letter from Ruth Callahan Landry. His hostility quickly turned to a mask of insult and hurt, but I'd seen the other before he'd squelched it.

And then I saw the truth.

Twenty-five

"Wait here," Simon said as he parked the truck. He climbed out, slamming the door hard enough to jar Micky's arm. The stitched-up gash began to throb beneath the tape and gauze, and the pain guaranteed she wasn't about to take orders to stay put. Not that she'd ever planned to. The minute she'd recognized Simon's cousin on the steps, she'd glanced to the side to check out Simon's reaction as he drove. It had not been pretty.

She'd been thinking of him as a fictional hero, an ex-military man guarding bodies in Afghanistan before assigning himself to guard hers. He'd become her make-believe version of who he really was, the same way he'd known her face on a billboard. But watching him watching King proved him both human and vulnerable.

He could've been a living rubber band, a coiled spring that breathed. She didn't think she'd ever witnessed that much tension without it resulting in a volatile blast. She didn't know King well, didn't really *know* him at all. She'd only met him two nights ago, and their conversation had been short.

Convicted felon or not, she didn't have to know him to want to warn him of what was to come. She was the one who could see Simon's knuckles as he gripped the steering wheel, the cords in his neck as he now held his chin high, the way his long dark lashes came down to hide the tempest in his eyes.

It was when she looked from Simon to King that she realized she didn't need to warn him of a thing. He knew what was coming. He'd been waiting. He was ready. Being here was his choice, one alpha wolf calling out another, one defending his territory from a challenger with the power to take it away.

Simon hadn't taken three steps before she opened her door. She saw him hesitate, but he didn't turn or look back. She was on her own, and for the first time wondered if she was being reckless, if she should be scared.

She was out of her element. A stranger in a strange land. There were rules here, unspoken laws she had no idea existed. One wrong step and she might find herself in over her head, water rushing up to swallow her whole. . . .

She loved it. The adrenaline.

The untamed beat of her heart.

She had never felt more alive.

"Kingdom," Simon said when he was four feet from the porch.

The other man pushed his body away from the steps and rolled to his feet, stepping down so they were on even ground. "Simon."

Micky wished for a video recorder, a phone with a digital camera; even a Polaroid would do. She wanted to capture the bravado that she knew in her heart wasn't a show but the truth of each man. They were so similar in size, in stance, Simon a hair taller, King ropier, rangy. Simon darker. King bronzed.

These two were the ones who deserved a billboard on East Houston Street. The thought of women unable to pass without shopping . . . what the cousins could do for Ferrer's line of male fragrances . . . The heart of Micky's creative genius began to race.

"I didn't know you knew the little lady here, cuz," King said, inclining his head toward her, offering her a wink. "Nice to see you again, Michelina."

Micky's, "Back atcha, Kingdom," earned her a scowl from Simon, who told his cousin, "I've known her about as long as you have, cuz."

"Are you keeping her hostage here, or feeding her bread and water or something? Because when I last saw her, she wasn't lookin' this haggard and worn. Should treat a gorgeous woman better than that, Simon."

"I've been through a lot since you last saw me." She opened her mouth again to explain about Lisa and the accident but only got as far as holding up her bandaged arm before Simon intervened.

"She's fine. She needs to get her packages out of the truck—"

"I'll be happy to get them for her," King cut him off to say as he moved toward her.

Simon blocked him before he took a second step. "She can get them herself."

Micky looked from one Neanderthal to the other. Neither one spared a glance for her. This time their posturing was too macho-macho man for her taste. Whatever issues had kept them at odds all these years, they could duke it out without using her as another point of conflict.

She moved to stand between them and said to Simon, "I can get them myself, but I'm going to let you do that," then turned to King and said, "If not for your cousin, there's a good chance I wouldn't even be alive to tell you that I don't give a flying fig what you think about the way I look."

And then she walked up the steps and let the screen door slam in punctuation behind her.

Twenty-six

At that moment, Simon couldn't really care about hurting Micky's feelings, but he was more than damn glad she had taken herself out of the way. He didn't know his cousin anymore. He'd often thought he'd never known him at all. But he did know he wouldn't be able to give his full attention to King with Micky around.

"She said you saved her life."

Simon gave a single nod.

"She get into some kind of trouble after leaving Red's?"

"She did." He understood King's curiosity. Micky wasn't from around here. She didn't fit in. But he didn't have to like the other man's attention.

"And you just happened along to save her."

"She saved herself, but I was here when she needed me to be."

King gave that some consideration before asking, "What was she doing here?"

"What business is that of yours?"

"Did you know her already? Before you saved her life?"

Enough. Micky was off-limits. Simon crossed his arms and faced his cousin directly. "Why are you here, King? Because if it's to talk about Micky, you can go."

"Micky, huh? Not Ms. Ferrer? Or Michelina?" King's mouth twisted into a nasty grin. "Staking your claim, cuz? Is that it?"

Simon took a step toward the porch. "Go home, King. This isn't getting either of us anywhere."

"You say that like we've got somewhere to go."

Simon kept walking, King calling after him, "What's going on with Le Hasard?"

Simon stopped, glanced back, hid the sense of loss he felt behind disinterest. "You're the last person I expected to care."

"I don't care," King said, then shrugged. "I'm just asking."

"If anyone should be asking questions, it's me. Not you."

King flung out both arms. "Then ask. It's not like I've never been willing to talk. You're the one who insisted we go through the lawyers for everything. Twenty years paying that retainer? I can see how that would turn your puss sour when you could've just picked up the phone. Of course, that wouldn't have done a lot of good considering how many times my service has been cut for nonpayment."

That did it. Simon walked back down the steps. "You mean the ninety grand I sent you for the well workover you never did wasn't enough to pay your phone bill?"

"Is that why we stopped speaking? Because I misappropriated funds for the well?"

Simon laughed humorlessly. "Boo, we stopped speaking long before you stole my money."

"Oh, right. That happened about the time you stole my land."

Simon hadn't been given the deed until his father had been declared dead, seven years after he'd gone missing. "Look back further than that."

King rolled his eyes. "This can't be about me making the touchdown that saved our asses from your butterfingers and won us state."

Yeah. That was it. "I haven't thought about high school since, oh, high school. I moved on."

"I hear the army's good about helping with that."

"You had the same choice I did." Simon found himself grinding his jaw. This wasn't getting them anywhere, but it was pretty much the way he'd seen their reunion going down.

"You're right. And I chose to stay close to home and keep an eye on the property your parents left to you."

"Making amends for burning what you could of Le Hasard to the ground?"

"You still think I set that fire?"

"I know it wasn't me."

"We weren't the only two there that night, boo. You were the one getting your pipes cleaned. You should remember."

Finally. He'd thought he was the only one not happy with Lorna's involvement. "What reason could Lorna Savoy have possibly had for setting your house on fire?"

"You tell me. And while you're thinking up a reason, think up one to explain what she got out of testifying against us." Then King added when Simon would have stopped him, "Besides immunity."

He had honestly put the whole incident behind him when he'd stepped off the bus into boot camp. Whether intended or not, Judge Terrill "Bear" Landry had given Simon the new life he would never have given himself—or recognized that he needed.

If not for the choice to enlist or serve time, he would've stayed in Bayou Allain, carrying on in his father's footsteps, working to make a go of the four thousand acres his mother's family had owned.

The obligation had hung over both him and King, yet King had been the one to come back, while Simon—the sole legal owner of Le Hasard—had paid the taxes and financed the improvements King's income couldn't meet.

It should have been the perfect and equitable setup, each cousin doing his part to keep the place in the family. Simon had never examined too closely his need to put what distance he could between himself and his Louisiana roots. So, no. Until coming here to settle the past, he'd never thought about Lorna Savoy's part in the trial—or in the fire itself.

He looked his cousin in the eyes, saw the toll the years had taken, saw how old King had become while Simon had been doing his own aging from a distance. "You've been here all this time. You know her better than I do."

"Are you asking for my theory?"

Simon nodded, headed back to his truck. "Want a beer?"

"Sure," King said, twisting the top from the longneck Simon offered. He sucked down a quarter of the brew before speaking again. "Doesn't it strike you as odd that Lorna and the judge are still thick as ticks on a hound?"

Bear Landry was a land man, Lorna a real estate broker. If their association went beyond business, Simon wouldn't know, but the business connection made perfect sense to him. "Not especially. I'm obviously missing something here."

King looked at him as if he were daft. "Lorna would never have been as successful as she has without Bear's help."

"Okay. And?"

"Why her? He could have chosen to help out either of the Callahan girls. Both were a hell of a lot smarter than Lorna. Or Marie Picard. Her family had connections Bear could've used. Even Cindy Robichaux would have made a better assistant. Who could look that girl in the tits and say no?"

Simon didn't say anything, just waited for King to go on—though he wouldn't deny his cousin had run a reasonable flag up the pole.

"Think about it. Lorna wasn't the brightest bulb in her class. The only connections her family had were to some very bad dudes I met in Angola. But she was malleable, and vulnerable, easy to manipulate. With the right clothes, hair, and makeup, she's hot enough, but it takes a lot of work to get her there." King took another long drink, wiped his mouth on his wrist.

Interesting. "She would've been desperate enough to jump at anything Bear offered."

"It would've been her only ticket to a better life."

"Kinda hard to believe she wouldn't have fucked up somewhere along the way, though. If she's been doing his dirty work all this time." That was a sticking point for Simon. Like King had said, Lorna wasn't all that bright.

"She knows how to do what she's told. And she knows how to keep quiet."

Two traits that would make her invaluable to anyone needing a fall guy. "What could she have gained by setting the fire? What could Bear have gained, for that matter?"

King reached for another beer. "The only thing I've come up with is that he wanted you and me out of the way. And he promised her the moon if she helped him make it happen."

It was a decent theory; it mirrored Simon's own, though neither cousin had come up with a motive. They needed more. "It's good, but it's not enough."

"Well, it's not like I've been sitting on my thumbs thinking it through. I've had crops to plant and tend and harvest and sell. Equipment to keep running since replacing it's been out of the question. Then there's the house I've been trying to get finished so I can get out of that goddamn tin can I've been baking in all this time. This place doesn't run itself, and the only manpower I can afford is my own."

"You ought to consider reducing your rates," Simon said,

tossing his empty bottle toward the burn barrel at the back of the house and reaching for another beer.

"Look, about the money—"

"Did you put any of it into the well? Did you buy new pipe? Arrange for water disposal? Anything at all?"

Beer foamed up the neck of the next bottle King opened. He sucked it down as if it were gold, then shook his head. "I had something come up."

"A gambling debt? A round-the-world vacation?"

"Sell the land, Simon. Put me off it. Surely that would give you ninety thousand bucks' worth of pleasure."

It was hard to believe this man was the boy Simon had grown up with, the one who'd been his best friend, his worst enemy, the one he'd fought with as often as he'd talked sports and girls. Then they'd always found their way back to a common ground. Now he didn't think they shared anything in common at all. And he couldn't deny the resulting sad twist in his gut.

He was through here. He'd had all of the past and of his cousin he could take. He'd been screwed over by Lorna Savoy and was getting nowhere figuring out what had happened to Micky, much less Lisa.

He headed for the porch, never looked back. "Good-bye, King."

"Hey! Can I have the rest of the beer?" King called.

Simon slammed the door on the question.

Twenty-seven

Micky hadn't been able to hear everything from the second-story window at the back of the house, though she'd given her best effort to eavesdropping. She didn't move after hearing Simon come in, waiting to see if he was going to seek her out or if he would take out his frustrations by pounding on the porch some more with his hammer.

She had no intention of hiding her snoopy nature, or denying her curiosity. In fact, if he did come looking for her, she planned to bombard him with questions about what was going on between him and his cousin. But only another minute or two passed before the kitchen door slammed on his exit and on all her answers.

She wasn't patient enough to let him work things out the way men seemed prone to do. If she expected him to tell her the raw truth rather than give her the rational explanation he reached after time alone in his man cave, she had to get to him before he'd put the incident away.

She scrambled down the stairs, dashed through the kitchen, and pushed open the door to the porch. Once outside, she heard the sound of running water. She followed the noise toward the storage shed that sat near the tree line at the edge of the clearing. On the far side of that structure and hidden from view was where she found Simon.

Naked.

At least she assumed he was naked, since he was standing under the spray of a shower. An outdoor shower. Naked. Water raining down. She suddenly couldn't remember why she'd come looking for him; she was too busy looking *at* him.

He had his eyes closed, his head turned up to the downpour, his hands slicking his dark hair away from his face. She could see the thick tufts of hair in his armpits, the wet mat of hair in the center of his chest, his spiky lashes like spider legs against his cheeks.

The enclosure's wooden fence stopped her from seeing anything below his first few ribs, though his legs were visible from the knees down, and his feet large enough to tempt her to open the gate for a peek at all the good stuff between.

"What do you want?" he asked.

She had no idea how she had given herself away—unless he could hear her heart racing, or feel the tingle in the well of her stomach, the suffocating belt of lust squeezing the air from her chest.

"What happened with your cousin?" she came up with as she climbed onto the stump of a long-ago felled tree to sit.

"He left."

"I saw that much."

"You didn't hear the rest?"

Damn him. "Only bits and pieces. Not enough to answer all my questions."

"He won't be coming around here again. That's the only answer you need."

That's what *he* thought. "You're not going to tell me about the money you gave him?"

"No," he said, sputtering water.

"You're not going to mend your broken fences?"

"I didn't bring enough tools."

"I'm not talking about property fences."

"Neither am I."

Apparently he wasn't into sharing his feelings. Or thinking confession good for the soul. "Did he take all the beer?"

"Every last bottle."

"And you didn't tell me you had an outdoor shower, why?"

That was when he looked at her. When he finally stopped being an island unto himself and let her see how much he wanted her and was struggling to keep her at bay.

She hadn't known a man's eyes could steal her breath from her body. That a man could look at her and grind everything she thought she knew about herself to dust. That desire could come alive and exist on its own, a being more powerful than she had ever pretended to be.

"Why do you think?" was what he finally said when she'd expected him to invite her inside.

He didn't want to make the first move. She'd never known a man who'd cared if she was ready, who'd asked himself if seduction was what she wanted. She'd known this man less than two days and had stopped counting the ways he'd surprised her. All she knew was that she was as comfortable with him as if she and not her one-dimensional self had been engaging him in conversation since the billboard had gone up.

"Because the woman you thought I was wouldn't care? But the woman I am wants nothing more than to strip to her skin and join you?"

He looked away, a visible tic in his jaw, another in his temple, his throat flexing as he swallowed his response. And then he gave up the fight, swearing to himself but loud enough that she could hear when he came to get her. He pushed open the enclosure's gate, stalked toward her bare and dripping, grabbed her by the wrist, and hauled her fully clothed with him into the small space and the spray.

It was the most caveman thing she'd ever experienced, a more intoxicating staking of a claim than any she'd ever imagined—and she had imagined plenty, but nothing like this . . . his hands holding her face, his fingers sliding into her hair, his wrists pressed to her temples as his mouth came down on hers.

This was the kiss she'd been waiting for all of her life, one that desperately tried to be tender and failed. She didn't care. Not about the effort or the outcome. She was too caught up in learning his touch, his taste, his mouth, his body . . . all the things he was feeling but wouldn't say.

His tongue played with hers, because when he'd pushed at her to open, she hadn't been able to say no. He tasted earthy and warm, like beer and water, and his lips pleased her. They were smooth and soft where they pressed against hers, and that came as a surprise. She'd expected hard, because he was hard, because he refused to take shit from anyone, because he insisted on things going his way.

But he was also hard in other ways. Oh, was he hard. His shoulders beneath her hands were like baseballs, his thighs bracketing hers like logs. And even wearing her clothes— granted, now stuck to her like her own skin—she could feel the hard length of his cock like a branding iron making his mark against her belly.

He let go of her mouth, moved his hands to the hem of her shirt, and pulled the shirt and her scarf over her head. She toed off her new sneakers, stepping onto the warm, wet concrete while he released the button of her jeans and unzipped them. She shimmied her way out of the heavy, wet denim.

He reached around and unhooked her bra. She would have

pulled off her underpants, but he had both of her breasts in his hands, squeezing, kneading, tugging at her nipples, molding her weight, and she couldn't think to move.

When he dipped his head, took her into his mouth, she grabbed at him to hold on. The pull of his lips, his teeth, the heat of his tongue, the late afternoon breeze, the stinging spray of water . . . they all combined into a flood of feeling that left her gasping and overwhelmed.

Her fingers slid from his biceps to his elbows. She shivered and moaned, closing her eyes and letting the water rain down on her chest as Simon dropped to his knees, nibbling at her belly as he slipped his fingers beneath the elastic of her panties and pulled them to the ground.

She stepped out of them, kicked them away, lifted her arms, and pushed her fall of wet hair from her face before spreading her legs for Simon's hands. He settled his mouth over her sex, slicked his tongue through her folds, sucking gently on her clitoris and bringing it to life.

She felt suspended in sensation. The water sluicing over her, the wind blowing in gusts through the trees around them. The warmth of the sunshine. The warmth, too, of his breath.

And now his fingers as he pushed one inside her, using his thumb as a complement to his mouth. Unreal. She was drowning. The things he was doing, the pressure, the length of his stroke, opening her, stretching her.

It was all too much, yet it wasn't enough. Having him this way felt too strangely detached. She wanted so much more than an orgasm. She wanted, she needed, to have Simon, his body pressed to hers, head to toe, and filling her.

And so she put her hands on his shoulders and backed away.

Twenty-eight

Simon looked up to see Micky shaking her head. If that wasn't a bucket of cold water . . .

"Don't get me wrong," she said, easing the sting with the softness of her voice, her fingernails stroking his wet hair from his face. "I'm about to burst out of my skin."

"Then what?" He gained his feet slowly, skating his palms from her thighs to her armpits before he settled his hands on her shoulders and stared down into her eyes. "What do you want? What don't you want?"

He knew he hadn't read her wrong. What she'd said about the woman she was . . . if she hadn't wanted this, wanted him, she wouldn't have come with him, wouldn't have helped him get her out of her clothes as if they burned her, wouldn't have let him kiss her, or kissed him back as if it was the only thing in the world worth doing.

"I don't want you to give me just an orgasm. I want you to give me sex." She kept her gaze locked on his and took hold of his cock. "I want you to give me you."

For a moment that seemed to go on longer than he should have been able to hold his breath, he did just that. Stopped breathing. Waited. He was pretty damn sure his heart stopped beating, too.

He'd fantasized about her fingers more than a few times, but the reality of feeling them wrapped around his shaft, of having her palm warm and cupped over the head of his cock, blew all his imaginings to hell.

This was Michelina, his Micky, the woman who was real and vibrant and couldn't have been more gorgeous standing in his shower had she been decked out in the dark jewels and glittery glossy colors of the billboard branded on his brain.

"Sex you can have," he finally said when he felt in control of his voice. "Me you can have, too. However. Wherever. As many times as you want. Except for this first time. I can't promise I'll be able to wait long enough—"

"I don't want you to. I don't need you to. I don't care if you promise me anything." She tightened her grip, teased his weeping slit with her thumb, smoothed his sticky release around his head to use as lube.

He groaned, dug his fingers into her skin. "I want to make sure you—"

"I will. Trust me. I'm as close as you are."

That he seriously doubted. If she opened her mouth just right, looked at him just so, he'd be done.

"Bet you a back rub that I'll get mine first," she said, and he swore her eyes promised she'd be rubbing more than his back and using more than her hands.

"I'll take that bet," he said, because no way was he going to blow his load until he felt her convulse around him. "You don't need to worry about being safe with me. I go into some really nasty places around the world, and I value my dick too much not to keep it in my pants."

She nodded, then reassured him. "I've got pregnancy covered, and my reputation is a lot more sexually active than I am. It's been a while for me. A very long while."

He shouldn't have liked knowing that as much as he did, but he couldn't deny his feelings. He was staking a claim, and he was doing so with his body. He couldn't think of what that meant beyond the moment. Being here with her couldn't be about the future. It was only about the now.

He grabbed her shirt from the shower's cement floor, spread it out on the utility shelf of one-by-eight planks attached to the enclosure's wall. Then he lifted her up to sit and stepped between her legs. The height was perfect. He hooked her knees over his forearms and let her guide him home.

She circled him around her opening, smearing her juices until he was slick with both of their fluids, then placing him where she wanted him and looking into his eyes. She waited, as if wanting to see his face the first time he pushed his way inside her.

He thought that this would be easy, that he could keep this casual, make it all about the sex, think of their encounter as the culmination of a fantasy living like reality for weeks in his mind. But he couldn't. It wouldn't work, his efforts at pretending that this didn't mean a thing, that it wasn't a beginning rather than an end.

He was too far gone to stop, and she was giving him no reason to want to, unless he counted her unexpected expression of hope. It was fierce, possessive, giving him as much grief as his own expectations, so he willingly, mindlessly, let his body have its way.

Holding on to her hips, he drove forward. She closed around him, a sheath so tight he could feel the texture of her flesh with each pulse of blood engorging his cock. He groaned, the rumble vibrating from his body into hers. He knew she felt it because of the smile that blossomed on her face, and he told himself the moisture welling in her eyes wasn't tears but the spatter of the shower.

The lie tore into his heart as he began to move, thrusting slowly, setting a steady rhythm, picking up the pace when her eyes rolled closed and the water beading in the small of his back was mostly sweat.

She came like a butterfly, tiny flutters of her pussy kissing the head of his cock. She shuddered, shivered, a strangely gentle release that floated around him teasingly, playfully, inviting him along.

He came like an elephant stampede, trumpeting, pounding, a brutish completion that nearly crushed him into a pile of broken bones. They collapsed, finished at the same time, leaving him to wonder how sex with a virtual stranger could be the best sex he'd ever had.

Twenty-nine

Chelle was standing at her kitchen counter, forming a mixture of crabmeat and seasoned stuffing into balls she would wrap with bacon and bake, when she heard King's truck rumble into her driveway and stop. She cringed when he cut the engine, jumped when he slammed the door.

She braced herself, waiting for him to materialize behind her the way he so often did. But he didn't, and when she finally saw him, it was through the window over her kitchen sink. He was standing downhill from her back porch, the grass up to his ankles, the moss from the live oaks hanging to skim his head.

She sighed, reached for a paper towel to clean her hands, then turned on the faucet and used soap. This was when it was the hardest to deal with him, when he was moody and broody, when he had a need to be with her but still kept her in the dark. This was why it was going to be so hard to send him away—because she knew she gave him something no one else could. She just didn't know what it was.

He didn't owe her anything. She had no right to expect him to confide in her, though she wished he would. Theirs wasn't an emotional relationship. Or it wasn't as far as King was concerned, and her wanting it to be was why she'd made the decision to tell him good-bye.

Drying her hands on a red-and-white gingham towel, she pushed open the kitchen's screen door and walked outside onto the porch, leaned against one of the column supports, and wrapped her arms around her middle, holding herself tight. She wouldn't be the first to speak, not this time.

He'd come to her house. Now he had to come all the way to her. Her pride was ragged, her willpower weak, but she'd given in to him for the final time. If there was anything here to salvage, King would have to be the one to dredge.

"I know you're there," he finally said, slurred, then lifted the bottle of beer she hadn't seen him holding and drained it dry. "I can smell you. On the wind. Your shampoo smells like honey. Your soap smells like peaches and almonds. It's all over you, that sweetness. It's in your skin, your hair, fresh, like an orchard."

He turned, looked up at her. Even from across the yard she could see that his eyes were red from emotion more than from the alcohol he'd consumed. She wanted to know what had happened, to ask him what was wrong. But she kept her promise to herself and didn't say a word, not a single one, though her heart, breaking, was filled with poems and sonnets and odes. There was so much she wanted to say.

"I've always liked that about you, Chelle, did you know?" He began walking toward her, not quite steady on his feet, his jeans and T-shirt dirty, though he couldn't have worked a whole day. The sun hadn't yet left the sky.

"Did I know what?" she asked, breaking her vow of silence. She really was incredibly weak.

"You have never smelled like you came out of a bottle, or like you bought the same scent dozens of other women pour on like they're watering grass, hoping it will grow."

He was talking about fragrances. Did his dejection have something to do with Michelina Ferrer? Had he finally met her, been snubbed, and come here to settle for the easy second best he was used to?

Uh-uh. She wasn't going to be anything but his first—if even that. She pushed off the porch column and turned back to the house.

"Hey, wait. Where you goin', *chère*?"

"I'm in the middle of making dinner. I don't have time to listen to you ramble—oomph."

He'd snuck up to the edge of the porch, reached out and grabbed her wrist, and spun her around. She slammed into him, his face at her waist. "What're you cookin'? Something hot and spicy? The way I like it?"

Weak, weak, weak. She was tingling between her legs when she should be pushing him away, keeping him at a safe distance; was there such a thing? At times she wondered if living on the moon would be far enough away for safety.

She held his head to her waist, his hair so thick, so soft, ignored his hands where they played so deftly with her ankles just beneath the hem of her skirt. "Crab balls and hush puppies and rice."

"Enough for two?"

For two, yes. Not for three, but for some reason she hesitated mentioning Terrill. "What are you doing here, King? Shouldn't you be working?"

"I could ask you the same thing," he said, tickling the backs of her knees with the mouth of his beer bottle.

She should have stepped away. She'd never been able to step away. That's why she had to tell him to go. "Lorna closed the office early."

And then she realized the import of what he'd just said. He hadn't known she'd be home when he'd come here. Obviously he'd seen her car when he'd arrived, but he'd come here without expecting to find her home.

He'd come because . . . why? For what reason? Was he looking for something intangible? That thing she gave him? That he got nowhere else? Had he come to wait for her to get home from work because he was in the mood for sex?

If so, why had he wandered deep into the yard instead of coming into the house? And what in the world was he doing with that longneck beneath her skirt? "King? Why aren't you working?"

"I am working," he said, lifting the hem of her tunic to blow on her belly.

She needed to get back to dinner, to get away from him. "That's not what I meant."

"You're not nagging me now, are you, *chère*?" He brought the bottle higher between her legs, rubbed it back and forth at her crotch. "Why would you be doing such a thing?"

She braced one hand on the porch column, found herself widening her stance, damn him. Damn him. "I'm not nagging. Just asking why you're here and not at work."

"I don't know why you'd be asking me that question when you're the one who had Red relay news that threw off my whole day." Taking hold of the fabric from inside, he tugged the waistband of her skirt down to her hips, kissed, nipped, and licked his way across her stomach.

He'd said something about news she'd relayed. Had she? She couldn't remember. What day was today? And was that his thumb toying with her clit? It couldn't be. It was too smooth, too hard and cold.

"You don't remember, do you? Or at least you can't remember just now. You can't think of anything but this," he said, sucking at her pussy through her skirt and her panties both, releasing her only long enough to pull the garments down to the tops of her thighs.

She was bare-assed on her back porch, letting the man she didn't want to see again slide his tongue, his fingers, the hard mouth of a longneck bottle through the folds of her sex. She threaded her fingers into his hair and pulled.

"What are you doing?" God, that squeak. Was that her voice?

"Making love to you with my mouth, *chère*. Making you forget."

She hadn't forgotten a thing. There was nothing she needed to forget. He, on the other hand . . . "I called Red and told him if he saw you to tell you about Simon coming by the office. He fired Lorna."

"Ah, you remember. Seems I'm not working hard enough here," he said, then shoved his tongue inside her, wetting her, readying her, pulling out to circle her clit while twisting the longneck into her sex and using it like a thick glass dildo to fuck her.

She knew dildos. She knew vibrators. She'd played with clamps and rings and plugs. She'd been with two men at once. She'd been with women. Her life in New Orleans had been work and sex, clubbing and sex, drinking and drugging and sex. Coming here had been in large part about getting her act together, and what had she done but hook up with a man who was all the men she'd been trying to escape?

That didn't mean she was going to stop him. In fact, she slid her hands down to cup her pussy and open herself further, playing there while he tongued her and fucked her until it became too much.

He pulled gently on the bottle to free it from her body, tossed it over his shoulder to the ground, and vaulted onto the porch. His hands were at his fly before she could get to him, and he was lifting his cock free at the same time she was stripping out of her skirt.

She wanted to taste him, to fill her mouth, to take him to

the back of her throat, but she wanted him inside her even more. She braced herself against the porch column, wrapped her hands around his neck, and jumped when he palmed her ass and lifted her. He was buried deep inside before she'd even locked her legs at his back.

He dropped his forehead to her shoulder and thrust like a piston, driving in and out with a stroke that was clean and deep and sure. She was strung so tight that she knew she'd be done in seconds, knew he would be as well. And she didn't care what he'd said the last time about keeping their sex about sex. She wanted him to know all of who she was, all of what she wanted.

She dug her fingers through his hair to his scalp and lifted his head, looking into his eyes as she came, bringing her mouth down to cover his before she had finished, before he had begun. She kissed him with her lips and her tongue and her tears.

She'd been prepared for him to fight her. Not for him to slow down, to pull back and stare at her, his eyes glassy and wet, to admit to so much pain.

"I went to see Simon."

"I'm sorry," she whispered, stroking his hair from his face, knowing he wasn't talking about the land but about the rift with his only flesh and blood.

"There's nothing good in my life."

"Shh," she soothed. "I know."

"This is the only thing I can give you."

"It's enough," she lied, burying her face against the side of his neck and holding him until he came.

Thirty

Micky would have been happy to stay in the shower the rest of the day, but Simon wouldn't let her. They *had* stayed quite a while; she was a real prune when she finally left the small fenced enclosure.

Before the water had gone cold, however, she'd discovered more of his scars, found a ticklish spot on the back of one thigh, learned that her mouth, as big as it was, was no match for his erection. She'd suspected as much the first time he'd pushed into her and hit bottom.

She honestly didn't remember sex being this good. She'd had fun, she'd had orgasms, but she'd had as much pleasure giving them to herself as she had receiving them at the hands, mouths, and dicks of men. The feel of Simon's body, his warmth, his fingers, the way he seemed to surround her, consume her . . . none of those sensations were in her experience.

What they'd done in the shower over and over had gone beyond fun and games. Their connection had reached a place so deep inside she knew it was her soul. Even when he'd hurt her—never on purpose—but when easing into her to do things she'd never known she wanted to do, even then the pleasure had been worth every sting of pain.

Of course, now she wasn't walking so well, and sitting wasn't as simple as it had been before he'd taken over her body. She yelped when the truck hit a bump in the road, grimaced as she searched for a comfortable position on the seat.

He glanced over briefly. "If the pharmacy's still open, we'll pick up more tape and gauze and do a better job covering up your arm. I never stopped to think about you not getting your stitches wet."

She hadn't thought about it, either. "It's not my arm that's hurting."

"Oh," was all he said.

She leaned forward and toward him to get a better look at his face. "Simon Baptiste. Are you blushing?"

"I'm sunburned."

Liar. And a funny one at that. "You are not. We weren't out long enough to burn."

"We were out almost two hours," he reminded her. "You're just lucky the hot water tank's the size that it is, and the shower is built to conserve the flow."

That had been nice, but not so much of a concern. She would have stayed with him had the water been cold; he had heated her up plenty. "If anything, I'm lucky that no one else dropped by to visit. And that I didn't need a wheelchair to get back to the house."

He cleared his throat, coughed. "I didn't know I was that rough."

"I'm not complaining. A girl needs a good horse fu—"

His hand came up to cut her off. "Don't even say it."

She had to laugh. "Surely all your preconceived notions about me have long been shot to hell."

He chuckled at that. "You have definitely made this the most personally interesting two days I've lived through in a while."

"What? After all those billboard conversations, there was a doubt in your mind?"

"There's always a doubt in my mind," he said, checking his rearview mirror. "That's why I never take a single day for granted."

Micky pushed her hair away from her face. "Well, you carpe diem quite nicely. More than nicely, if you want to know the truth. And I'll have to agree with you on two days that stand out more than any other lately."

Simon didn't respond right away, as if weighing how well he could control this particular topic, if he could keep the intensity, the potency that had had him hauling her into the shower, in check. "I'd think with the life you lead most of yours would."

"It's a lot less glamorous than it looks, I promise." Still shivering at the memory of seeing him give in, she didn't mind the segue. "All you have to go on is what you see from your patio."

"I've enjoyed the view and the conversations." He hesitated, cleared his throat. "But nothing beats live and in person."

"That's good to know. I'd hate to think you found guarding my body a waste of time."

He was quiet for a long moment, and she wasn't sure what she'd said wrong—if anything—but then he glanced toward her and said, "I'm not in the bodyguard business anymore. Not exactly."

Full disclosure? She blinked, uncertain why he was telling her this now, if it should set off any alarms, or if it even mattered. "What do you do"

"I work for a private firm. We take on cases that fall through the cracks of law enforcement jurisdiction."

"Is what you do legal?"

"Depends on whom you ask," he said with complete seriousness.

She wondered why he suddenly felt compelled to admit the truth, to reveal something that she couldn't imagine him making public knowledge on a whim. Was that job what had brought him to Louisiana? Was he here to do more than check on his house and his cousin?

Was he doing something clandestine he didn't want anyone to know? A small tickle crawled up the back of her throat. "You know, I think you're starting to scare me."

He didn't soothe or hesitate but jerked the truck over to the side of the road, shoved it into park, and shifted on his seat to face her. "What have I done to frighten you? Tell me. I want to know."

She shook her head. "It's nothing you've done. Unless you count the bodyguard lie. It's more how you pick and choose what you want me to know. And the fact that I only have your word to go on that things are as you say."

"They are. They're as real as everything that's happened the last two days."

Had what happened been related to his visit? Did he know more than he was telling her? "So, you making fun of me and crime TV was about covering up your own expertise in fighting the bad guys?"

"I didn't tell you this to prove that I know what I'm doing. I told you because I want you to know me." He dropped his gaze, shook his head, rubbed at his eyes before looking at her again. "I told you because I need you to understand what happened between us can't ever be anything more."

She wasn't sure what he was trying to tell her. "Any more sex? Or any more than sex?"

"The latter. The first, too, if it makes it easier."

He seemed as confused as she was. "Easier for whom?"

He shrugged. "You, I guess."

"Right," she said, then snorted. "Because you weren't the one who nearly snapped my wrist dragging me into your cave. I'm surprised you didn't grab me by the hair."

"I didn't mean to hurt you."

She wanted to ask him if he was talking about her tender wrist specifically, or if that included her aching bones and the raw and swollen flesh between her legs. Then again, maybe he was tossing it out there to cover anything she might later find broken or bruised.

Like her heart.

"Are you kidding? I'll be as good as new in no time, walking like I've never spread my legs for more than my annual exam."

"Micky. That's not what I meant."

"So you don't care if I can walk straight?"

"Of course I care. I—"

She cut him off with a wave of one hand. "You might have actually done me a favor. Papi sees me waddling like a stuffed goose, he'll be too mortified to foist me off on an unsuspecting groom."

"That's not funny. Micky—"

"You know, it's probably a good idea if you do put me on the next flight home since I'm not needed here. I'll hire my P.I., he can work with your man and Terrill, and maybe someone will actually find Lisa before it's too late." There. She'd given him an easy out. A way to get rid of her without having to worry about hurting her feelings.

He didn't take it. Instead, he opened up and unloaded. "What Terrill is going through waiting for word on his wife? I don't have that in me. Putting on a good front, remaining civilized and human. I'd be ripping into anyone who crossed my path. And Terrill is only a deputy sheriff in a sparsely populated Louisiana parish.

"I work around the world and come up against people who would gut a woman I loved in front of me for fun. Not to get me to talk. Just to prove that they can, and that they can get away with it. That they could flay me open without ever touching me at all. That's why I told you the truth of what I do. I want you to know who I am."

He took a deep breath, stared for a moment out through the windshield before looking back at her, his face still taut but his voice softer. "That's why as much as I wish things were different, it's a hell of a lot safer for both of us if I keep getting drunk and jacking off to your billboard instead of falling in love with you."

"That billboard's not going to stay up forever, you know," she told him after a long tense minute of being unable to breathe, of doing nothing but listening to the crumbling of her heart, which ached for the life he'd just told her he led as much as for the one she was losing.

"I know."

"What are you going to do then?"

"Move."

She wanted to laugh. She wanted to cry. She had met the most amazing man, and what she'd shared with him was already over. Just like that. The blink of an eye. "There will always be a hot new face in that spot."

"Last time it wasn't a face."

"Lucky you."

"And it wasn't a woman."

"Oops, sorry."

"Having another dude's package in his boxer briefs staring me in the face every morning isn't my idea of a good way to wake up."

Again she wanted to laugh, again felt herself fighting tears. This wasn't fair. It wasn't fair. She didn't want to go home without him. "I dunno. I could get off to it, er, used to seeing that every day."

Simon shook his head. "You're a hell of a woman, Michelina Ferrer."

When he leaned toward her, she held up one hand. "Don't give me a kiss-off, Simon. Just take me to New Orleans and let me catch my flight."

He nodded, faced front again, and started to shift into

gear. He was stopped from doing anything by a Vermilion Parish Sheriff's Department patrol car sliding across the road to cut them off.

Before Simon could do more than get his window halfway down, Terrill Landry was gesturing and shouting at him over the roof of his car. "Follow me! Now!"

Thirty-one

Simon never considered defying the deputy sheriff. Terrill had extended no greeting or explanation for the stop. He hadn't verified Simon's identity. And though Simon knew who the other man was, neither had Terrill offered his own name or credentials. Any of those could have, should have, given Simon pause, but it was the expression on the deputy sheriff's face that made up Simon's mind to follow.

Whatever Terrill wanted with him, it was no small thing. The deputy had appeared nearly manic, shouting, gesturing. The only thing that came to Simon's mind was that something had happened to King.

But when they turned off the state highway and into Bayou Allain, instead of heading for the hospital or the jail, Simon decided that was enough. He needed answers. And his need grew to mammoth proportions when Terrill drove past the business district and into the residential section of town.

"What the hell?" Simon murmured under his breath.

"This is the street where I came looking for Lisa," Micky offered as they pulled to a stop in front of a small cottage with a wraparound porch and the biggest azalea bushes Simon had ever seen. "But this isn't his house."

"Say what?"

She pointed across the street. "He lives over there."

Simon's need to know had reached a boiling point. And the temperature rose even higher when he climbed from behind the wheel and realized his cousin's truck was parked in front of Terrill's car in the drive.

Where the hell were they going?

"You don't know who lives here?"

"No clue," Micky said, rounding the front of the vehicle.

"It's Paschelle Sonnier's place," Terrill responded after slamming the cruiser's door and coming over to where they stood.

Lorna's secretary. That didn't tell Simon much. "What's King doing here?" he asked, his gut tightening until Terrill said, "He dates her. Paschelle."

King was almost forty. Like Simon. The girl he'd seen in Lorna's office wasn't even thirty yet. But he *had* seen her, and he knew his cousin, and he had more than a strong feeling that there wasn't a whole lot of dating going on.

"Is something wrong with King?" Simon asked.

King had left Le Hasard carrying more than a six-pack after their earlier encounter. Simon glanced over at his cousin's truck, looking for evidence that he'd been in an accident, found none, felt . . . relieved.

"Nothing more wrong than usual," Terrill said, taking the four porch steps in two strides. "He's surly and miserable and mean. Oh, and not quite sober."

Simon followed, hearing Micky behind him, his irritation mounting, his patience growing thin. If there was nothing wrong with his cousin, then what the hell—

"I really hate bringing you here like this," Terrill began, "the neighbors being as prone as they are to minding everyone's business but their own, but I didn't want to move all the boxes to my house, since they were already here—"

"Boxes?" Micky asked before Simon managed to make

sense of what Terrill had said. "I'm Michelina, by the way. Micky Ferrer. Lisa's friend from college?"

Terrill stopped in front of the door, his hand halfway to the knob, and judging by his blank expression, apparently having trouble putting her into context. "I'm sorry. I don't get it. You're Micky and you're here?"

"Didn't your father tell you?" she asked as Simon moved close and took hold of her elbow. "I talked to him Wednesday night at Red's."

"Wednesday night? I was there Wednesday night," he told her, looking even more confused.

"I wasn't there long. King pointed out your father so I could ask him about Lisa."

Terrill scrubbed one hand over his jaw. "I don't get it. How did you know she was missing?"

"I didn't. Not until your father told me."

He looked from Micky to Simon and back. "Did you two come down here together?"

Simon shook his head. "If you've got snoops for neighbors, the story can wait until we're behind closed doors."

Terrill still seemed lost, but he rapped sharply on the door before pushing it open. Simon ushered Micky in front of him, bringing up the rear as the three of them entered a small living room hardly meant for five adults and a dozen boxes that smelled like dirt and old bread.

"I think all of you know each other, unless Micky and Paschelle haven't met," Terrill said, playing host.

Sitting on the floor, her back to the sofa, where King sat sprawled, Paschelle raised a hand in greeting.

"They were both at Lorna's office this morning," Simon said, turning to Terrill. "Now, are you going to fill us in on what we're all doing here?"

"It's a party, cuz." King slapped a hand to his knee. "A mystery dinner theater. Isn't that what they call it when the host gives his guests the clues they need to solve a crime?

Except there's no dinner with this one. Chelle only made enough for two."

"We were actually on our way to New Orleans," Simon told Terrill, ignoring King. "We were going to grab a bite, and then Micky's catching a plane. If this is some kind of game, you go ahead without us."

"Wait a minute," Micky said, stepping closer to Terrill and giving Simon her back before he could stop her from asking, "Does the crime have to do with figuring out who ran me off the bridge over the Allain bayou?"

Paschelle gasped. Behind her, King moved his hand to her shoulder and sat forward. Terrill's expression darkened. "Ran you off? What're you talking about? The car that went off the bridge was leased to a Jane Mitchell from New York."

"I know. I use that name when I travel on personal business." She rattled off Jane's address, cell phone and social security numbers. "I was the one in the car when it went into the water."

"That doesn't make sense," Terrill said, pacing, shaking his head. "As soon as we got the accident call Thursday morning, we started searching. We were all over that place. How did you get out without us seeing you?"

"Because I went in twelve hours before."

"And because it wasn't an accident," Simon added. "She got out and made certain she wasn't seen by you or the thugs who ran her off the road."

"What are you saying? Why would anyone want to run you off the road?" Terrill asked, disbelief sharpening his features and his tone of voice.

Micky shrugged. "You tell me."

Simon made sure he had the deputy's full attention. "She obviously made someone at Red's uncomfortable with her questions about Lisa's whereabouts. The accident was less than an hour after she left the bar."

"The only people she talked to at Red's," King offered, "were me . . . and Bear."

"You think my father did this? Wait, wait." Terrill collapsed onto the edge of a folding chair set in front of the boxes. It nearly buckled beneath him. "God, I can't believe I'm saying this, but it makes so much sense. Especially with everything else."

"What everything else?" Simon asked, having realized this was real and not any kind of game.

"The mystery dinner theater, boo," King said. "The one without the food."

Simon scrubbed both hands down his face, wondering what the last few days would have been like if he'd stayed in New York, spent the time off holed up in his apartment, heading to Katz's when his stomach couldn't deal with his empty fridge any longer.

Then he realized that if he hadn't driven up to his house on Le Hasard the moment he had, Micky might not be standing beside him. He wouldn't have spent two hours with her lush and wet body all over his. Bear Landry and his goons might have gotten away with her murder if Simon hadn't come to face the man who'd been a thorn in his side for too long. It was time he and King put the past behind them.

To do that he had to go back to the beginning, to start over and let none of what he knew get in the way of the things he needed an open mind to learn.

A mystery dinner theater, huh?

He took a deep breath and a seat on the edge of a blue corduroy recliner. "What's the deal with the boxes? And is there anyplace in town that delivers food? I can't think on an empty stomach."

"No delivery, but I've got the makings of crabmeat omelets," Paschelle offered, jumping to her feet. "Will that work?"

Simon nodded. "It'll more than work. Thanks."

"No problem." She waved a hand as she climbed over boxes to get from the couch to the kitchen. "This stuff is all y'all anyway. I'm just a fly on the wall."

Once Paschelle was gone and Micky had settled on the far end of the couch from King, Simon looked from his cousin to Terrill and asked, "What stuff is she talking about, and who makes up the y'all?"

"The y'all is the three of us who grew up here," Terrill said, kneeling in front of the small square coffee table and the open box on top. "Maybe Micky, too, if Bear really did try to shut her up, son of a bitch. He's always been one, but goddamn if he's hurt Lisa . . ."

"Have you confronted him?" Simon watched the other man struggle to pull in a breath. "Are you dealing with suspicions, or real evidence?"

Terrill looked up. "I haven't confronted him because what I wanted you to see I only ran across this afternoon."

"In these boxes."

"In this one here, if we're wanting to be exact." Terrill reached inside for a single sheet of paper. "Before Lisa went missing, she'd been working on the Landry genealogy. These boxes have been in Bear's attic for years. Lorna's handiwork, I'm sure. He's never been organized, and she's the only one who's ever worked for him."

"Even after going into business for herself?" Simon glanced at King, remembering their earlier conversation about the unlikely pair.

"She may have her own office and her own business," King said, "but she still works for the judge. She's always worked for the judge."

"If I can interrupt," Micky said, looking at each man in turn before going on. "You said Lisa had been working on the family genealogy."

Terrill nodded.

"And she was going through these boxes?"

He nodded again.

"Are you thinking she uncovered something in his files that your father didn't want known?"

"That's what I'm thinking now. At first I thought she'd gone asking questions of someone she shouldn't have. Or even been caught looking through public records someone thought should be private."

"What changed your mind?" Simon asked.

Terrill rattled the paper, handed it to Simon as King sat forward and said, "Looks like Le Hasard might not have been in the family as long as we thought, cuz."

What the hell?

Simon frowned at King, looked down at the parchment he held—a handwritten transfer of ownership passing the four thousand acres in question from a Ross Landry to Zachary Benoit, his and King's great-great-grandfather, as payment for winnings due in a poker game. It was signed by three witnesses.

Priceless. Seriously priceless. Simon rubbed at his forehead, then started to laugh. Micky snatched the paper out of his hand to read it for herself.

"So one of your grandparents," she said to Terrill, "bet the farm and lost it to one of their grandparents? Is that what this says?"

"That's what it looks like to me." Terrill returned the paper to the box.

"Except if that's the original," King mused aloud, "why's it in a box of Bear's things instead of on file with the parish's property tax assessor's office?"

"I imagine because Zachary Benoit never had a chance to file it. He was found with a bullet between his eyes the next day," Simon offered in response, having noticed the document's Christmas date. "I did a family tree in fifth grade. I remember my mother telling me that he'd been found the day after Christmas, and that no one ever learned who killed him."

"But if the transfer was never filed," Terrill said, changing his mind midsentence. "It had to have been. The deed's in your name now, right? You've been paying taxes on the place?"

"It's mine," Simon said. "But this is the first I've ever heard about the property having belonged to a Landry, or been lost in a poker game."

"Finding that out wouldn't have been enough to get Lisa in trouble, would it?" Micky asked.

"Not unless there's a reason Bear doesn't want it known that the property used to be ours. I didn't know," Terrill said, looked at Simon then King. "You two didn't know."

"And so you're thinking the reason it's been kept secret might be in all this stuff?" Simon asked

"Far-fetched?" Terrill asked.

Simon didn't think so. "Well, look at the big picture. Lisa was working on the Landry genealogy. The boxes she was digging through turned up information none of the remaining Landry or Benoit descendants knew—"

"With the possible exception of Bear," Terrill reminded him.

Simon nodded. "With the possible exception of Bear. And now Lisa is missing."

Micky picked up his next thoughts. "And when someone outside the small circle Bear controls shows up and asks about his daughter-in-law, she's run off the road."

"I guess that would make the question, what exactly did Lisa discover?" King asked, and Simon responded, "And how far would Bear go to keep the information from getting out?"

Thirty-two

Micky didn't like to think of herself as a wuss, but she couldn't take it anymore, this speculation over what might have happened to Lisa, what she knew, what she could be going through even now—wherever she was, if she was still alive.

All of those unknowns were getting to be too much, especially when she thought how things might have been different if she'd made the effort to stay in touch with her friend, if she hadn't let her own life get so out of control that she forgot about Lisa and what they shared.

Then she wondered if her coming here was the very act that might have put the wheels in motion to save Lisa from her fate. It was all too much to process on an empty stomach, or with her body continually reminding her of the afternoon spent naked in Simon's arms. Even the short walk to the kitchen to offer her help to Paschelle had Micky grimacing. And, unfortunately, she hadn't put on a full happy face before the other woman turned.

"Are you okay? Is it your arm?"

"You wouldn't happen to have any gauze and tape, would you?" she asked, gladly latching on to the topic. "We were on our way to the pharmacy when Terrill found us."

"I think I might still have some." Paschelle wiped her hands and crossed the kitchen, opened a door that led into a small bathroom. After banging a couple of cabinets, she returned with the supplies.

"I taped King back together not long ago. He was drunk, missed the steps, hit his head on the corner of the porch," she said, gesturing to her own hairline. "Super Glue and butterfly bandages. Stitches might hurt, you know."

Knowing, Micky smiled. She sat at the table topped in red Formica and began to unwrap the gauze she'd reused after drying it in front of the upstairs fan.

Paschelle joined her, wincing in sympathy. "That's going to leave some kind of scar."

"I know. I'm sure it won't make my people happy, but the way I see it, they're lucky I'm alive." *My people?* Had she really just said that?

"*You're* lucky you're alive. Especially since you survived the fall *and* escaped from whoever it was who rammed you."

Micky arched a brow. "Are people talking? Do they know it wasn't an accident?"

Paschelle opened the box of gauze pads, not looking the least bit chagrined that she might have listened to gossip. "All I know is what I've heard from y'all and most of it just now. I don't plan to mention it to anyone. The only people I talk to are Lorna and King. He obviously knows, and I'd rather Lorna not know that I do."

"You work for her. Are she and Judge Landry as tight as the guys think?"

"He's always at the office, yeah," she said, nodding. "But I've worked for her only a couple of years. I'm not the best person to ask."

"You're not from here?"

"I guess I am now," she said, retrieving a pair of scissors from a kitchen drawer. "I grew up in New Orleans."

"Were you there during Katrina?" Micky wondered what the other woman might have lost.

Paschelle nodded. "Partied like it was nineteen ninety-nine, then left the city when it should have been too late to get out, and ran out of gas in front of Day's Dress for Less."

"And you just stayed?"

"I just stayed. Didn't have anywhere else I needed to be." She added, "And then I met King," her face coloring slightly with the admission.

Micky had noticed Simon's lack of comment when Terrill had mentioned King and Paschelle dating. She'd met him at Red's before meeting Simon. She understood his appeal—base though it was. She also understood Paschelle blushing. If King was anything like his cousin . . .

"You know, when you came into Lorna's office," Paschelle said, snipping off several lengths of tape, "I couldn't place you until the judge said your name. Do you know how beautiful you are? I mean, all made up in your ads, you're stunning. But you don't even need the clothes and the color and the jewels and the hair. Look at you. Jeans, sneakers, a baseball jersey, and a ponytail. You're hot dogs and apple pie and still drop-dead gorgeous."

Micky was used to compliments. She was always appreciative, but Paschelle's words left her speechless and humbled and embarrassed when she thought she was past feeling any of those things.

And then she wondered if it was the billboard more than anything giving Simon hell. If he wasn't able to see her as herself. If he felt more of a responsibility to keep her out of harm's way—and out of his life—because of who the rest of the world thought she was.

"Thank you," she finally said. "I'm enjoying being incognito. If not for the circumstances, I'd be enjoying it even more. I don't get a break from the public eye very often."

"God, why would you want to? Live here, like this, instead of traveling the world, meeting the people you do?"

The most interesting person she'd met in years she'd found here in bayou country—even though he lived half a city away. She couldn't believe this was all they were going to have, this madness, this mystery. This attempt on her life, a fate that might be worse for Lisa.

"Do you know Lisa? Have you two met?"

"Sure. She lives right across the street."

Of course. Small towns. Friendly neighbors. Even the nosy ones were probably just looking out for their friends . . . and might not be welcoming of a stranger who showed up looking for one of their own when that one had gone missing.

But Paschelle was Lisa's neighbor, too. Micky's pulse picked up as inspiration struck. "Do you know the other people on the street?"

The other woman nodded briskly, her razor-cut hair swinging as she began to unroll the gauze. "Sure. To say hi to. Mrs. Callahan always gives me tomatoes and cukes from her garden. I pay Mr. DuPont to mow since the yard is so big and he has a tractor."

"I'm sure Terrill has questioned them already, but do you think they'd talk to me if you introduced me? Lisa and I went to school together. She's been my best friend for years."

Paschelle looked up. Her eyes widened. "And you might think of something to ask that Terrill hasn't?"

"It's a dumb idea, isn't it? I mean, either they saw her leave with someone or alone, or they saw someone take her."

"Assuming they saw anything at all."

"Like I said, dumb."

"Not necessarily. Mr. DuPont has been visiting his daughter in Houston since Monday morning. I've been collecting his mail. It's late, but if you want, we can walk it over and see if he saw Lisa that day."

Micky was already reaching for the scissors and the long length of gauze. "You finish Simon's omelet. I'll patch up my arm. If we could find something that would help . . ."

She couldn't even put what she was thinking, what she was feeling, into words. "Just cook. Go. Cook."

"Yes, ma'am," Paschelle said with a smile.

Thirty-three

The omelet helped, but Simon had just about run his last lap for the night. Out of the dozen boxes, they'd knocked back six filled mostly with documents related to Bear's business as a land man. They'd run across a few newspaper clippings, too—most were stories detailing cases over which he'd presided while on the bench and had been dropped down loose inside—but nothing seemed out of the ordinary or rang anyone's mystery dinner theater bells.

Simon pushed up from his chair and stretched. King had headed for the kitchen and another beer twenty minutes ago. Simon decided he'd better grab one for himself before they were all gone, and offered to bring one back to Terrill.

"No, I'm good," the deputy said. "I'd like to finish up a couple more boxes, and at this point even one brew's liable to do me in."

Simon glanced at the clock on Paschelle's sound system. Midnight-thirty. He was so close to being done in that no amount of beer was going to make any difference. "I'll be back to give you a hand in a few."

Terrill waved him off without looking up from the files. Simon made for the kitchen, finding it empty, and frowning as he pushed open the screen door onto the porch, where he found only Kingdom. No Micky. No Paschelle.

"Where are the girls?" he asked, not worried, but not exactly thrilled to find them gone.

"The *women* walked over to one of the neighbors' houses to take him his mail Chelle's been picking up. I expect they'll be back in a few."

Kinda late for visiting neighbors, to Simon's way of thinking. "Is that what you're doing out here? Waiting?"

"Seemed more productive than digging through boxes thinking any of Bear's shit is going to help Terrill find his wife."

That much they agreed on. "No, the boxes aren't helping. At least not yet."

"You'd probably get a quicker answer to what Bear's been up to if you sweet-talked Lorna Savoy. And you wouldn't have to get your hands dirty. Now your dick's another matter," King said, gesturing with his empty longneck. "Unless you've found it a good home with your Ms. Ferrer."

Simon wasn't about to discuss sex or Micky with his cousin. That wasn't part of making amends. "Hearing what Lorna has to say isn't a bad idea."

"I've been known to have a few good ones."

"The orchard was a good one," Simon said, an olive branch, a peace offering.

It took King several moments to respond, as if he were weighing Simon's intent. "That was a tough loss. The trees were just up to producing a good amount of the Satsumas when Rita blew through. Damn hurricanes. It'll take the new trees a while to get up to speed, and then all we can do is hope no more bad bitches pick Louisiana to come ashore."

King had said we. All *we* can do is hope. And not a smartass remark in his short speech. Maybe he was as tired as Simon was of their war. Maybe one battle at a time they could end the thing for good.

"Funny when you think about it," King said. "Me wiped out by Hurricane Rita, Chelle by Katrina the month before. And here we both still are."

"Humph. I didn't know about Paschelle and Katrina."

King nodded. "She was a bartender in New Orleans. And now she's answering phones for Lorna."

"She doesn't like it?"

"It's not about liking it. She needs a career. Doing interior design or whatever it's called. Hell, she needs her own television show. Like Martha Stewart. Or Raechel Ray."

Simon snorted. "You a fan?"

"This from the man who has *Buffy* DVDs in his truck? At least my Rachel can cook. Your girl fights monsters. Though a slayer might come in handy for taking care of the judge."

Ridiculous or not, Simon wasn't going to argue. They needed something. "If it turns out Bear *is* responsible for whatever has happened to Lisa, someone's going to have to straitjacket Terrill to keep him from doing damage to the old man."

"I say let him. Son of a bitch has ruined more lives than he's turned around, if he did any turning at all during his days on the bench. And Terrill being his son, I'd say that gives him more rights than most. Especially if this Lisa thing goes south."

All Simon could think about was how it could have been Micky, how he would never have known her, how he wouldn't have been here to save her if he hadn't picked this week to get over himself and grow up.

He would never have suffered Terrill's worry, but he would have missed out on the pleasure of Michelina Ferrer. He wasn't sure how he felt about the trade-off. "Let's hope it doesn't. That we turn up something before it's too late."

"Are you guys talking about Lisa?" Micky asked, trudging across the yard with Paschelle. "Because we learned something from Paschelle's neighbor, though I'm not sure how much help it's going to be."

The relief that washed through Simon at hearing her voice left him reeling. And it wasn't the news she'd delivered. It was nothing that simple; it was the complexity of knowing that she was safe, that while she'd been out of his sight, no one had rushed up behind her and rammed her off the road.

King was the one who stepped into the awkward silence as the women climbed onto the porch. "What did the old guy have to say?"

Paschelle moved to his side. "Mr. DuPont left for Houston Monday morning and said he nearly backed his car into Lisa's. There's hardly any traffic during the day, so he wasn't looking at the street as much as he was the pollen on the back window of his car."

"Pollen?" Simon prompted, as if making the effort to get back in the game hadn't cost as much as it had.

"It's nasty and yellow this time of year, cuz. Or have you been gone long enough to forget?"

Simon ignored King's dig—if it was one—and said, "I remember. I was just trying to make the connection between Lisa and pollen."

Micky came to stand in front of him, placed her hand at his waist. "He said he was thinking that he needed to stop and clean the window before leaving town, and he backed out of his driveway and into the street and didn't even see Lisa's car until she swerved to miss him."

"And she was leaving her house?" Simon asked, adding after Micky nodded, "What time?"

She looked from him to Paschelle. "He said ten, right?"

"Between ten and ten-thirty," the other woman responded.

"And what time did Terrill or anyone last talk to her? Before that? Do we know?"

"You'll have to ask him, boo," King said, nodding toward the deputy sheriff as he pushed open the screen door.

Simon started to, then stopped when he saw the look on the other man's face and the yellowed newspaper clipping in his hand.

"I don't think this is what Lisa found, but it might have something to do with someone—maybe even Bear—wanting to get you away from the bayou." His expression grave, Terrill handed the article to Simon.

It was from a small newspaper published in another parish, one that didn't have much of a circulation, one he wouldn't have paid attention to at eighteen had he been home to see it. He scanned it only briefly, taking note of the date.

He didn't need to see more. He needed time, space. He needed a crowbar and five minutes alone with Bear Landry to get at the truth. If this crime, this betrayal, this . . . violation was the judge's doing—and he had very little doubt about that—the bastard had just made things as personal for Simon—and King—as for Micky, Lisa, and Terrill.

He let Micky pull the clipping from his hand. Then she walked to the far end of the porch beneath the overhead fan, where the light made it easier to see, and read the text out loud.

" 'The Calcasieu Parish Sheriff's Department is asking for the public's help in identifying a man whose body was found on the banks of the Sabine River. The man was approximately forty years of age, six feet tall, one hundred seventy pounds. His primary identifying marker is a tattoo in the center of his chest that resembles two Bs.' "

Her voice shaking, she stopped there, though the story went on to offer details about the distinctive wound from the blow that had killed the man. It was information that cut Simon to the quick, that nearly doubled him over.

Behind him, he heard Paschelle ask, "Is that 'bees' like insects, or 'Bs' like letters of the alphabet?"

This was one answer Simon had. One he wished he hadn't found this way. One he wasn't sure he'd wanted to find at all. He turned back to the others. He and King were the only ones still alive who'd ever seen the tattoo, hidden as it was beneath a mat of dark chest hair.

"One B is for Benoit, my mother's family name," he finally said. "The other is for Baptiste."

Micky gasped, and before King was able to get his hand on her shoulder to stop her, asked, "You know who this is?"

He nodded. "My father."

Thirty-four

It was close to two a.m. by the time Micky and Simon made it back to his house and up the stairs to bed. Paschelle had offered them her guest room. Terrill had offered the same. King didn't have a room to spare in his trailer-for-one but had given Simon his hand and pulled him into a hug that both men seemed reluctant to break.

Terrill had chosen that moment to head home. Paschelle had gone inside to clean up the kitchen, telling Terrill the boxes in the living room were up to him. This time, Micky hadn't had the strength to give the other woman a hand but had walked out to Simon's truck to wait.

He'd joined her ten minutes later, looking as if he wanted to bite off her head for the way she'd disappeared. She'd braced herself, but he quickly shut down, seeming totally spent. She imagined that he was, that he didn't have the energy—emotional or physical—to do more than fly on auto.

He remained silent for the entire drive, and once upstairs, he barely grunted when she tugged away the sleeping bag he'd been prepared to crawl into and pushed him toward the bed. She refused to let him sleep another night on the floor.

They'd been as physically intimate as possible. Sharing a bed, both of them fully clothed and wrapped up in sleeping bags, wasn't a problem. Not tonight when so many others demanded their attention and time.

Side by side in the dark, the night breeze cooling the room, the light from the moon sneaking in to sweep the shadows from the corners, they were both beyond tired, both in desperate need of sleep, yet not surprisingly both still wide awake.

And since she didn't see that changing before morning came, she turned to face him, laid a hand in the center of his chest, feeling his heart beat through his sleeping bag and into her palm. "I'm so sorry you had to learn about your father that way. That was so wrong. So unfair."

He released a deep sigh. Her hand rose and fell with the motion. She left it where it was, wanting even that tenuous connection of knowing he was there beneath her touch, of knowing he couldn't deny her presence.

"He disappeared right after graduation. That wasn't a surprise. He'd told everyone he'd had enough bad luck to last any man a lifetime. My mom, she'd died three years before." Simon cursed softly. "She didn't die. She killed herself. She couldn't take her sister, her twin, King's mother, not being with her anymore. Left the rest of us to deal with her suicide on top of losing King's parents in an auto accident two years before."

Micky couldn't speak. It was beyond words, beyond even a whisper, her ache at what he'd told her. What was going through his mind, as he relived the pain? What had gone through his mind then, as a boy of eighteen, barely a man, the loss of his parents so senseless?

"I knew he was dead. He'd been declared dead legally, but I knew we would eventually find out what had happened to him. It was so long ago, that's the thing. That's what's so hard." He shook his head on the pillow of his wrists where he'd raised his arms and crossed them. "I guess I wanted to think he was out there keeping tabs on me, making sure I didn't get into more trouble than I already had."

"The fire?"

"Yeah. That was the big one. I enlisted only because it was that or spend four years in the pen with King, and that would never have worked. There was so much hate between us. Neither one of us would have made it out alive. Until today, I'd always thought he'd been the one to set it."

She propped up on her elbow to see his face, wondering about all the things the two men had said today that she hadn't been able to hear. "But you don't think that anymore?"

"We were there at his house, both of us. It was graduation night, and we'd hit all the local parties. None were worth hanging around any longer than we did, so we went home to get wasted. Out of the blue, Lorna showed up."

Irrational or not, Micky wasn't liking where this was going already. "Was she in your class?"

"She's older. A couple of years," he said, pulling one hand from beneath his head and rubbing at his eyes. "She went off with King. I bunked down in the extra room. Next thing I knew, she was crawling up between my legs and taking me out of my shorts with her mouth."

Really. Having met the other woman, Micky could have gone the rest of her life without knowing that.

Simon went on. "I don't remember all of it. But I do remember waking up hearing her screaming that the house was on fire. I ran outside with my dick wagging and didn't stop to put on my pants until I was halfway across the pasture."

"And you thought King set it."

"He went to jail for it. Didn't deny it. Never said a word."

This wasn't really a good time to play devil's advocate, but . . . "Maybe he thought you set it and didn't want to rat you out."

"Yeah. Like I didn't want to rat on him."

So he *had* considered the possibility. "Could it have been Lorna?"

"It doesn't make sense. I mean, I can't think of a reason, but she was the only other one there." He paused, staring at the ceiling, blinking as he thought. "I don't know that it matters, really. Not anymore."

Micky was done with the advocate thing. Now she was going to nag. "It matters because it's been a thorn between you and King all this time. And with your father gone, really gone, isn't King the only family you have left?"

Simon didn't respond.

She pushed. "Isn't that why you loaned him the money?"

His brows came together in a frown. "I thought you couldn't hear us talking."

She pushed again, harder, refusing to be distracted. "Isn't it?"

"He told me that the money was for a workover of the well our fathers used to operate. Nothing he's tried to do with the place has paid off, or given him enough of an income to put the cash aside himself."

"If there's still oil there, then you had to have believed he could do it. You took a chance on your cousin, he let you down, that's that. It's not the end of the world. Or a reason to cut him out of your life."

He didn't say anything right away, as if his thoughts had gone elsewhere, to the oil, to his cousin. She didn't have a clue, so he surprised her when he finally said, "That's what it means, you know. Le Hasard. It means chance."

Apropos, she supposed, considering he'd come to own the place because of a poker game played long ago. And he'd taken one on his cousin. So why couldn't he take a chance on the two of them?

He could lose her to a reckless driver—one with no ulterior motive or evil intent—any day, out of the blue, no warning. Wouldn't their time together be more precious because of knowing that?

"I'm glad you gave him one," she finally said. "He seems so . . . lost."

"What's lost is my ninety thousand dollars," he said with a snort.

Uh-uh. She didn't believe this was about the money. The money was a diversion, keeping him from dealing with the fact that getting rid of what stood between him and King would cost him even more.

"What did he do with it?" she asked.

Again with a snort. "He didn't tell me. I could find out if I really wanted to know, but it stopped being important. It doesn't matter."

He didn't want it to be important. He didn't want it to matter. He didn't want to face the possibility that his estrangement from his cousin had been a mistake. "Seriously. You don't want to know," she said.

It took him several seconds to respond. "About the money, no. But I do want to know if that's all you plan to do with your hand."

He was being a man. Changing the subject. And for the first time *to* sex instead of away from it. "You told me that this afternoon was all we could have," she reminded him, wanting to hear him argue his way out of a trap he'd laid. "That you didn't want to risk us becoming more deeply involved."

"I don't. At least the involved part. But the deep part is sounding pretty good."

"Is that so?" She wouldn't say no to having him deep inside her. She wouldn't say no to having him any way at all. She just wanted him to give them a chance.

He lifted her hand, tossed back his sleeping bag, returned her hand to its resting place. Only this time instead of coarse fabric, she felt the triangle of his chest hair, which was like strands of fine silk to the touch.

"It's so," he told her gruffly. "But see for yourself if you don't believe me."

"Oh I believe you. I just don't . . . believe you. But I'm more than willing to dispel what doubts either of us might have," she said, leaving it to him to sort out her meaning, because she was certain he was lying to himself about not wanting to be involved.

She eased out from beneath her sleeping bag, slid to the foot of the bed, then up between his legs. He had obviously undressed before she had finished up in the bathroom; while he was wearing nothing, she was still wearing her jersey and socks, and, well, everything but her jeans.

His skin was warm, the hair on his calves and thighs soft, that surrounding his penis and balls bristly. He was already erect when she took him into her mouth. He pulled in a sharp breath, shoved out a string of curses that encouraged her, whether that was his intent or not.

The head of his cock was full in her mouth, slick with beads of salty moisture, and hot to the touch of her tongue. She lapped at the flat of the top, teased the seam where it split the underside, caught the ridge between her lips, and held him there as she sucked.

He had a mouth on him, her Simon, the words coming out enough to make her blush. Giving him this pleasure was exquisite, the feel of his flesh in her hand, against her tongue, the arousal that swept up her body. But there was more, so much more, the desire to have him in her life that took hold of her heart and squeezed.

She couldn't breathe for the way she wanted him, couldn't breathe for the sharp sob caught in her throat. He seemed to realize her struggle, raised up on one elbow and reached out, wrapped her hair around his wrist to tug her close.

"C'mere, *chère*," he said, and she followed his lead, crawling up his body to straddle his thighs. "Don't think about it. Not about any of it that's not right here, right now."

But it *was* right here, right now, didn't he know?

"I'm so tired. I didn't know I could be so tired." She was exhausted and emotionally punch-drunk, not to mention dealing with the physical aches that still twitched from time to time.

"We're both tired. We both need sleep." His hands were at her chest, fingering the buttons down the front of the old-style jersey. He released them quickly, parting the front of the shirt, soothing her nerves with soft murmurs and shushing sounds. "And I can let you go, though you gotta know it's the last thing I want to do."

"What's the first?" It was all she could ask.

"Get you naked."

"Do you need help?"

He shook his head, the moonlight glinting off the glossy strands of black in his hair and the green of his eyes. "The journey's as much fun as the destination."

"So I've heard." She let him skim the shirt off her shoulders, leaned forward, her hands on the mattress as he reached for the clasp of her bra.

When her bare breasts were inches from his face, he said, "Have I ever told you how much I love your tits?"

That made her smile. "Don't most guys love tits?"

"I don't know from most guys, *chère*. I only know that I could eat you up for hours."

"I don't see anyone here stopping you," she got out just as he plumped her breasts together and began to tease her nipples with his tongue.

And so it began, her fall. Into oblivion. Into mindless sensation. Into love. He sucked gently, then with enough force to make her squirm, before he pulled back to blow on the flesh he'd so thoroughly wet.

While he played there, she lifted her bottom up off his thighs, slipped a hand between her legs to pull away the crotch of her underpants, then, using the heel of her palm, she found the pole of his erection and lowered herself onto his shaft.

She took him in slowly, gripping him, rotating her hips as she slid to the base. The head of his cock nudged the entrance to her womb and stayed there, pulsing, waiting as if deciding between holding on and letting go.

"Woman," he growled. "Do you have any idea what you do to me?"

She knew what he did to her. That told her plenty. "I want hours of you. Uninterrupted. With time to sleep wrapped up together. With no apologies for indulging in pleasure. Hours of nothing but this."

"I can't . . . I can't say anything. I don't know how you put that into words."

This . . . emotion. It did that to her. A rush of warmth that grew to swaddle her, cotton and down and comfort. All the things he made her feel. All the things she felt for him.

Did he know?

She rode him like the fine stallion he was, thick and muscled and prime. She tightened around him as she came up, opened as she slid down, ground her clit against the wide base of his shaft, the hair above tickling.

He held her hips, guiding her, reining her in as if he feared that his thrusts might drive her away, that if he let her go she would fly. And oh, but she flew, all over him, coming apart as he bucked up into her, as he spilled his seed as deep inside her body as he could.

They took forever to finish, neither one wanting to return, to lose what they'd found, finally giving in to sleep that was swift to take them, though unable to pull them apart.

Thirty-five

Simon had barely made it downstairs the next morning when a loud knock sounded on the door. Before he made up his mind to answer, the knock came again, an insistent banging he wasn't going to be able to ignore. He started to cross the room, stopped as the door opened and his cousin, as jumpy as an addict, walked in.

Simon turned toward the stove, picked up the aluminum drip pot sitting on the back burner. "Coffee?"

That was all he had the energy for. After the hell of a long day yesterday turned out to be, he'd expended his reserves on Micky in bed, and four hours' sleep hadn't left him anywhere close to recharged—funny, since he could go for days on nothing but catnaps on the job.

Seemed something about Bayou Allain, or something about Micky, was draining him drier than he'd been in a while. Or maybe it was finally getting away from the cave of his studio and letting the tension of the last month go. More than likely it was a combination of all of the above, and he was going to wear himself out trying to piece it all together without the help of caffeine.

"Yeah, sure, I guess," King said, pacing the small room.

Simon wondered if what his cousin really wanted came in

a bottle with a long neck, but being too familiar with that devil himself these days, he didn't offer. Neither did he prompt the other man to find out what had brought him here so early. King's agitation was obvious, but no more so than the sludge in Simon's brain.

He put water on to heat, dumped ground coffee in the metal basket, reassembled the pot, then leaned against the counter to wait. "You been up all night?"

King snorted. "You making conversation, or do I look as dog shit bad as I feel?"

"Dog shit?" Simon shook his head, took in the tension keeping the other man moving, began to feel it himself. "Wired is more like it."

"I'm just waiting for you to wake up enough for me to tell you what I found."

What the hell? "Found? In Terrill's boxes?" It had to be. What else would bring King over here this early? "I'm awake. Talk."

"It wasn't in the boxes, no. I gave up on those before everyone left. It was too needle in a haystack. I don't know how Terrill managed to find the things he did. Two bits out of thousands, most written in legal speak that had my eyes crossing like T-Beaux Gentry's."

Meaning he didn't look at much of anything closely. Meaning who knew what all he had missed.

"I wanted to see what else I could find about the Landrys owning Le Hasard."

It had been the middle of the night. King could have done his digging only one way. And he'd beat Simon to it, since Simon had planned to contact SG-5's ops center after coffee and before Micky got out of bed to see who was in the office and what they might have time to find out.

"And where did Google get you?" Simon asked as the water began to boil. He poured it into the top of the pot and inhaled deeply as the fresh brew began to drip.

"Some interesting stuff, boo," King said, the legs of a kitchen chair scraping the floor when he spun it around and straddled the seat.

"Interesting how?"

At the sound of Micky's yawning question, Simon turned. She walked into the kitchen pushing her hair from her face, rubbing sleep from her eyes, and wearing nothing but the baseball jersey and crew socks she'd worn to bed last night.

Granted, the shirt came down to the middle of her thighs and covered all the things he didn't want King to see. But it was impossible not to remember her body on top of his, milking his, loving his, and not want to heave her over his shoulder and haul her back up the stairs to his bed.

Not a reaction that was going to make it easy to put her on a plane later today.

"King was just about to explain. We were waiting on the coffee."

"Is it done?" She gathered her hair into a tail with one hand, leaned over the stove and inhaled deeply.

"Almost." He, on the other hand, was sizzling, as was the glare he shot toward his cousin, who was busy checking out Micky's ass.

She straightened, turned to face King, and leaned back into Simon's body as if this were commonplace, the two of them here in this kitchen, a couple, together, at home. He couldn't believe how fiercely the desire for that very thing ate at him from the inside.

King finally had the decency to clear his throat and stare over Micky's head at Simon. "I did a search on the history of the property, tax records—and you are the legal owner, boo—past liens, and other filings. Found some stuff about the loss of the orchards and grazing land in the storm, and other stuff about Smokin' Aces."

"Smokin' Aces?" Micky asked, moving away for Simon

to fish three Styrofoam cups from the box of supplies on the counter he'd never had time to unpack.

"The well on Le Hasard," he explained, pouring the coffee, handing her two cups, carrying his own along with the creamer and sugar to the table. King took his black, blowing across the top before sipping but still scalding his tongue.

"Shit," he yelped, but sipped again, growling when Simon laughed. "Anyway, I also found a Web site that describes treasures that have never been found."

"Like buried treasures?" Simon asked.

"Pirate chests? Bags of gold from stagecoach holdups? Diamonds and jewels from train robberies? Unmarked bills from bank heists?" Micky added.

Both men looked at her before Simon told his cousin, "She watches too much TV."

King went on with no more than an absent nod, an elbow on the table, his cup in his other hand. "One of these treasures, one there isn't a lot of info on—and trust me, if it was there, I'd've found it. The Internet is a seasonally employed man's best friend."

Simon arched a brow at that, but King didn't wait for him to comment. "Anyway, one of these treasures is a cache of gold coins a Confederate soldier stole before the Union seized New Orleans. They hunted for him, and his body found in what is now Vermilion Parish."

"What about the gold?" Micky asked before raising her cup to her mouth.

Simon thought about the coin his father had found on Le Hasard and carried with him for good luck. A grin pulled at his mouth. "It's still there."

"How do you know? For that matter, how would Bear know?" Micky asked.

"Did I mention the soldier's family's name?" King asked.

"Landry," Simon and Micky said as one.

King grinned. "That's got to be what Lisa discovered. Either where the gold is or how to find it."

"And why Bear doesn't want anyone on the land," Simon said, striking the table with his fist. "The poker game has nothing to do with any of this. He just wanted us out of his way. But if he still hasn't found the treasure—"

"And he wouldn't still be here if he had—"

"Then Lisa obviously never told him what he wanted to know."

"Meaning," King concluded, "that she's too valuable for him to have hurt her."

"He's got her stashed away somewhere."

"Any ideas?" King asked on top of Micky's, "We've got to find her!"

"So where do we start?" Simon asked.

They started by splitting up. Micky went to find Bear and keep him occupied with more seemingly innocent questions about Lisa—though with King this time, not on her own—while Simon headed to town. Lorna knew he was coming by for his money. It was the perfect time to get her to talk.

To make that happen, he needed to see her alone. Not only alone without Bear putting words in her mouth and pulling her strings, but alone without Micky there to remind Lorna that she wasn't thirty years old anymore.

Getting what he wanted out of Lorna would be a tough sale with another woman around, no matter how much he would have preferred having Micky with him. It wasn't about not trusting King, but about wanting to see for himself that she stayed safe and out of harm's way.

He was glad to have King for backup. Not thinking things were going to get so complicated, he hadn't called in another

SG-5 operative to help. If this entire scenario was about finding a buried treasure, then he'd truly underestimated Bear Landry's level of sanity. No man in his right mind would threaten a member of his family to increase his material wealth.

Oh, sure. It happened all the time. Like he'd said. No man in his right mind. And not much of a man at that, to Simon's way of thinking. He wanted an example of a man? He had only to look to Hank Smithson. Or to any member of the Smithson Group team.

Looking at King is what hung Simon up. And a big part of that was recognizing that he, most of all, had let his cousin down. Having watched from a distance he'd known King was struggling. He'd seen what he'd tried to do with the land. He'd witnessed him fail time after time after time—whether the fault of money, Mother Nature, or the man.

Simon had been in a position to help. He hadn't. He'd let a single incident from their past—granted, a big, fat, nasty one—get in the way of doing the right thing, seeing to the needs of his family.

It had eaten at him. All this time it had eaten at him. And until he'd seen his cousin again, he hadn't known how much. He thought they might finally be on the road to making amends. Their first meeting hadn't been stellar, but during the last two, the tide had seemed to change.

Whatever he had to do to keep it rolling, he would, drawing the line at enabling. But the rest . . . There wasn't a single reason to keep him from offering Kingdom a hand. And if some of that was the result of being here with Micky, well, so be it.

Caught up in his thoughts, Simon almost didn't see the truck that flew past him headed the other way—and driven by Lorna Savoy. She was going east, into the sun, which sat like a fireball in the sky above the road. He doubted she'd seen him through the glare off her windshield.

He pulled over, made a U-turn, maintained enough of a distance between their vehicles to keep his New York plates out of sight, and then followed her all the way to the parish library in Abbeville.

Thirty-six

Since most of Bayou Allain's business district closed for the weekend, Micky and King had no luck finding Bear at his land office in town. They checked to see if he might be at Savoy Realty, but Lorna's place was closed, too. Strange, Micky thought, for a Realtor not to be working on a Saturday. She could only hope Simon was having more success.

Even so, she wasn't overjoyed with the idea of his questioning the other woman. And, yes. It was a silly possessive response based on nothing but the story he'd told her of Lorna crawling into his bed twenty years ago.

Well, that and the way Lorna had seemed desperate for a repeat performance when she'd seen him in her office lobby. At first, Micky had been too caught up in the drama to pay much attention to the woman and her claws. But when Lorna had grabbed him to keep him from walking out the door . . . grr.

Micky had no reason to be jealous. No matter the night they'd just spent, Simon wasn't really hers. She'd known him for two days, and he was about to put her on a plane. One did not *belong* after two days.

So why did she feel like she did, to him? That he did, to

her? And that if she never saw him again, well, she would curl up in a ball and just die?

This emotion was new and frightening, and her biggest fear was that she wasn't going to have a chance to explore its potential, to nurture it, to watch it grow, to enjoy the full beauty when it blossomed into what she knew would last forever.

King made a sudden, screaming U-turn, taking up most of the street, sending Micky flying into her door and oncoming cars off the road. There were only a few, but he just kept driving. The honking didn't faze him a bit.

She looked over at him wide-eyed. "What are you doing?"

Her question didn't faze him either. "Bear's not in town. It's too early for him to be at Red's. Next stop? His house."

They were in this together, yet he was running plays on his own. She wondered if he knew there was no "I" in team. "We're supposed to keep him from getting to Lorna before Simon does. If she's at his house, there's not much we can do."

"True, but I figure it can't hurt to see what the old guy is up to. I'd like to know how much you showing up alive after the bridge thing really spooked him."

Again, making it about what he wanted instead of what best served the plan. "He saw me yesterday. If it spooked him, I'm sure he's gotten over it by now."

"Then we'll spook him again," he said, waggling both brows like he was in junior high and getting ready to hijack the school's public-address system.

She rolled her eyes, but she couldn't help thinking his being a jerk was mostly for show. "You like this, don't you? Stirring up trouble. Running people off the road." She pointed behind them toward the town they'd just left. "Did you even hear those cars honking?"

He rolled his shoulders in a careless shrug. "They'd honk

at me if I was driving to church. That's how they are, how this place is."

Or his behavior deserved such reactions. "Then why do you stay?"

"Are you kidding? He laughed, a wicked sound of enjoyment. "With good ol' cuz paying the taxes on the land and not charging me a dime in rent?"

She faced forward, crossed her arms, glad he wasn't the cousin she'd fallen for. His recklessness scared her. "He needs to charge you rent."

"Oh-ho. I see whose side you're on."

"It's not about sides."

"Then what's it about, *chère?*" he asked, his voice silky. "You just met the both of us. He just happened to be the first one to get in your pants. If you hadn't run out that night at Red's, I can guarantee you wouldn't be sitting all the way over there hugging that door right now."

"I'm hugging the door so you don't kill me with your driving," she said, ignoring his cocky cheek.

"Whatever you say, *chère.*"

"What about Paschelle?"

"What about her?"

"I don't think she'd like me sitting any closer than this."

"Aww, Chelle and me, we're just friends with benefits." He cast her a dangerous glance. "And a man can't have too many friends."

He was so full of shit, but she couldn't help but wonder if he was using that shit to cover up things he'd never told Simon. Micky had met Paschelle. A cute girl, but one smart enough not to be taken in by a man who looked like King. She had to see something more.

Micky wanted to know what it was. Not for herself, but for Simon. She wanted this thing between the two men to go away. She wanted the two of them to have each other, to know each other, to be family. To not be alone.

Papi was everything to her. Her mother had gone away so long ago that she was nothing but a collection of memories. But Papi. Micky's chest tightened. She knew she was holding on too tight, using him to keep men at a distance because he loved her for herself, just the way she was.

"Well, what have we here?" King asked, and Micky returned from her musings to look up.

They'd driven onto what she assumed was Judge Landry's property, but they hadn't stopped at his house. King had kept going, and all Micky saw was fields.

Fields, and the tree line beyond edging a plot of uncleared acreage. Fields, the tree line, a plot of uncleared acreage . . . and a vehicle driving through the first, toward the second, and into the third.

King looked at her. She looked at him.

"You game?" he asked.

"Why not?" she answered.

So they followed Bear into the woods.

Thirty-seven

Bear pulled his International Scout up to the tarpaper shelter that squatted on the edge of Snickers Bayou. He'd sent Lorna to the parish library's Abbeville branch to get the Landry family Bible held there on display, and he couldn't do what he needed to do until she got here. He cut the engine to wait.

Lorna had argued that the Bible was considered reference material. It could be viewed only on the premises. It was not to be removed. He'd told her to get it anyway, dumb bitch. If he'd had any idea of its true value, he would never have made the donation, and that made him just as dumb.

Unless he was psychic, he couldn't have anticipated the hunt for the treasure would heat up as it had. And though Lisa had wound up at the center of it all, he had never wanted her hurt. What he'd expected was that she'd tire of having very little water and even less food and eventually tell him what he wanted to know. She hadn't come close.

Once he'd revealed to her his part in her kidnapping and what her freedom would cost, she'd said she'd die before she'd tell him a thing. Said she knew he'd be forced to kill her anyway. Said she wanted to enjoy thinking about him living the rest of his life still searching.

He hadn't told her he'd been doing it since his childhood. Bear's father had told him the treasure story—though like his grandfather before, his old man had written off the tale of the treasure as legend. Bear hadn't been so quick to do the same.

Finding something that incredible was a dream. He'd been an only child with nothing much to do and acres to roam. Bayou Allain had not even been the speck on the map then that it was now. There hadn't been any boys in school who lived near enough to be regular playmates. He'd played soldiers and cowboys and pirates with his imagination instead.

Harlan Baptiste's coin was the first bit of evidence proving the treasure's existence. After seeing the piece for himself, Bear had no doubt that the cache was buried on the land Zachary Benoit had won from Ross Landry in that poker game decades before.

Until Lisa started her genealogy project, Bear hadn't realized he'd been holding on to a piece of the puzzle for years. He'd found the slip of paper in his father's effects. It was old, brittle, and looked as if it had been used to record Morse code. He'd thought the markings meaningless. They weren't meaningless at all.

He'd come close to suffering a stroke the day Lisa had asked him to meet her at the main branch of the parish library. He'd always liked the girl, didn't mind indulging her whims, so had driven to Abbeville to meet her for lunch.

She'd taken him to see the Bible afterward. It had originally belonged to one of his forefathers, had been passed down through generations and lost—only to be unearthed when he'd razed an old barn on his property.

What Lisa had found in the binding made the cost of

tearing down the structure and having the rubble carted off worth every penny. The letter hidden between the back parchment and the leather cover explained the purpose of the markings. And to think how close he'd come to throwing the doodlings away.

After he'd fed her the story about his never having taken the rumors seriously, so never sharing the legend with his son, she'd suggested they work together to find the gold and surprise Terrill and the town. And since she had her own reason for keeping the secret and wouldn't have to be coerced into silence, he'd gladly gone along.

During one of their afternoons at the library, she'd asked him what he knew about Harlan Baptiste. That wouldn't have been so bad if she hadn't also shared her theory, showing him both the article about a body being found in a western Louisiana parish and the photo of his own father holding the cane Bear still used every day that appeared to have made the markings on the dead man's face.

How she'd made the connection between the article, the photo, and the missing Harlan Baptiste, he'd never know. What he did know was that he was not going to spend the rest of his life behind bars. At that point, with what he'd thought covered up all these years unraveling and the treasure finally so close, there'd been only one thing he could think of to do.

Get her out of the way.

He'd arranged for the kidnapping, and once she'd been secured in the shelter, he'd paid the man he'd hired half the promised amount. The rest of the money would be delivered and Lisa set free as soon as he had the gold coins in hand and was safely out of the country.

He knew he'd be implicated, accused, even indicted in both the kidnapping and the murder. For that very reason he'd chosen to make his new home on an Indonesian island with no extradition treaty or agreement.

Lisa was never supposed to know he was involved. It was only when he'd grown stumped working the codes on his own that he'd become desperate enough to reveal his involvement. He'd needed her help. She'd refused to give it, leaving him no choice but to raise the stakes.

Having tired of waiting for Lorna to show, he now grabbed the gun from the seat beside him, climbed down from the Scout, and headed for the shack's door. It was time to finish what had been started.

When he shoved the door open, Lisa squinted against the sudden assault of light and scrambled up from where she was lying on the cot to sit in the corner and lean on the flimsy excuse for a wall.

He stayed where he was, keeping the light in her eyes, his shadow to the side. "I thought you might like to know that a friend of yours came to visit. She's still here, actually, thinking she has a hope of finding you."

"Who?" she croaked out.

"Michelina Ferrer," he said and watched her eyes widen slightly, the pulse in her neck jump, her throat flex as she swallowed. She showed no other emotion and said nothing, brave little soldier that she was.

He went on. "I've decided that if you don't tell me what I want to know, I'll kill her instead of you. Then I'll kill your parents."

She sucked in a shallow breath, grated out one word. "No."

He gestured with the barrel of the gun. "You can be responsible for those three deaths, or you can forget about the death of a man you didn't know."

"I won't be responsible for anything you do."

"Of course you will. You're the one with the means to stop me. I don't know why I didn't think of it sooner. I guess I thought that you'd come to your senses, that the threat on your life would be enough." He paused, watched her use her shoulder to brush her hair from her eyes, added the final bomb. "I suppose I could add Terrill to the list."

"He's your son." She stopped, coughed, tears spilling from her eyes. "You wouldn't."

She didn't know what he was capable of. "I would."

She pushed her way to the edge of the cot, wobbling as it creaked beneath her. "Once you get a taste for murder, it never goes away, is that it?"

He knew what she was talking about, what had started all this. He glanced down the rutted trail, looking for any sign of Lorna. Seeing none and growing impatient, he glanced back. "Harlan Baptiste was an accident. I never meant it to happen. It was self-defense."

Lisa shook her head. "It can't be both. And I doubt his son or his nephew would see it as either considering what you did with the body."

He didn't owe her an explanation, but they had time; he offered one just the same. "I had just sentenced his boys. He came to the house that night. He'd been following the trial, had seen the news that they would be going away. He came to beg me to reconsider, but it was too late."

"You wanted the boys off the property, didn't you?" She cleared her throat, coughed again, but she never asked him for water. "With Harlan having made it clear to the entire town that he wasn't coming back, Simon and King were the only thing keeping you from having free run of Le Hasard. You were probably responsible for the fire, too."

"That land should have been mine," he told her, tightening his fist on the stock of the gun. "It was lost to that family in a poker game. They didn't know anything about oil. That well they drilled? A waste." He'd seen the geological surveys. He knew what pooled beneath the land. "The gold is the least they owed me for that oil."

She glared, her eyes narrowed to slits, her bound limbs shaking. "You're insane."

"Maybe. But you're sitting there, and I'm the one who's going to make sure you have no family left."

She was silent for a minute, and he saw the surrender that washed over her before she said, "I need the Bible. There's no other way."

"Lorna is bringing it," he said, feeling a thrilling rush of blood through his veins.

"And you're going to kill her, too?"

He ignored the question. "Are you going to show me how to read the markings in the Bible?"

She nodded.

That was all he needed to know. He could take it from here. He had no need of Lisa, of Lorna, of anyone. Once he had the Bible in hand, he'd be on his way to living the rest of his life as he pleased.

Yes, he had money, he had power, but he also had obligations weighing him down—not to mention the murder of Harlan Baptiste twenty years ago now rearing its ugly head. Unlike complicity in arson, there was no statute of limitations on murder.

He wasn't taking any chances.

"It's about time," Bear muttered to himself, relieved at hearing Lorna arrive. Or at least he was relieved until he realized what he was hearing was an engine more powerful than the one in the truck Lorna drove.

Thirty-eight

Micky glanced at the small shack that was nothing but four walls and a roof covered in tar paper. There were no windows on either of the sides she could see from where King had stopped the truck. She couldn't see the third at all, though she doubted it was designed any differently, and she assumed the door was on the fourth, facing the water.

"This isn't someone's house, is it?" She wasn't so entitled that she knew nothing of poverty, but this . . . no one should live like this.

The shake of King's head brought relief. "It's for hunting. Not room for much but a cot and a lantern, but I just don't think that's what Bear's out here to do. Or all that there is inside."

They were idling close enough on the rutted trail that anyone in the place would be able to hear them, but they hadn't known they'd come up against this sudden dead end. "If Lisa's there, and he knows we're here . . ." She didn't want to think what the judge might do, what might be happening even now.

"He knows," King said, letting off the brake and rolling slowly forward. "We might as well say hello."

Micky's stomach pitched up and fell down with every bump King hit. She knew it wasn't the ride as much as the anticipation of what they'd find—and what would happen when they came face-to-face with Bear.

She doubted Simon would have sent her off with his cousin if he'd thought for a minute this was where she'd wind up, at the terminus of what was no more than a rutted dirt path heading into the unknown.

Once King had pulled up beside Bear's vehicle, he shifted into park and left the engine running. A shock of his hair, golden brown where Simon's was black, fell over his forehead and into his eyes. He shook it back with a cocky movement, reached for his door handle, stopped.

Micky wasn't sure what to do. She was taking her cues from him, trusting his instincts—this was his turf, his bayou—but even he seemed hesitant to move. "Do we go in? Wait and see if he comes out?"

"This is feeling even more wrong than I thought it could," he admitted, sending her stomach tumbling again.

They didn't have a phone to reach Simon or Terrill, and though Simon knew they were off to find Bear, she couldn't imagine he'd know about this place, to come looking for them here if he had news, or to find out what they had learned. No one would think to come looking for them here.

No one had thought to look here for Lisa.

Micky wondered if she was the only one wishing they'd taken the time to figure out a way to keep in touch. Then she noticed the radio beneath the dash of King's truck. She gestured toward it. "Please tell me that works."

He nodded. "It works."

"Do you have a gun?"

Another nod. "Under the seat. A shotgun."

She wasn't sure if any of this was making her feel better. "Should we take it?"

He glanced over. "I'm not so sure we're going anywhere."

She met his gaze. "To see if Lisa's inside? We can't just sit here."

"I'm thinking we can. He knows we're out here. We know he's in there. It's like a game of chicken. Whoever gives in first, loses."

"That might work. If this was a game."

"Life's a game, *chère*. We're just the pawns."

Just what she needed. A Cajun philosopher. Eyes closed, she took a deep breath, then rolled her gaze toward him. "Could you at least get your shotgun out from under the seat? In case we need it?"

"Oh, we're going to need it, but I think it's too late."

At that, she turned to look through the windshield. The judge walked toward them, holding a gun that looked more like something she'd expect to see in the hands of a Marine on patrol in Iraq. She started to wonder if Simon had such a gun but found herself cringing as Bear began waving it around.

"Turn off the truck and get out!" he shouted, his face an unhealthy beet red. "Both of you! Now!"

The windows were up. His voice boomed that loudly. She opened her door. King opened his. They climbed down at the same time, forcing Bear to switch his attention back and forth. She followed King and his lead, walking two steps behind him, walking slowly, slowing even more and hoping he was using the time to plot and plan, because she was fresh out of ideas.

Just as she realized they could have seriously made use of the sort of expertise—legal or not—Simon had, they rounded the front of the cabin. She'd been right about the location of the door. It was standing open—and Lisa was inside!

Micky gasped, rushed forward, ran into the barrel of

Bear's gun. That didn't stop her from calling out, "Lisa! Are you okay? Are you hurt?"

The light inside was dim, but it was enough to see that Lisa wasn't okay. She was sitting on the cot King had guessed would be there, her knees drawn up, her ankles and wrists bound.

She wasn't bloody or bruised, not that Micky could see, but she was so obviously exhausted and haggard that Micky couldn't stand what she was seeing, or help what she did.

She swung. On Bear.

Arms flailing, she struck out, screaming. "You bastard! You monster! I'm going to kill you! I swear—"

Bear swung back. With the gun.

He caught Micky in the ribs, flung her by the arm through the door. This time when she screamed, it was from pain. She crumpled to the shack's dirt floor, aware of Lisa behind her coughing as she tried to speak.

Micky wanted to tell her to stop, not to strain her voice, to waste her energy, that King would get them out of here, that Simon was on the way. She didn't say any of it, because she couldn't draw a breath. There was dirt in her mouth, a hammer pounding railroad spikes into her side.

"Tie her up," Bear ordered.

Micky sensed King at her feet binding her ankles, then pulling her wrists between her legs and roping them tight. She couldn't move. She thought he'd leave enough slack for her to work her way free.

She wanted to yell at him, to ask him what he thought he was doing, to get him to admit that he was on the wrong side, betraying her, but when she managed to get one eye open, she saw that he didn't have any choice. Bear was standing over him pointing the gun at his head.

"Can't do much better of a job, boo," King said, giving

her a reassuring wink and squeezing her fingers before turning to look up at the judge.

"Good," Bear said, slamming the stock of the gun into
King's head. He collapsed next to Micky, bleeding all over
the ground.

And that's when she started to cry.

Thirty-nine

Simon ditched his truck in a pint-size clearing twenty feet inside the tree line and followed Lorna on foot. The road was nothing but two tracks cut by the repetitive grinding of four wheels traveling back and forth over time.

He could jog as fast as she was driving, and moved at a steady pace, sticking to what he gauged to be her blind spot. Even so, he kept under the cover of the brush, taking no chance of being seen.

There was only one reason he could think of for Lorna to have driven all the way to the library in Abbeville, gone inside for less than ten minutes, then driven out to the middle of nowhere without noticing he was behind her the entire way.

Bear was waiting.

He'd obviously ordered Lorna to the library for something. Simon couldn't think the old man was out here wanting a book. It had to be a document, a copy of a record of . . . what?

The only thing that came to mind, that kept coming to mind, prodding and insistent, was the information King had found about the treasure on Le Hasard.

Simon couldn't believe it, but at this point the why of

Bear wanting something didn't matter. All that mattered was the *what* Lorna had brought. Seeing movement up ahead of the truck as it slowed, he ducked low behind a thick growth of foliage.

"It's about goddamn time, Lorna," Bear said, jerking open her door before she'd come to a complete stop.

"It's a long round-trip, Baby Bear." She reached back, grabbed her satchel.

Simon hadn't noticed the bulk when she'd clutched it to her chest as she'd run to her truck. Maybe he'd been wrong. Maybe it *was* a book. One she'd had to keep hidden. One she'd stolen. But why?

He went back to thinking of documents and records. What in the hell was Bear doing? What could he possibly need from the library that he couldn't get anywhere else?

Bear grabbed Lorna's satchel, dug inside for what looked to Simon like a Bible, and tossed her bag to the ground.

"Hey, B.B. That's my best Dooney and Bourke."

"I don't care if it's sewn from the Shroud of Turin." He turned and headed back toward the shack, leaving Lorna to retrieve the satchel and scurry after him.

"Wait. Baby Bear, wait."

God, what a whiner. Simon wondered how any woman could allow herself to become so pathetic, so controlled and dependent, then realized whom he was looking at, and who her controller was.

He shook off the distraction and crept closer, keeping low to the ground, his steps steady, stealthy, and soft. He figured the sound of the vehicles driving up had driven away the birds in the area, but he didn't want to chance startling any that might still be around into flight.

Using first King's truck, then Bear's Scout for cover, he moved into position where he could see the front of the shack. Lorna stood in the doorway. Bear was inside, as he hoped were Micky and King and Lisa.

He could hear Bear talking, his words directed at some-one other than Lorna, and when she shifted to the right, Simon could make out the shape of a body on the ground. He saw what looked like a piece of white clothing, which would most likely make the body King's.

Except the hulking shape he was seeing appeared too large to be just his cousin, meaning he was looking at more than one body. He was looking at either Lisa or Micky, and since he knew for certain only one of the two was here . . .

Goddamn.

God fucking damn.

He couldn't panic. Even if he couldn't slow the blastoff speed of his pulse, he couldn't panic. Number-one rule. He had to assess the situation calmly, make his move—if there was one to make—based on what he knew.

Not what he hoped.

Not what he guessed.

Not on emotion.

Lorna was an easy mark. He wrote her off. He had yet to see a weapon, but he couldn't think of any other reason King was unmoving on the ground. The other body . . . it was too dark for him to see motion of any kind.

Bear was his objective. That was it.

He reached for his Smith & Wesson, released the safety, returned to the rear of Bear's Scout. He could cover the area from there to the back wall of the shack in seconds, scope out the other side, and make for the front. Kick out Lorna's legs, send her to the ground. Pivot on Bear and aim to shoot. To kill if he had to.

Gun at the ready, he pulled in a deep breath—only to be stopped by a shout and Lorna's cry. A scuffle. Banging. A weak female voice. Silence. He breathed. In and out. In and out. Waited. Waited. Sweat sizzled down his spine. Dripped into his eyes. And still he waited, maintained his position, strained to hear more.

Finally it came. The sound. Not a voice, but footsteps, heavy, in no hurry at all. Simon crouched low and slipped from the Scout to King's truck, peering through the windshield from the passenger's open door.

Bear didn't look anywhere but straight ahead. He jerked at the Scout's tailgate, grabbed a gas can from the vehicle, and returned to the shack. He started at the back, pouring the fuel along the base of the wall.

Simon moved before it was too late, crossing the open space at a full-out sprint. He was at Bear's back, his gun behind the other man's ear, before he had straightened from his task.

"You've got a thing for setting fires, don't you, boo?" Simon grabbed the can and tossed it away, patted down Bear's pockets, found a book of matches and a lighter. "Hedging your bets?"

Bear smirked. "Why do you think I sent Lorna to suck your dick twenty years ago? A smart man always does."

Simon spun him around. "Goes to show that you are one dumb ass. Let's go."

Forty

"I cannot believe you're here," Lisa said to Micky while leaning into Terrill's body, his arms wrapped around her waist, her hands on his hands, her voice weak and scratchy but so full of joy. "I mean, I am *thrilled* that you are, but it's just so impossible. Want to know the first thing I thought after realizing it was you?"

"What?" Micky asked, grinning.

"Your father is going to kill you as soon as Greta finishes doing you in."

Oh, it felt good to laugh. "I hope that wasn't the first thing you thought."

"Yeah, well, it was the first thing I thought after I realized we weren't going to die together."

It had been a pretty hairy scene, Micky had to admit. And it was something Simon did all the time, stepping into the unknown, putting himself into dangers far worse than what had happened today. But then so much more *could* have happened, and wasn't that what he was afraid of? Why he wanted to send her away?

She looked over at him now, where he was talking to the other deputy sheriff, the parish sheriff himself, and two officers from the Louisiana State Police. How any of them had found this place in the back of beyond boggled the mind.

Even more boggling was how lucky she, Lisa, and King had been that Simon had shown up when he had. He'd been too late to save Lorna. Bear had broken her neck. He hadn't wanted the rest of them to get off so easily, he'd said. But Lorna had deserved that consideration.

No, Bear had wanted the crime to be so horrific that more attention would be paid to the gory details and the loss of a celebrity than to hunting down the criminal. He knew that that's what the public would remember, that Michelina Ferrer had died in a fire, an excruciating, disfiguring death.

Thinking about it now, she shuddered, and then she caught Simon looking her way. The words he was speaking were for the ears of law enforcement, but his eyes were all for her. He gave her a small shake of his head, inhaled deeply, and pressed a fist to the center of his chest.

She read relief in the expression, saw even more, an emotion deeper and incredibly telling in his eyes. She wanted to get him alone, crawl all over him, touch his nose and his elbows and the soles of his feet. She had to know that he was all right. That he was hers.

Funny, when she was the one who'd been hog-tied and manhandled, when she was the one who'd thought she was going to die. The one who had wanted to see him one last time if she had truly met her fate.

"Hey, Micky," Lisa said.

"Yeah?"

"I gotta know."

"What?"

"What are you doing roaming the swamps with that outlaw Kingdom Trahan? I mean, I know you were looking for me, but with King?"

Micky pulled her gaze from Simon, gave her attention to

her friend. Her entire face felt as if it were smiling. "Do you know how good it is to see you? All in one piece at that?"

"Stop avoiding. Answer."

"And do it so I can get my wife out of here and to the hospital," Terrill said, as the sound of an ambulance siren could finally be heard.

He was right. Lisa was dehydrated, tired, weak, and so deathly wan, and so Micky did. "King's not so bad. At least now that he's got his cousin to keep him in line."

Lisa's eyes twinkled as she grinned. "I can't believe you of all people are the one taming the infamous Simon Baptiste."

"You've heard of him?"

Lisa winked. "*Chère*, everyone in Bayou Allain knows of Simon Baptiste. Even those of us new to the swamp."

Before Micky could respond one of the officers assigned to guarding Bear yelled, "Fire!" hell breaking loose as all heads turned to see flames licking up the walls of the shack—the shack where they were holding the judge while they took all the witnesses' statements.

No one stopped to question how he'd started the fire while in handcuffs, though Micky assumed he'd knocked over the lantern. They just ran. Terrill scooped Lisa up in his arms. Micky followed, seconds later feeling Simon at her back. King and the officers brought up the rear.

No one ran far, the whole group stopping when it became evident that there was no longer anything volatile inside to explode—or no chance of the person who'd set it surviving the blaze.

Forty-one

Chelle hadn't really planned to say her good-byes to King in front of an audience Sunday morning, but she couldn't deny the sweep of relief she felt at driving up and finding one waiting.

That was the thing about these long dirt roads. Sneaking up on people was out of the question. Not that she'd ever been able to sneak up on King the way he'd done to her.

Strange, that was one of the things about him she was going to miss the most. She didn't want to think about missing the sex. Their affair—and that's all it had been really, all any of her relationships had ever been—had held such promise for more.

She'd felt things for him she'd never felt for a man. What she'd felt was love, felt, too, that as strong as it was, he surely returned more than her passion. She'd assumed wrong, put feelings into his heart instead of taking him at his word that he had nothing to offer.

The beer bottle on the back porch had been the last straw. She'd given him anything he wanted. He'd hidden everything from her. That was what she couldn't handle, seeing what she had in his eyes, the emotion that contradicted the words he had spoken. He did have something to give her. He just hadn't yet let himself do it.

She pulled her car to a stop alongside his truck. It took a really deep breath for her to climb out, one that left her light-headed. When she looked up again, Simon and Micky were gone. Only King was there, his arms crossed over his chest, his backside braced against the edge of the porch, his booted feet crossed at the ankle.

A big white bandage covered one side of his forehead. So typical. Too tough to admit he needed more care and observation than what he could get with tape and gauze. She wondered if this time he'd sat still for the stitches.

Then she started to sweat. "Did I scare off Micky and Simon?"

King gave her that trademark grin of his, all wicked and knowing and raw. "I'm the scary one, *chère*. You ought to know that by now."

The scariest part was that she did. She swallowed, walked as close as she dared—which still left five feet between them—and kept her hands in the pockets of her skirt so he wouldn't see them shake. "Were they afraid I was going to get all weepy saying good-bye?"

"Is that what you came to do?"

Which one was he asking? Was she going to weep, or going to say good-bye? "I'm assuming they'll be heading home soon. I wasn't sure if I'd get another chance to see them."

"To see them before they left? Or before you left?"

He just stood there looking at her, his comments goading her to admit she was walking away from Bayou Allain, walking away from him—even though it was something he already knew.

"I have to go."

She swung her hands back and forth, her skirt swirling

around her ankles. She thought of how many times he'd found his way beneath the yards of fabric she wore, either pushing them up or pulling them down. She really had to stop her thoughts from drifting.

"I'm surprised it took you this long to figure it out."

Now he was making her mad. Was he doing it on purpose? "Figure out what exactly? That I don't fit in? That I'm not wanted?"

"Is that what you've felt here? Unwanted? And here I thought I was wanting you plenty."

"That's not what I meant."

"What then, *chère*? Explain it."

She shook her head. She didn't need this from him. "No. I don't think so. I'm just going to go."

She was only three steps from her car when he caught her. He took hold of her elbow, but he didn't spin her around the way she expected. Instead, he moved to stand in front of her, to face her, still holding on.

"You're too good for this place, Chelle. Not unwanted." His face had gentled. The look in his eyes was one she'd seen only in her dreams. She hadn't thought he had it in him, that compassion. "There's a huge world out there that you need to see before you even try to fit in here. With me."

"I'm not too good," she began, hating the sting of tears welling. King stopped her from saying anything more with a finger pressed to her lips.

"You are the best woman I've ever known, Chelle—"

"The easiest, you mean." Because that he couldn't deny.

"That, too," he said, his thumb tracing her lips, her cheekbone, her temple. "If I could keep you here in my bed—"

"Or on the porch, in a parking lot, at the side of the road—"

"In my *bed*," he emphasized, "forever, I would. But you'd wake up one day and realize you were wasting your life screwing me when you could be making it with some Harvard MBA."

"It wasn't just screwing."

He cupped her face, dropped his forehead to hers. "I know."

"This is so hard, King. It shouldn't be this hard."

"Doing the right thing usually is."

Did he really believe that? Was letting her go hard for him at all? Would she be able to walk away if she knew that it was?

"I don't even know where I'm going," she said with a small laugh.

"You'll figure it out."

"What if I don't?" She lost everything in New Orleans. She had no one. She was truly on her own. "What if I mess up? What if I end up being stupid?" She couldn't help but worry. She was so close to having everything go right after it being so wrong for years.

"You won't." His hands were in her hair, threaded there, holding her. "But if you do, you call me."

"You don't have a phone!"

"I'll get one. Call Red. I'll give him the number."

"Oh, King," she said, closing her eyes so he wouldn't see how sad it made her to lose him.

He didn't speak but brought his mouth close and touched it to hers, his lips, then just the edge of his teeth, then the tip of his tongue. She opened her mouth and kissed him with all of her love, with the parts that wanted to hit him for being so crass and vulgar, with the parts that wanted to soothe the little boy hiding inside the man.

It was so easy to tell him how much she would miss him, so much easier to do it this way—lips pressed, tongues wet and seeking, hands gripping to bruise—than with a verbal explanation.

She was the one to finally step out of his embrace and into the future. Her eyes were as damp as his were red when she kissed her own fingertips and placed them on his cheek. He held her wrist for longer than she should have stayed, but then he let her go. He even opened her car door, closing it once she'd gathered her skirt inside.

"It's for the best, Chelle," he said.

"I know," she answered, and this time it wasn't a lie.

Forty-two

"That's it? You're just going to let her go?"

King watched Chelle drive away, the back end of the Mustang obscured by the dust thrown up by the car's wheels. He didn't have an answer for his cousin's question. He didn't know what to say.

Was he going to let her go? Had she been nothing to him but a fine piece of ass? Could he have had more with her if he'd ever given half an effort to finding out? Was he going to let her go?

He shrugged, not sure of his voice.

"How far up your ass is your head? The girl is mad for you."

Woman. Not girl. "She's mad, period. Living here as long as she did when she had nothing tying her to this hellhole."

"She had you."

"And now she doesn't. *C'est la vie.*" King wasn't going to talk about it anymore. He had other things he needed to say. Things he'd been holding on to a lot of years. "It's good she decided to go."

"Good for her? Or for you?"

"Both, for certain. I've got some things to deal with, and they'll go down easier this way."

"I don't know, boo." Simon glanced toward the house, where King knew Micky waited. "Alone isn't always the best way."

"You've had some experience with that then." King didn't even know what it was that Simon did these days, what it was that made it possible for him to come up with ninety thousand dollars when King had asked. That was the distance between them.

Simon nodded. "I have. After the service, I worked places that put me in a lot of danger. Then I took a position that sent me into even worse. I never wanted to bring anyone else into that. Felt it would be too hard to lose them, selfish to put them in harm's way just so I wouldn't be alone. And so I was. I am. I was."

Interesting. "How did she get you to change your mind?"

"By showing me the other side. I'd rather have what time I can with her than no time at all. The thought that she could've died kills me, but it doesn't take away how being with her lifts me up."

After a long quiet moment, King said, "And she feels the same."

Simon laughed. "If she doesn't, I'm going to be in a world of hurt."

More hurt than doing time for a crime he hadn't committed. More hurt than hating the one man who'd been there for him through all their years of silence. King wondered if it was too late to go after Chelle, but his heart knew it was too soon.

"About the money—"

"It doesn't matter—"

"I have a son." The words were out. The relief, monstrous.

"I didn't know . . ."

King laughed once. "Neither did I until three years ago. He's thirteen now."

"I've got all the usual questions, King, but you telling me what you want me to know is probably best."

He wanted Simon to know everything, but even King hadn't gotten that far figuring it out. Getting answers had been worse than realizing how much he regretted the things he'd missed.

"She was a woman who put me up for a while. Before I got the trailer moved in, the water well and septic dug, the electricity working. I met her at Red's. Gina. I honestly can't remember much more."

Simon frowned. "The money wasn't for a lawyer, was it? To set visitation rights, or fight for custody?"

"Oh, hell no, boo. I'm not father material. At least . . . not then. Probably not even now. For a while it looked like my adventures in parenting were going to be over before they got started."

"He was sick."

King nodded. "I knew he was mine when she showed me his picture. Remember that one Ma used to tease me about? In third grade?"

"Where your ears looked like a jackrabbit's poking up through your hair, and your shirt was inside out?"

"That's why my wardrobe's nothing but white Ts. And I tear off the tags. Hard to tell the difference," he joked, then sobered. "Besides, I got used to wearing the same thing all the time in the pen."

"I never asked you about any of that, about those years."

"Nothing about it to say."

"What's his name? Your son."

"Calvin. Cal." Just voicing it . . . God, his throat. His heart.

"Is he okay?"

"He's getting there." King didn't mention how many nights he'd spent in waiting rooms at the Texas Medical Center, never going into the boy's room, seeing glimpses of tubes and monitors and a tiny body swallowed up by sheets and blankets when he'd walked by the door.

"He couldn't have got the treatment he needed here. He had to go to Houston. His mother had raised some of the money, barbecue fund-raisers and bake sales, and then donations from friends and families from his school and church. His grandparents."

"But it wasn't enough."

"I don't know why she thought I could get it," he said, choking on his laugh. "If he'd never got sick, I'd never have known he was out there. I don't know if it would've been easier that way."

"Sounds like he's got a lot of caring folks around him."

"He does. A great father, even. Just not me." Damn, but that was hard to say.

"Does he need more? Do you?"

"I'm not asking for more, Simon."

"I know. But I'm offering."

"Well, keep your offer. I've got the trees about to produce, and I'm going back to Delcambre to work with a shrimper I know until then. I'll save what I can. If Gina doesn't need anything more, I'll put it aside. A college fund maybe. Or one day I might have enough to really do a workover on the well."

"And somewhere in there you'll go after Paschelle?"

"Not sure I'll have time."

"Then you make time. Make time for me, too. Twenty years is long enough for this Hatfield-and-McCoy bullshit."

"We're family, boo. That analogy doesn't work."

"It works if you know what I mean, and that I'm serious."

"I do. It's nice knowing someone out there who has my back. Next time I go after a judge who's a criminal as well as corrupt, I'll do it on more sleep and less booze. Maybe then I won't need the save."

"It's what I do," Simon said with a shrug that reeked of humble.

But that was it. King wasn't going to press for more, for answers Simon didn't want to give—even if he'd had his fill of secrets. "You do it well, cuz. I hope they pay you what you're worth." He dug into his pocket, spun his keys around on one finger, and palmed them.

"You heading home?" Simon asked.

"Figured I've kept you long enough. You've got some miles out there calling your name." He headed for his truck, stopped and turned as a thought struck him. His grin nearly split his face. "And I've got a buried treasure calling mine."

Forty-three

"Are you ready to go back to New York?" Simon asked after slamming his truck's tailgate and closing the bed cover over his stash of supplies.

Micky stood there watching him, her hair in a ponytail, a smile on her face, a sparkle in her eyes that a few days ago he took as a warning to keep his distance but now was a beacon beckoning him.

"It doesn't matter if I'm ready or not, does it? I came to see Lisa. I've done that. It's time to go home."

Nothing about her accident, Lisa's kidnapping, Bear's death, how close she'd come herself. She made it sound like the days she'd been here had been a relaxing vacation rather than the truth of what they were. The attempt on her life didn't even seem to faze her.

He wondered if the shock would hit later, if it would send her to seek counseling, or if she had sectioned off those memories, that experience, and lopped it off like overlong hair.

He wanted to know the truth of how she was doing, how she was dealing. He didn't want to put her on a plane. "Was your father glad to hear from you? That you're okay, and on your way back?"

"He never knew I wasn't okay. The physical accident-on-purpose part anyway. He knew the underpants thing was a symptom of a much larger problem. He told my intended that there would be no wedding, so at least I got his attention."

"Or the pictures did, anyway."

"According to Jane, the pictures were dark and blurry and incredibly grainy even after they were cleaned up. The ass could have belonged to anyone wearing that skirt."

He doubted Michelina Ferrer would have been seen in public wearing something so easily purchased as she wore now. He looked at her again in her twelve-dollar sneakers, her twenty-dollar jeans, the oversized black polo marked down to half price because of the sun-bleached streaks on the shoulders.

He couldn't believe she was the same woman from the billboard, the one who'd stared down into his tiny patio and refused to let him give up, who'd told him that he'd only been doing his job, that Stella Banks getting hurt was the sort of collateral damage no one could prevent or anticipate, and that if Eli McKenzie was man enough to deal, he'd better be.

He nodded, trying to remember what she'd just said, or what his life had been like a week ago without her. "Good. That's good. I'm glad."

"Glad about what?"

"I don't know. I mean, I do know. I'm glad about a lot of things. It's just—"

"What?" she asked, coming closer. "What are you glad about?"

Ask him something easy. "That Lisa was found safe. That she and Terrill are going to get the hell out of here." Micky had told him she'd convinced them to come to New York, at least for a while.

"I'm glad about that, too," she said, smiling. "They need to be safe, to be with each other away from here."

Away from their loss that was wrapped up in so much anger and pain. He got that. "I'm glad King's going to stay on at Le Hasard. At least for now."

"Until he goes after Paschelle, you mean."

"Yeah. I was thinking he won't be sticking around here long."

"But you'll still keep the property."

He nodded. He had to. "I'm glad I finally know the truth about my father." Though with Bear gone, he would never know the why.

"I am so, so sorry about that." She was close enough now to wrap her arms around him, and she did, holding him, her head on his chest, where it fit like his favorite thing to wear.

He glanced up at the house. "I'm glad I saw this place again. It'll be easier to tear it down knowing what bad shape it's in."

She looked into his eyes. "When did you decide to do that?"

"Just this morning. It seemed to fit. Putting an end to the past. Starting over."

"Then you're ready to get back to work?" She paused, letting her fingers walk up his spine. "Or does that not mesh with the starting-over thing?"

He remained silent, enjoying the feel of her fingers on his back, her breasts flat against his chest, her hips in the cradle of his. He was used to this already, used to having her at arm's length when he reached for her, used to her making him think with the way she prodded and questioned, nudged and provoked.

He was already used to her making him happy, to thinking of her as his own. "I'm going back, yeah, but I'm not in a big hurry."

"Understanding boss."

He'd like her to meet Hank, and one day the rest of the guys. But they could wait. He wasn't ready to share her. "He's the best."

"You've never thought of changing careers?"

He'd been in the service of his country under Uncle Sam's eye for twelve years, in the service of its people in one way or another since. He'd never thought of doing anything else. Anything safer. Something that would keep the woman in his life from worrying about him.

That didn't keep him from asking, "You got something in mind?"

"Actually, I do." She backed out of his embrace, walked in a circle around him. "Ferrer is introducing a new male fragrance next year. Trieste. We're just now beginning to work on the ad campaign. That's actually why I want Lisa in New York. She's advertising brilliant; don't ask me what she was doing down here in the swamp."

"Uh, making a life with her husband?" Simon reminded her, feeling as if he were being sized up like a porterhouse.

"Besides that." Micky easily waved him off. "Anyway, she could have commuted. Or telecommuted at least. If she'd been busy working for me, she wouldn't have had time to get involved in the Landrys' genealogy—"

"And Bear would have gotten away with my father's murder."

She stopped, stared at him. "Then you admit that good can come out of dangerous situations."

"It usually does," he agreed, having brought down enough bad guys to know.

"And being in life-or-death situations doesn't always mean innocent people die or get hurt."

He saw what she was trying to do, where she was going— which was okay since he'd already done a bit of working it out for himself. "Not always, no. But it can happen. It happened to you."

"I didn't even know I was in a dangerous situation, and I got through it anyway. A few bumps and dings, but basically unharmed."

"Yes, but you were lucky."

"I was also resourceful. I know how to take care of myself. I just want to make sure you know that."

"I know it."

"Good, so then you can do some test shots, see how you look on film and in pixels, and if that doesn't pan out and you have to go back to your life as a spy—since I'm assuming that's pretty close to what you are—at least we won't have to worry about us."

"Us?"

"Yes," she said, emphatically adding, "Us. I called Jane from the hospital. She's looking for an apartment for me. I told her to start on the Lower East Side."

Ah, what she did to his heart. "You don't belong there."

"But you're there. And that's where I want to be."

"I can afford to move. I just stay there for the flavor."

She tilted her head and considered him slyly. "You wouldn't miss the billboard?"

"You won't be there forever. I'd rather have the real you."

"I can get you a print so you'll have me to talk to when I'm gone."

"We haven't even picked out china and you're leaving me already?"

"Traveling gone. Not leaving-you gone. Unless you can get time away to come with me."

"I've seen a lot of the world already. I like the idea of staying home."

"You haven't seen it with me. And I'm a lot more fun to be with than your *Buffy* DVDs."

"What's up with everyone disrespecting my girl Buffy?" he asked, though he had to admit he was liking this sassy Michelina, the business tycoon, the go-getter. He could imagine having her boss him around in bed. He could imagine liking it. What he couldn't imagine was letting her go.

"Here's the thing, *cher*," she said, and his heart began to pound, his body to tighten. "*I* want to be your girl."

"And you want me to be . . . your bodyguard?"

"Yes. And my confidant, my best friend, my lover. My man."

It was time for sharing what he had on his mind. "Are you set on catching your plane?"

She shook her head. "Not really. At least not today."

He slapped the truck's front quarter panel. "How about a road trip? Camping out. Sleeping under the stars. Showering outside. Naked."

"You know I'll have to give up the nature girl act once we're home."

"In public, sure. But in private? The nature-y-er the better." He opened his door. "How do you feel about getting naked in my truck?"

"Now?"

"The sooner the better."

His pants were around his hips, hers around her ankles, and he was inside her before either of them could breathe.

"Is this going to be happening a lot during the trip?"

"It had damn well better, *chère*. It had damn well better."

If you like this book,
you've got to try Amy Fetzer's latest,
FIGHT FIRE WITH FIRE,
out now from Brava . . .

"**Y**ou don't have time for that."

Instantly Riley scooped up the pistol and spun on his knees, aiming.

A figure stood near the blown-out entrance. Shit. He hadn't heard a thing.

Still as glass, the man's head and shoulders were wrapped in dark scarves over a once green military jacket, now a dull gray like the weather. The only skin exposed was his eyes. Around his waist, a utility belt sagged, and the sniper rifle was slung on his shoulder, the weapon held across his body, ready to sight and fire. Yet he stood casually, without threat.

"If I wanted you dead, I wouldn't have wasted bullets to see you two safe and alive."

The sniper, Riley realized with a wee shock, was a woman.

She advanced with easy grace, stepping over piles of rubble to hop down at his level. Her rifle looked all too familiar.

"Yes, it's American," she said, noticing his attention. He lowered his weapon. She stood a couple feet away, staring down at Sam. "He doesn't look good." She unwound her head scarf and a braided rope of shiny dark hair spilled down one shoulder. She met his gaze. Beneath arched brows, whiskey-colored eyes stared back at him.

"Sweet mother a' *Jaasus.*" She was younger than him.

"I get that a lot." She gestured at Sam. "What do you need to do?"

"Set his leg again and get a tighter splint on it."

She nodded as her gaze bounced around the interior. "Let's get busy. I don't know how much time we have."

Though the pop of gunfire was lazier now, Riley wasn't ignoring the help, or the danger of staying put too long. He instructed, glad Sam was unconscious or he'd be screaming to the heavens. After unbuckling her utility belt, she got behind Sam, her legs and arms wrapping his torso and hips as Riley grasped his calf and ankle. On a count, he pulled. Even drugged, Sam arched with silent agony. Riley ripped the flight suit more and pushed the bone down, forcing it to align closely. Blood oozed from the gash. He met her gaze and nodded.

"It's set. Well . . . better than it was."

She eased from Sam and unclipped her canteen, offering it.

He cleaned his hands and the wound, then Riley worked against the cold. With the needle poised over Sam's flesh, he shook too much to stitch. "For the love of Mike." He dropped the needle, sanding his hands, blowing on them. She quickly grasped them both, wrapping her scarf around them, then brought his fists to her lips. She breathed hotly against the fabric, and Riley felt the warmth sting his icy skin. She rubbed and breathed, her gaze flashing up. He felt struck, her soulful eyes hiding so much.

"Better?"

He nodded, unwound the scarf. "The rest of me is a bit chilly still."

It took a second for that to sink in and she made a face. He chuckled, then said, "Get yourself on the other side, woman, and let's make some quick work here."

She snickered to herself, yet obeyed, holding Sam's skin

closed as he stitched. She still wore gloves and though she was dressed warmly, he noticed everything was cinched down, nothing to catch, and her rifle would collapse. It was a weapon he'd seen in spec, a prototype of the MP5. Not in production, yet she had one. And if the bodies outside indicated, she knew how to use it. It was at her right, by her knee with a bullet chambered.

"You're Company." CIA. Probably attached to NATO.

He had to give her credit, she didn't look up or make even a single nuance. If she was any good, she wouldn't give anything away.

"Tell me how an Irishman got to be in the Marines."

Okay, he could go that direction. "I was a runner for the IRA and my older sister caught me. Dragged me home by my ear, she did." His lips curved with the memory as he took another stitch. "My parents, fearing for my immortal soul, sent me to America to live with relatives." He shrugged.

"So dodging bullets comes easy, huh?"

"Yeah, I guess."

Then he went and chose a career in it. He glanced at Sam, knowing this would cost him what he held dear. His Marine enlistment. But he couldn't let the one man who treated him like a friend instead of his superior die in the frigid Serbian forests.

"I saw the jet go down."

His gaze briefly slid to hers.

"He was doing some amazing flying before the missile hit. I've been behind you for a day."

"So you're the reason the patrol didn't catch up to us?"

Bless her, that blank expression didn't change a fraction.

"Thank you for our lives." He clipped the thread. "I'm Riley." He held out his hand. She bit off her glove and shook it. Her skin was warm, her palm smooth and dry.

"Safia," was all she offered with her disarming smile.

He wondered why someone so young was in the field

alone. She helped him work the inflatable air cast over Sam's upper thigh, then wrapped him in rags and curtains Riley'd found to keep him warm. Sam's fever would spike and he had to get him some antibiotics. He'd used his last just now.

The woman unwound from the floor, strapped her belt back on, then dug in her pack like a purse and blindly reloaded her magazines. He recognized C4 packs and some gadgets he didn't. She was a little fire team all by herself, he thought, smiling. Armed, she went to each opening. He reached for his gun when she disappeared out a gap in the wall. He waited, chambering a bullet and aiming.

Tell me I can't be that much of a sucker. Icy wind spun through the building. Seconds ticked by. She reappeared and stopped short, then cocked her head. She smiled almost appreciatively, and he lowered his weapon. She moved to him with an elegance that defied her crude surroundings and the two pistols in her belt. Her exotic features and tanned skin puzzled him. Without head scarves, she looked completely out of place.

Then the radio hooked on her belt buzzed and she brought it to her ear, listening. The language sounded Albanian. She didn't make contact, only listened, then said, "We need to go.

Kathy Love's done it again with her sexy paranormal,
DEMON CAN'T HELP IT,
available now from Brava . . .

Jo breathed in slowly through her nose. What had she just agreed to? Seeing this man every day? She pulled in another slow, even breath, telling herself to shake off her reaction to this man's proximity.

Sure, he was attractive. And he had—a presence. But she wasn't some teenage girl who would fall to pieces under a cute boy's attention. Not that cute was a strong enough word for what Maksim was. He was—unnerving. To say the least.

But she wasn't interested in him. She decided that quite definitely over the past two days. Of course that decision was made when he wasn't in her presence.

But either way, she should have more control than this. Apparently should and could were two very different things. And she couldn't seem to stop her reaction to him. Her heart raced and her body tingled, both hot and cold in all the most inappropriate places.

"So every morning?" he said, his voice rumbling right next to her, firing up the heat inside her. "Does that work for you?"

She cleared her throat, struggling to calm her body.

"Yes—that's great," she managed to say, surprising even

herself with the airiness of her tone. "I'll schedule you from
8 A.M. to"—she glanced at the clock on the lower right-hand
corner of the computer screen—"noon?"

That was a good amount of time, getting Cherise through
the rowdy mornings and lunch, and giving him the go-ahead
to leave now. She needed him out of her space.

If her body wasn't going to go along with her mind, then
avoidance was clearly her best strategy. And she had done
well with that tactic—although she'd told herself that wasn't
what she was doing.

"Noon is fine," he said, still not moving. Not even
straightening away from the computer. And her.

"Good," she poised her fingers over the keys and began
typing in his hours. "Then I think we are all settled. You
can take off now if you like."

When he didn't move, she added, "You can go get some
lunch. You must be hungry." She flashed him a quick smile
without really looking at him.

This time he did stand, but he didn't move away. Instead
he leaned against her desk, the old piece of furniture creak-
ing at his tall, muscular weight.

"You must be hungry, too. Would you like to join me?"

She blinked, for a moment not comprehending his
words, her mind too focused on the muscles of his thighs so
near her. The flex of more muscles in his shoulders and
arms as he crossed them over his chest.

She forced herself to look back at the computer screen.

"I—I don't think so," she said. "I have a lot to do here."

"But surely you allow yourself even a half an hour for
lunch break."

She continued typing, fairly certain whatever she was
writing was gibberish. "I brought a lunch with me, actually." Which was true. Not that she was hungry at the moment. She was too—edgy.

"Come on," he said in a low voice that was enticing, coaxing. "Come celebrate your first regular volunteer."

She couldn't help looking at him. He was smiling, the curl of his lips, his white, even teeth, the sexily pleading glimmer in his pale green eyes.

God, he was so beautiful.

And dangerous.

Jo shook her head. "I really can't."

He studied her for a moment. "Can't or won't? What's the matter, Josephine? Do I make you nervous?"

Jo's breath left her for a moment at the accented rhythm of her full name crossing his lips. But the breath-stealing moment left as quickly as it came, followed by irritation. At him and at herself.

She wasn't attracted to this man—not beyond a basic physical attraction. And that could be controlled. It could.

"You don't make me nervous," she said firmly.

"Then why not join me for lunch?"

"Because," she said slowly, "I have a lot of work to do."

Maksim crossed his arms tighter and lifted one of his eloquent eyebrows, which informed her that he didn't believe her for a moment.

"I don't think that's why you won't come. I think you are uncomfortable with me. Maybe because you are attracted to me." Again the eyebrow lifted—this time in questioning challenge.

And be sure to catch Lucy Monroe's new book,
WATCH OVER ME,
coming next month from Brava . . .

"Dr. Ericson."

Lana adjusted the angle on the microscope. Yes. Right there. Perfect. "Amazing."

"Lana."

She reached out blindly for the stylus to her handheld. *Got it.* She started taking notes on the screen without looking away from the microscope.

"Dr. Ericson!!!"

Lana jumped, bumping her cheekbone on the microscope's eyepiece before falling backward, hitting a wall that hadn't been there when she'd come into work that morning.

Strong hands set her firmly on her feet as she realized the wall was warm and made of flesh and muscle. Lots and lots of muscle.

Stumbling back a step, she looked up and then up some more. The dark-haired hottie in front of her was as tall as her colleague, Beau Ruston. Or close to it, anyway. She fumbled with her glasses, sliding them on her nose. They didn't help. Reading glasses for the computer, they only served to make her feel more disoriented.

She squinted, then remembered and pulled the glasses

off again, letting them dangle by their chain around her neck. "Um, hello? Did I know you were visiting my lab?"

She was fairly certain she hadn't. She forgot appointments sometimes. Okay, often, but she always remembered eventually. And this man hadn't made an appointment with her. She was sure of it. He didn't look like a scientist, either.

Not that all scientists were as unremarkable as she was in the looks department, but this man was another species entirely.

He looked dangerous and sexy. Enough so that he would definitely replace chemical formulas in her dreams at night. His black hair was a little too long and looked like he'd run his fingers through it, not a comb. That was just so bad boy. She had a secret weakness for bad boys.

Even bigger than the secret weakness she'd harbored for Beau Ruston before he'd met Elle.

She had posters of James Dean and Matt Dillon on the wall of her bedroom and had seen *Rebel Without a Cause* a whopping thirty-six times.

Unlike James Dean, this yummy bad boy even had pierced ears. Only instead of sedate studs or small hoops, he had tiny black plugs. Only a bit bigger than a pairs of studs, the plugs were recessed in his lobes. They had the Chinese kanji for strength etched on them in silver. Or pewter, maybe. It wasn't shiny.

The earrings were hot. Just like him.

He looked like the kind of man who had a tattoo. Nothing colorful. Something black and meaningful. She wanted to see it. Too bad she couldn't just ask.

Interpersonal interaction had so many taboos. It wasn't like science, where you dug for answers without apology.

"Lana?"

The stranger had a strong jaw, too, squared and accented by a close-cropped beard that went under, not across his chin. No mustache. His lips were set in a straight line, but they still looked like they'd be heaven to kiss.

Not that she'd kissed a lot of lips, but she was twenty-nine. Even a geeky scientist didn't make it to the shy side of thirty without a few kisses along the way. And other stuff. Not that the other stuff was all that spectacular. She'd always wondered if that was her fault or the men she'd chosen to partner.

It didn't take a shrink to identify the fact that Lana had trust issues. With her background, who wouldn't?

Still, people had been known to betray family, love, and country for sex. She wouldn't cross a busy street to get some. Or maybe she would, if this stranger was waiting on the other side.

The fact that she could measure the time since she'd last had sex in years rather than months, weeks, or *days*—which would be a true miracle—wasn't something she enjoyed dwelling on. She blamed it on her work.

However, every feminine instinct that was usually sublimated by her passion for her job was on red alert now.

GREAT BOOKS, GREAT SAVINGS!

When You Visit Our Website:
www.kensingtonbooks.com
You Can Save Money Off The Retail Price
Of Any Book You Purchase!

- **All Your Favorite Kensington Authors**
- **New Releases & Timeless Classics**
- **Overnight Shipping Available**
- **eBooks Available For Many Titles**
- **All Major Credit Cards Accepted**

Visit Us Today To Start Saving!
www.kensingtonbooks.com

All Orders Are Subject To Availability.
Shipping and Handling Charges Apply.
Offers and Prices Subject To Change Without Notice.